THE
TAXIDERMIST'S
LOVER

POLLY HALL

THE
TAXIDERMIST'S
LOVER

CamCat
Books

CamCat Publishing, LLC
Brentwood, Tennessee 37027
camcatpublishing.com

Hardcover ISBN 9780744300376
Paperback ISBN 9780744303810
Large-Print Paperback ISBN 9780744300420
eBook ISBN 9780744300390
Audiobook ISBN 9780744300406

Library of Congress Control Number: 2020949408

Cover design by Rena Barron / Maryann Appel.
Book design by Maryann Appel. Illustrations by Rebecca Farrin.

5   3   1   2   4

FOR MUM & DAD

"YOU ARE A WONDERFUL, complex, fucked-up mess," you once said to me. Sometimes when you passed these judgements I would flinch, as if the words were darts or sharp tools piercing my skin. That old saying—sticks and stones may break my bones, but words will never hurt me—does not make sense. Words can be the most damaging of all things; they have life, power, intensity. Just as this place, our home, shapes us into new beings over time.

The world has frozen around us with icy precision. A closing in and sealing off, like a scar healing shut over an abscess. It is a process occurring at a rate immeasurable to the human eye. This peat-packed land of water, leat and marsh has been isolated and stilled. Everything waits.

But out of that stillness comes a word, born from circumstance. The word? Unfurling. For nothing is truly still, is it? Even ice contracts and expands, creaks and crystallizes. It has a voice of its own, speaks in eerie groans like the split trunk of an old willow in the wind. It lives and breathes. It transforms.

The roads are compacted like a skating rink, and the biting wind entraps breath as fine particles, each molecule of heat visible as it cools. Bodies become tense. Cruel black ice shines with no sign of thaw. Condensation makes window panes translucent, weeps in solemn drips as if yearning for change. The light here is movable; it shifts like the surface of water. Candlelight moves, and I want to touch the flames.

I want to send a message to the starlings for them to draw in the sky for you. Can you see? One tells another, then another, then another, a whispered message from wing tip to wing tip. They rise up from where they sleep in the reed beds to the misty sky to create an aerial display. Murmurations over this Summerland rustle like ash falling slowly onto china dishes. I throw my will around their swarming mass as if they were sardines in a frenzied run across a faraway ocean. I make them turn and separate into darkened shapes—a heron diving; a wave crashing; confetti lifting to form the shape of a bride; a heart; a pine tree; and the letters one after another to spell, I – L - O - V - E – Y - O - U.

ANUARY

Do you remember January as I do? I see it as the death of one of many beginnings, or could it have been the beginning of the end? Depends how you look at it. I know that things were never quite the same after you started mixing up the species.

"You need to specialize," I said, "find a niche—I hear cased mammals are making a comeback. Or how about mystical menageries?"

You looked at me, your moustache twitching slightly with amusement.

"A crabbit or a stox?" I offered.

"What?" you huffed.

"A crabbit is a crow crossed with a rabbit."

I could see you mulling over the combinations in your head, picturing the sleek iridescence of the crow's breast feathers set against the smooth down of an American Albino rabbit.

"And a stox," you guessed, "is a stoat crossed with a fox?"

"No. A stork actually." I imagined the body of a red fox, its flame-orange fur contrasted with the angelic white of a stork's wingspan; a flying, majestic vixen.

"A stork—yes a stork!" The cogs were set in motion. That was when I knew you would not return to the pampered pooches cradling their favorite toy on their favorite cushion, their cute little necks twisted in a final gesture of compliance. Or the coarse hair of a stag, tongue lolling in shock from the gunshot that sent it on its final rut to the afterlife.

There was a woman who came to you once with a bald Pomeranian. It had been petted so much after its initial taxidermy that the fur on its head had worn thin. It looked like a tonsured monk from the Middle Ages. Do you remember, you said you were in tune with the ancient Egyptians and that mummification was an art? Yet your art was more powerful, as the creature was exposed to air when you'd finished it, sometimes handled.

I had not always been interested in dead things. But they seemed to be interested in me, even from an early age.

Growing up among the wetlands of Somerset, I had plenty of opportunity to mix with the wildlife, dead or alive. It became a part of my life, a part of me. The ground was black and wet; it smelt of woeful solitude. As a child I'd collect the bones of animals I found on the compost heap and line them up on my bedroom shelf alongside plastic toys, or poke a carcass with a stick to test if life could be reanimated by my interference.

When we were nine, Rhett found a bloated badger puffed up like a balloon in the field at the back of our parents' house, so using a kitchen knife I set about dissecting it. I wanted its coat for a hat. Imagine the badger's head sitting upon my own like a shamanic warrior. As I sliced down its belly (a movement I'd witnessed on a TV crime drama) I pierced the viscera and the putrid gases puffed out. A river of maggots escaped from the grey snake of its intestines onto the grass. Rhett was all for leaving it to rot but, undeterred, I thought if I could flay enough of it successfully, I would have my hat and parts of the badger would live on instead of decaying by the ditch.

But this was a child's fantasy. I had not even learned to spell the word taxidermy then. Of course, I had seen stuffed animals at the museum, or peering out from the walls of old stately homes we had visited in the school holidays. But the act of preserving was not one I had been taught at such a tender age. So, I made it up, much to my mother's disgust, and a few days later the rotting flesh from the inside of the badger's skin putrefied and infused the house with the scent of sweet decay.

I'll never forget her face as she looked at the jagged pelt, rough edged, where my knife had cut it away from the carcass, random feathers sewn crudely to the rim. She tried to hide her horror with a look of vague disappointment. Her little girl did not play with dollies like normal little girls; her little girl cut up dead animals and collected their parts to display as trophies! Even though all the remains were removed from the house, I still felt that badger near me. He lumbered toward me as I slept, then nosed about my room in the dark.

I learned that badgers preferred the dark. They showed their true nature to me in ways you cannot imagine. They would tramp through my head, uprooting my thoughts with their powerful heads and stocky bodies. These were earth dwellers, underground burrowers. They were nocturnal and peaceful, unless provoked.

My mother's disapproval did not put me off interfering with nature. Even in my dreams I would steal the wings from birds and try to fly, or grow the lithe legs of a hare so I could race across a moonlit field. Mostly my dreams consisted of sinking into the wet-black below my feet, right up to my neck, and I'd wake just before my head was covered in darkness.

But always, day or night, I'd hear them, those creatures that had starved or frozen to death or been poisoned or killed or died of natural causes. I heard them like a sort of electrical static that got louder, especially if the hunt was galloping across the fields or if the pheasants were flushed up to the sky in a bountiful bouquet. Each creature had their own unique signature; they all seemed to know their place in the scheme of things. I longed for that certainty. That was how I became sure that when feathers were ruffled, dead did not always mean dead.

◆━━◆━━◆

January was the time you religiously took to your workshop, almost every day, with a renewed purpose—to create something so unusual it would be talked about in circles way past your final breath.

It was your devotion to the work that drew me closer to you, the preparation spelled out with lines of jars and tools; it was scientific, medical, and precise, not like my childhood efforts of wild abandon with blunt cutlery. Each of the stages you went through would lead to a final perfect representation of what once lived. I admired you as I would admire any artist, although your medium was grotesque. It stank. You messed with nature.

I think that's what got to us in the end. You were dealing with life, not death. Each specimen had to be renewed, like Jesus molding new life into Lazarus; you used your hands to replicate the living. Everlasting life. Even then, I witnessed the madness creep up on us and slip under our skin.

◆━━◆━━◆

That long month. Somerset was groaning and moaning under an oppressive grey sky and endless dark nights. After the Christmas lights had been packed away, the decorations stowed in the loft for another year among the spiders and dust, we got back into the daily pattern of our lives, a pattern I had fallen into so effortlessly in those few months since we met. For us, it was a great month for resolution with all those dark hours, thinking about what to do when the sun finally appeared to warm our skin once more. We were thinking about our future—planning, dreaming.

"I'm tired of stags," you said, as we ate venison for the fourth night in a row. It was the week after New Year. We stayed at home for that too, munching our way through pretzels and marzipan-laced stollen and a freezer full of meat. My stomach felt heavy from all the rich food I'd consumed. It was just as well I had the sort of metabolism where I never seemed to put on weight no matter how much I ate. Annoyed the hell out of you. Chunky Pepper was what they called you, wasn't it? Your childhood nickname. But I always thought we were a perfect match—you with your steady hands, me with the flighty grace of a starling. You could look at me as if seeing through my clothes, penetrating my core. I had never softened in the sights of any man before you. I usually moved too fast, letting those leering fools snap at my ankles like nasty dogs. Nothing pleased me like your strong hands on my body. Your hands, even your unkempt beard and severed finger, seemed perfect to me. You knew exactly where to touch me; your fingers palpated my skin and smoothed back the faint lines and dimples with a pressure you had mastered through your work.

You had already begun to diversify into more non-domestic animals: chinchillas; iguanas; a snow leopard that had belonged to an eccentric octogenarian; even a celebrated mirror carp that had allegedly lived for over thirty years in a local fishing lake. The fishermen had affectionately named it "Wonky Fin." It took pride of place in the clubhouse, gazing dry-eyed from a glass cabinet at the lake where it had once swum. I had watched you preserve it and paint the varnish on the scales to make it appear water-bound once more. But it cried. I never told you that. That cold fish cried at the injustice of being born again into a dry body, instead of swimming away to the great lakes in the sky.

"The eyes," you said, "they never quite show what was once inside." You would place the polished nuggets of glass onto the mount last of all, preferring the naked frame of each animal blind until you had finished sculpting and stitching the skin over layers of structure, blow-drying the fur, or primping the feathers, sometimes fixing with hair lacquer. *"Welcome to my boudoir!"* I could hear your throaty chuckle echo around the workshop when I delivered cups of coffee.

I loved your darkness. The way you clipped and snipped, slicing the fascia and sinews, while our dogs sometimes looked on with an expression of awe and fear. It smelt like the depths of a cave in your workshop, and the dense metallic odor of organic matter would infuse your clothes and hair.

When we made love, I'd somehow taste the essence of the creatures you'd been handling—the quick, acrid bite of a fox, the feathery scratch of an owl, the smooth perfume of someone's beloved pet cat. At mealtimes I watched you dissect the food on your plate, as if delaying the sensation of taste. You'd carefully chew in silence, mulling over the constituent parts, preferring your meat without seasoning, plain and rare. "I like my meat to taste of meat," you told me.

<hr />

Once there was a man who kept goats in his backyard. He didn't name the goats; they weren't pets after all. He ate every part of them: the legs, liver, kidneys, blood, even the fat encompassing the intestines. He just clawed it off with his bony fingers and chewed it up, raw. I fantasized about us doing this. We could enact a sacrifice to the gods, drink the blood, dance naked under the moonlight. There was something honorable in rearing and dispatching your own meal.

<hr />

The landscape had only changed a little since my childhood. More intensive farming methods, more houses, and more sophisticated drainage continued to pump the water off the land and into the rivers, but the contours and ridges looked much the same.

Our county, just a car drive from Stonehenge, was famous for being mystical Avalon. We were in the middle of the hinterland, the Somerset Levels, the Moor, Land of Apples, Land of the Dead. The marshes reclaimed from the sea still haunted the place with watery whispers from withy beds, and mist rose up from the rhynes like smoke from a mariner's pipe. Here we chose to live among the vernacular of widgeon and teal; the loose earth low and slaked with moisture. We lived on borrowed ground, peat shifting beneath us, as if the bodies of buried beasts wanted to reform their ancient bones from the earth itself and resurface to taste the air with moistened tongues.

Even in the cold density of January we sensed the shift of seasons. The flight of lapwing and starling reminded us of impermanence. Their wings were flashes of light in the grey mornings as they rose like an idea suddenly surfacing.

So, January became not so much of a drag as an exploration along an unmapped road. And where you went, I would follow, an enraptured devotee of your world of grisly body parts—heads, legs, claws, beaks, feathers, scales, all catalogued and preserved then reinvested into new imagined creatures. You inspired me to use my skills as an artist, so I started sketching out ideas for you; I had studied art but was more accustomed to drawing portraits and bowls of fruit, the things I could study with my own eyes, not these bizarre monstrosities that bombarded me at night in my dreams, as if mislaid blueprints of evolution were exhumed after millions of years. I had daydreamed about becoming famous like Frida Kahlo but mostly I ended up in jobs that didn't fulfil me; waitressing, bartending, packing crisps in a factory. I was working at a call center for an insurance company when we met. I never dreamt I'd find my life filled up by another person.

We started with the crabbit, my original idea, a crow's head attached to a rabbit's body adorned with the bird's black wings. It now sits on our mantelpiece as a reminder of those early, naïve days. I felt it watch us, trying to make sense of its own identity. Am I crow? Or am I rabbit? Its confusion was obvious to me, as if fur and feather, claw and paw, were never meant to be conjoined.

⊷━━◦━━⊶

To the south of our house, your workshop nestled at the bottom of the garden. The soft glow of an electric bulb denoted your presence, a beacon, but also a "No Entry" sign for any unwelcome interference. The lit-up interior said to me, "I'm working in *my* world among *my* things—give me space." I understood your need for solitude in your cave-like retreat, a place away from our shared home; it was yours alone. Not ours. What I'm trying to say is: I know how you worked. Having worked in lively places where people talked all day, every day, I found this quiet world with you a dreamy paradise.

We both were seeking solitude after all the layers of affection were stripped back, much like the way you peeled back an animal's skin with precision, flaying the tough sinews and fascia with sharp tools, turning it inside out, revealing, exposing it and ultimately becoming intimate with its form. Its unique essence was mastered by your hands. This couldn't be shared—it was personal. That is why I thought you'd understand my own needs. My solitude was not sought in the cool confines of a workshop but in the expanse of another place—the dark recesses of my imagination.

⊷━━◦━━⊶

I suggested a website for your business, but you looked at me as if I were suggesting you sell your soul to the devil. *That* seemed unnatural to you. Too removed perhaps?

"Who would see it?" you asked.

"Everyone."

"Everyone who knows me?"

"Yes—well, everyone who uses the internet and searches for you. Or for taxidermy."

"What—strangers too?"

"Yes—everyone!"

"What's the point of, say, people in China seeing it—"

"The point is . . ." but by this stage in our discussion you could probably sense my exasperation. "It's what people do! It's how people communicate!"

"Well, I don't."

"No. I know!"

So, we left it at that, just an understanding that there was no point in persuading you of its efficacy, especially as I was not even convincing myself. Selfishly I wanted to protect you from the rest of the world and all its lies, deceit snarled up in layers of data clogging up pages and pages of computer screens, forever there, eternal but dirtied, unverified, and open to abuse. Perhaps the internet was a form of afterlife preserved in a graveyard of dumped information. Perhaps you were right. Perhaps I was my own worst enemy.

Besides, if you had spent less time working on those creatures, you would perhaps have discovered that my world was coming undone. I felt turned inside-out like the skin of a dead rabbit, waiting to be filled, stuffed fresh and preserved, put on display and admired—*how life-like, don't the eyes follow you about the room?*—those that are new to the craft always look at the glass eyes first, just to check that the specimen is really dead. Or maybe to see if any remaining life clings on.

What I'm trying to tell you is that January was about the time when I found him. He seemed to appear at the top of all the search engines when I typed in: best taxidermist in the world.

Felix De Souza—a name that would become etched on our psyches, a name that signified doom. But being the petulant Scarlett that I was, how could I resist? And what Scarlett wanted, Scarlett got. From that moment I became consumed by his whereabouts, thinking that you too could achieve such international acclaim. His youth was an asset but no match for your experience. Knowing he existed gnawed away at my brain like one of those parasites that eats you from the inside.

＊＊＊

Once a year, in Somerset, a custom called wassailing is carried out to encourage a bountiful apple harvest for the coming season. A gun is fired to scare away malevolent spirits and a wassail queen soaks bread in cider as an offering to the apple gods and goddesses. I knew about it before I met you, of course, but many didn't if they were not from the rural areas.

This was my first wassailing ceremony. We were wrapped up in thick coats and woolen scarves. In fact, the only piece of skin showing was the strip across my eyes below my hat and above my scarf-covered mouth.

You held my hands encased in padded mittens—I felt upholstered together and sweaty underneath all my layers, waiting by the door for you to fetch your gun. But I knew it would be cold in the apple orchard at Penny's place. At least it wasn't raining that night.

"Do we really have to go?" You knew Penny made me feel uncomfortable, as if she had some kind of ownership of you.

"I'm the one firing the gun this year. Come on, you'll enjoy it once you get there. There's cider! And a hog roast!" You tried to tickle me under my arms, but I had so many layers of clothes it just felt like mild pummeling.

I couldn't believe how many people were there. It was a beautiful night; the clouds had been blown away and a cold serenity seemed to open up the sky like a velvet sheet dusted with glitter. My neck hurt from looking at the stars, searching for a shooting one. I was about to ask you if you'd ever wished upon a star, but we were interrupted.

"Henry darling." Wafts of sickly perfume met my nostrils before she appeared, pushing through a group of people exhaling clouds over plastic cups of mulled cider. Her face was painted with ivy leaves that spiraled up her cheeks to the corners of her eyes and down her neck, as if a reptile were trying to gain access to her wrinkled cleavage.

"Penny." You nodded a clipped greeting and stood by my side to face her. This reassured me, to know where your loyalties lay. I knew she was itching to touch you as she edged closer. Her sagging bosom heaved over the neck of her dress as if something in her chest were trying to break free.

"Can I have a word about the proceedings?" She whispered like it was some kind of conspiracy between you two. You were only to play a small part, firing your gun into the air. I had watched you replace the lead shot with corn for safety, an old trick of yours you'd learned from your father.

"It will still knock you down," you told me sternly, "but you'd survive." I had no doubt you would not hesitate to use it for protection. A small shudder ran through my bones.

The wassailing ceremony began and Penny, crowned with a wreath of dark green leaves, led the parade to one of the apple trees in her orchard that had been decorated in twinkly, solar-powered lights. She looked severely underdressed for the weather but insisted on wearing a long silk gown and a velvet cape. Then, as self-appointed Wassail Queen, she dipped a hunk of toast into a jug of mulled cider, placed it carefully on one of the branches and suggestively sucked her fingers while looking at you. I felt like a voyeur.

"She's a bit serious, isn't she?" I whispered to you when she poured the rest of the cider around the base of the tree.

You shushed me, and I felt a pang of jealousy. I wondered if you had in the past shared more with her than a cup of cider in a freezing-cold field. I took a swig and let the warm spiced liquid sink down to my stomach. It shouldn't have mattered to me, but she'd known you for longer than I had. It wasn't even that. You seemed to have this common acceptance of each other. Perhaps you loved her?

Penny signaled to you with a nod and you fired your gun to the sky to ward off the evil spirits. Even though I was expecting it to be loud, the shot still made me jump. I saw her snigger and scowled in her direction, but she was too busy rousing the crowd into a wassail song.

> *Old apple tree we wassail thee*
> *And hoping thou will bear*
> *For the Lord doth know where we shall be*
> *'Til apples come another year.*
> *For to bear well and to bloom well*
> *So merry let us be*
> *Let every man take off his hat*
> *And shout to the old apple tree.*
> *Old apple tree we wassail thee*
> *And hoping thou will bear*
> *Hat fulls, cap fulls, three bushel bag fulls*
> *And a little heap under the stairs.*

You nuzzled your beard into my neck and whispered, "Time for bed, Miss Scarlett." Penny may have had you wrapped round her little finger, but I had you every night. As I looked again toward the branches of the trees and up above to the big indigo sky, I felt your heat reach me beneath my clothes and the effects of the cider creeping up my legs. How did I get so drunk?

The day after that night I felt invigorated. No hangover, surprisingly. We had probably burnt it off in bed. We had stripped off and launched naked under the covers as soon as we arrived home. The patchwork of warmth from your hot hands on my cold skin, and your tongue still sticky with cider, made me sink into a weighty sleep.

In my dreams you were chasing me round and round an apple tree, and Penny was laughing, hands on her hips taunting me with a bust that was more fitting on a twenty-year old. We were all naked. The crabbit was hopping and flapping its wings beneath the tree and Felix was spraying warm cider from a champagne magnum over my head. I woke to find you kneeling upright on the bed beside my face, pumping a heavy erection. As I refocused my eyes, a globule landed on my cheek.

"I didn't want to wake you." You were out of breath from your exertions and sat back on your haunches gazing at me. The covers were pulled down below my waist and my naked body felt chilled. I sleepily reached for my face, the stickiness already sliding down toward the pillow.

"Here let me . . ." you wiped a tissue across my cheek, tossed it to the floor, then pushed your tongue into my mouth. As you slid down next to me, I could still feel your dampness fading against my thigh. You leaned over to kiss me again, but I felt a pang of anger. Even though we had shared every inch of ourselves the night before, this seemed like an intrusion into my dreams, an infiltration of my mind. I turned my head away, trying to catch glimpses of Felix from my dream, but you continued to nibble at my ear.

"You looked so sexy, so still." *The crabbit hopping and flapping.*

"I was sleeping." *Felix, perfect in every way, splashing champagne over me.*

"Did you enjoy it last night?" you continued kissing my neck, my weakness, sending shivers through me.

"My first wassail," I said.

"A wassail virgin!" *Hat fulls, cap fulls, three bushel bags full!*

My fixation on others was just my way of proving how much I loved you. I hope you believe me. But the noises in my head grew louder. The crabbit was angry. *Am I crow or am I rabbit?* It squawked and squealed with all its might. I thought my head might explode.

<hr />

When you went down to your workshop, I fetched my laptop and clicked straight onto the internet. *Felix De Souza.* His website said he had trained as a sculptor at the Royal Academy before providing blue chip art to galleries and private collectors. It certainly looked expensive.

The magnificent coiled silkiness of a boa constrictor with wings mounted on a granite plinth, its mouth wide in attack; some sort of rodent with chicken's feet and a snake as a tail. As I flicked through his portfolio, I felt a surge of jealousy; I wanted you to show off your work like that. Whenever I looked at your creations, I felt as if they were still alive, or an essence of them had been carried through the veil of death and lived on. Your crabbit signified such an important breakthrough; it really worked. But Felix's site showed even more bizarre combinations. He seemed to mix up wild and domestic species to create almost alien-looking creatures. I know it went against all your training, but I also knew you could do it.

We all do things we don't want to, and I thought participating in an exhibition would be perfect in the spring, something to work toward with healthy competition. That was why I suggested it to you. Partly because I thought you deserved it. Partly because I thought it would be a way to expunge my stupid fascination with Felix, by meeting him in the flesh and setting him against you, as if comparison would cure me of my obsession with things that weren't mine to possess. Should I have stopped meddling and accepted things as they were? Nothing and nobody would ever come between us.

"I'm not sure about this." We were sipping wine and admiring the crabbit on the mantelpiece. The crow's dark head and wings were fixed onto the white rabbit.

"Alice in Wonderland gone wrong?" I said.

"No, it's not the combination. More that it doesn't feel right."

"How do you mean?"

"When I stuff a whole creature—I mean without mixing it with another species—it seems pure somehow. These hybrids seem unnatural."

"But you said yourself, the market is dwindling. It's all high-brow conceptual stuff nowadays." I sipped some wine. "I've entered you into a show."

"What do you mean?"

"The Spring Show. I've entered you. As an exhibitor. There's plenty of time to build your portfolio."

"What show? What portfolio?"

I couldn't tell you then that I knew Felix was a part of it, but at the time I thought it would be good for you. For *us*. I knew it would have to be your idea and you would distance yourself from me while you considered it.

I was surprised when you agreed with minimal fuss. I thought you complied to indulge me, and it pleased me indeed. We set about devising a strategy. Every morning we would wake, make love, then walk the dogs together before breakfast. Sometimes we would make love mid-morning if you were feeling aroused by the ideas we talked about. It seemed to be a routine we fell into rather easily. I drew up a spreadsheet with timescales and sources for specimens. My sketches took up so much time that I felt the creatures swim inside my head. Some I'd never heard of before, but excitement ran through me at the prospect of you experimenting. Pangolin? Uakari? Capybara? The searches for legal imports and laws around the protection of species, even extinct animals, needed certification, and the postage seemed extortionate. Nevertheless, we were not deterred. You had ways of acquiring the animals. I became your assistant as well as your lover.

I couldn't help going back to what you said about the creatures not being pure once you had disassembled then stitched them together as something new. You felt it too, didn't you?

CHRISTMAS DAY / TODAY

Early Morning

Our home has been trimmed up. Red and gold tinsel drape the picture frames and curtain rails. Paper chains are tacked to the ceiling beams, and a new batch of halogen lights are set to slow-fade and flicker so they reflect on the window and make me think of musical notes ascending and descending on a scale. We have a real tree this year rather than the synthetic one that you keep boxed up in the loft. This glorious tree has been installed in the lounge, not too close to the log fire, so it has space to breathe and retain its needles. It's a Nordman Fir, bushy and voluptuous, as if Narnia has arrived in our home. At any minute a horny Mr. Tumnus will appear, scarf adjusted at a jaunty angle tickling his bare chest, with a couple of beavers jostling in his wake. You sort of remind me of a manlier Mr. Tumnus, or maybe I'm confusing him with a centaur. Yes, you're more of a centaur–strong legs like a horse, tough muscular back and proper chest hair I can burrow into with my long, cold fingers.

The pine needles look blue-rinsed and shimmer a hue so ancient that I want to cry with joy. You've lit a scented candle, hints of cinnamon and cranberry mixing with the other scents. Its flame casts shapes on the wall like the probing tongues of lizards. The smell reminds me of the Christmas cake my mother used to set on the table, steeped in brandy, fruit packed tight like glistening beads, loaded with promise. I am drawn to the flicker of the candle. I am drawn to the top of the tree.

I start at the top and work my way down the branches. A star, five-pointed and silver, twinkles and reminds me of the eyes set in the heads of your stuffed creatures. It is only reflection; there is nothing genuine about it—artificial and fraudulent. But I am enthralled by its status, all the way up there, elevated on high. Where is the angel? Did we not have an angel among our decorations? One of those hermaphroditic, symmetrical beauties with blonde hair and spread wings and arms, but no feet. Angels don't need to walk when they have the gift of flight.

To fly I need only to lift my thoughts higher than that tree. I lift my mind, and my body seems to follow. There is freedom when I place my will above the confines of my form. By the way, angels are not sweet, trumpet-blowing lovelies like the ones on Christmas cards—no—they breathe fire, spit earth, cast demons from the shadowy pits of valleys and stagnant lagoons. Listen to me talking of angels like I'm some authority. There are no angels here.

⊷━━⊶

It's early in the morning. You are clattering around in the kitchen, metal banging against the ceramic top of the cooker, utensils rattling as you begin to prepare the Christmas feast. I have always loved your way of cooking, impulsive yet diligent. A turducken seems a bit extravagant for just the two of us, but I half expect Rhett to appear at the door empty-handed as an urchin. Most years he tends to make his way back to me, as if by being twins we have some natural homing device fitted to each other. Flesh and blood belong together at Christmastime.

Christmas wouldn't be right without traditions and routines. Every family has them. Some of ours have merged and evolved, like what food to eat and when; others are devised or re-invented, like the order in which we open gifts and the patterns of the day. For one day of the year, it's as if everyone else's home has become an enigma. Unless you have the code to enter their world, you'll be lost in translation. I'd imagine most people expect us to be quite eccentric on Christmas Day; they may be right this year.

Bread sauce, cranberry sauce, stuffing (ha!), gravy, mustard—all these delicious liquid accompaniments to what is only one meal of the year. But it is a meal charged with expectation. That's probably why Rhett always turns up; he knows he'll get fed. And the sprouts will take center stage, glistening like green bullets in butter and sprinkled with tiny cubes of crisp pancetta. Christmas without a momentous meal is like me without you. Unthinkable.

So, this is our second Christmas together on the Somerset Levels. Preparation is key to a perfect day, you always say. Tree—tick. Decorations—tick. Food—tick. Booze—tick. Christmas music playing in the background—tick. And enough logs to see us through if this deep freeze doesn't thaw like the Christmas I spent in Poland with my family as a child. The thickest drift of snow in decades, great white waves wedged up against the walls of the house, as if a truck had tipped it there on purpose. We were holed up for over a month before it melted. We couldn't even open the front door, so Rhett and I ended up climbing out the upstairs window instead and slid down the roof. Mother and Father together and in love. Our family grew close, laughter and mealtimes shared in the big house my father had rented for work. That year really did feel like Narnia. We made up stories holding a flashlight under the duvet like a giant billowing tent, nibbled biscuits and pretzels, we were even allowed to sip hot vodka. No pretzels this year, and no Rhett. Yet.

I soon forgot the snow when I returned to England, let the memory melt into grey sludge and trickle away down the drain. There were other years in the UK when I felt the similar effects of that childhood snow. It was fleeting. Cars soon returned to the once-blocked roads, and the momentary inconvenience of a bit of bad weather was shoved to the back of everyone's minds.

For us children it was a novelty. I felt sorry for the animals during those harsh winter months, some bound in hibernation burning their body fat like oil lamps. Those winsome dormice tucked up in burrows and even the stinky, robust badgers having a hard time of it. I can feel their pain more than ever now. Each squeak becomes a roar to me. Their cries prick me like sharp needles.

It's the damp I worry about this Christmas. After all the rain this year, we may as well have grown webbed feet and gills, evolved into creatures that swim—amphibi-sapiens. You'd like that, wouldn't you? A new species to tinker with? Mermaids and mermen inhabiting the Somerset Levels. I am tingling, thinking about your hands at work. Do you remember how it all began in January? You were really fired up then. I like to think I still ignite your passion. I do, don't I?

Henry Royston Pepper. How could I not love you with a name like that? My spicy peppercorn. You are my true love, my confidante, my savior and all those clichés we toss about when our hearts get stolen. So here we are at home, alone, on Christmas Day—our favorite day of the whole year.

FEBRUARY

The weather girl, in a tight-fitting blue vest, flourished a bare arm toward the map of the British Isles. I didn't normally watch television in the mornings but I felt grotty so was lounging about after breakfast before you went off to your workshop. Cartoon clouds and perfectly spaced diagonal droplets of rain swept across the screen in regimental fashion as the time fast-forwarded across the bottom to forecast the gloomy day ahead. Most of the weekend would be under a low front—*squally showers and a brisk wind from the west, turning north-westerly. Followed by gales overnight.*

"Gone with the Wind, Miss Scarlett." You winked at me, kissed the top of my head then let the door slam behind you. I flinched; the gales made me jittery. You calling me Miss Scarlett reminded me of Rhett.

My name was a source of ridicule for most of my childhood. The fact that my parents named my twin Rhett made it all the more embarrassing. It was Mother who had latched on to Scarlett O'Hara as the brave, resourceful woman, and Rhett Butler, the rebellious rogue. She thrived on longing, an old-fashioned romantic at heart. She used every opportunity to fuse us together, like those fancy-dress parades she insisted we join or the matching cardigans she knitted for us. I was used to being dressed up like a mannequin. I'm sure you could tell.

My parents were immortalized by the fact that they were dead, and the very few memories I had were kept tightly encased in a part of my mind reserved for family access only. Although you are family to me, you know what I mean, it's never simple, is it? Do we decide where we belong? Or is it decided for us?

The windy weather tied me in knots. One moment a calm lull like an exhalation, then a door slamming hard like a snapped jaw. Relentless, buffeting madness. The dogs felt it; "wind up their arse," you would say as they deftly slinked about the yard, tails up, darting about then crouching down as if they could stalk the invisible currents of air.

You had decided to work all weekend, which suited me. My head was thumping. I was worried about Rhett. We were connected even when apart, a shared ancestry and subconscious connection. No matter how far he travelled geographically we were always close. We were together from the very beginning, do you understand? Perhaps you don't. You never had brothers or sisters.

Even the air pressure seemed to affect me, especially when it rose and fell so frequently, as if I were being squashed between two sheets of metal.

Later in the day, I retreated to have a lie down like a bird taking shelter from the storm. The sound of pellets on a tin roof woke me. It sounded rhythmic though, like someone urgently knocking at the door. If I ignored it, I thought, I could block it out or it would eventually cease. But it *was* knocking. Sharp raps on our front door. Ours was not a house that was en route to anywhere except the marshes and the fields; any visitors had to make a determined effort to find us.

The knocking continued, so I threw on my old, sloppy cardigan over my pajamas, slipped my feet into my boot slippers and ventured downstairs, half hoping whoever it was would have given up and gone to find you in the workshop by the time I opened the door.

"He's dead." Penny stood on the doorstep, arms wrapped about her cashmere coat and the wind fighting against the pins in her hair. Even in her disheveled state she had an air of old-school glamour. I focused on her through a haze of headache. The pulsing returned to my temples. She continued to speak as she pushed her way past me and stepped over the threshold, fingering her windswept mop of blonde hair as if it were candyfloss.

"Henry not at home?" She asked, looking down her nose at my pajama bottoms, which were frayed and torn at the hems.

I caught the door just before it was about to slam again and shut it tight against the wind. Penny was pacing around the kitchen, eyes darting about for an answer to her own question. She didn't want me, she wanted you. I stood my ground waiting for an explanation, feeling my hackles raise as she slid her fingers across the work surface and inspected for dirt.

"Henry's working," I told her.

"Darling, I've not slept a wink."

"What's happened, Penny?"

"I told you—he's dead!"

"Who?"

"He's in the car—I put him in the deep freeze overnight. I hope I've done the right thing."

"The deep freeze?"

"Congenital heart defect," she continued by way of explanation. Her cool, matter-of-fact manner replaced the mock grief offered on the doorstep.

"Really?" I couldn't believe she was talking so freely about putting someone in the deep freeze.

"Yes. None of the others ever had anything like that. They always seemed so fit."

I knew she'd had a few partners in her time—groomed, compliant types—but the way she was speaking disturbed me. I could not imagine how she even lifted his body. Did she cut him up? My head thumped loudly in my ears.

"Kyrano and Virgil are pining," she was babbling now. "I've got to keep their spirits up. We've got three dog shows coming up. Poor little pumpkins. Parker was running around bright as day last week."

Then it all became clear.

"Parker?"

"Yes, darling. Parker, of course. He was my favorite, although we shouldn't really have favorites. He was my prize-winning boy." She sniffed loudly and dabbed at her nose with a lace-edged cotton handkerchief. It had an embroidered letter "P" in red cotton at its corner. Parker? Penny? Pepper?

"Oh," I said, "Parker the Poodle!"

"Of course, dear. He's always been a poodle. Now, where is Henry?" She seemed to snap out of her grief and peered behind me as if I might be concealing you in the room somewhere.

That was the weekend before Valentine's Day. I know this because you said you'd work all that weekend and we'd spend the next together. No work—just us together.

I should've known it was the start of something complicated. Penny had been breeding poodles for years and of course Parker wasn't the first to die. But she'd never had any of them immortalized through taxidermy before. Perhaps what she really wanted was attention, for you to comfort her with your strong arms wrapped around her, but I sure as hell wouldn't disturb your work for her. Just turning up like that in her flashy convertible, wanting you to drop everything for her. It made me livid. Her thin smile was plastered with a shade of lipstick I can only describe as neon tangerine. It matched her nails and that thin line of flesh inside her lower eyelids.

You must have had some kind of forged trust with her, for her to turn up with her beloved prize-winning poodle expecting to jump to the front of the taxidermy queue. What kind of hold did she have over you? Why had I even bothered to get out of bed? You must've heard her arrive too. It was as if you wanted me to answer the door to her. As if you wanted to prove you had nothing to hide from me by letting her barge into our sanctuary unannounced. She never wanted to speak with me normally. That day was no different; I was but a signpost to your whereabouts. I told her where to find you and she scurried out, leaving me to catch the door again before it slammed.

From the window I watched her retrieve Parker from the boot of her car, a not-quite-frozen package, wrapped in what looked like a silk bed sheet. That was when I saw you come up the path from your workshop and walk up to her. She tossed her head back in that way she does when she's flirting, handed you her dead dog and offered you her cheek. It looked like she was passing a child from her arms to yours. Was it instinct or habit that made you linger as you kissed her? You must've known I could see you both whispering to each other as the trees whipped their bare branches above you. I took another two pills and went back to bed.

<hr />

The next week I felt cleansed. The weather had calmed and the sun was shining. Inside, behind glass, I could close my eyes and pretend I was sunbathing on a beach. Outside, the winter still had its grip upon the landscape and the air was crisp and fresh. You took my hand and led me down the path toward your workshop, where you had spent most of the morning. The hedgerow rustled with dead leaves embraced in its skeletal frame, but new life was beginning to shoot through the dark layers of bramble, and a blackbird chattered noisily across the grass. I breathed deeply as if to distil the afternoon breeze into colors that I could draw upon when the darkness descended.

"Don't peek or you'll ruin it," you whispered while guiding me through the doorway. I knew the route even with my eyes shut, but you held my shoulders from behind as if I might stumble, your hands tightly gripping me.

The smell of your domain hit my senses—the usual scent of animal skins, and the sticky resinous glue that lingered like molasses in the air. It was a musky smell, an afterword to real life, which seemed to settle like a well-read elegy on the benches and floor. It was like breathing in fragments of your imagination. You closed the door, so the cool air did not intrude and we were enclosed in your private space.

"Happy Valentine's Day!" you boomed, and I took this as your cue for me to open my eyes.

There before me on your bench I saw the bowed heads of two stuffed swans nudging together in perfect symmetry, like one of those hearts drawn as a doodle—the perfect gift for Valentine's Day. White, serene, austere. I tried to take in what my mind could not comprehend. There were swan heads and necks, but not swan bodies. The heads and necks of two swans rose up from one newly imagined round globe of a body. As my eyes re-focused, I could see that they were not just swans, but swans with fur.

Positioned among the soft feathers of the globe was a small heart-shaped swatch of white fur. I could tell you wanted to experiment with the texture. Swans combined with a poodle—not just any old poodle—you had used part of Lady Penelope's prize-winning pooch! A quick stitch job and a remnant of Parker's coat had been mounted onto what looked like a perfect feathered sphere. Personally, I think you could have used Parker's body, but I understood she was waiting for him to be returned complete. It just looked a little, well, crude, but I never would have told you that then. Something lurched inside me. You had taken something precious from her and given it to me. That was love, wasn't it?

"How did you dream this one up?" I gently ran my fingers over the silky orb-shaped body beneath the swans' curved necks as you stood there, a grin lighting your face as you held it out like a trophy to be awarded. The texture of Parker's fur in a heart shape was ovine; it jarred on my senses, contrasting with the sleekness of the swan's feathers. It was a beast of one color but two origins. The masculine fuzz of fur had been fixed onto the bulbous ball, the size of a football, set against the feminine gloss of swans' necks rising above it. It had no legs. Long-necked and legless, it looked top heavy; a white ball with only the red of the bird's beaks offering an airy kiss to one another.

Valentine's Day offered more than just roses or chocolates or heart-shaped soft toys with cutesy smiles. My true love, you, only you, would surprise me with a *swoodle*. Feathers and fur belong on a catwalk. They say, "Look at me, I'm gorgeous." But white feathers and white fur—really? I was speechless. My card to you and homemade rose chocolate hearts were boring in comparison to this gift. It was safe to say no one had ever given me real swans as a gift before (especially stuffed ones).

"Is it legal?"

"Scarlett—spoil the mood, won't you!"

"Sorry, I just thought swans were—well, you know—protected."

"It's illegal to kill them. But I didn't kill them." You set the swoodle carefully down on your work bench and stood back to admire your creation.

"What, you happened to find two dead ones?"

"They must've flown into the power lines—it happens. I'm fairly sure they didn't suffer. And they are a pair, so just think of them having died together, like Romeo and Juliet."

"Romeo and Juliet did not fly into overhead power cables!"

"Do you like it though? Say you love it, Scarlett." You suddenly grabbed me round my waist and squeezed.

"Thank you, Peppercorn." How could I not love something created by your masterful hands? Yet it unnerved me in close proximity. Two swans combined with a poodle; in life these species would not mix. I could tell the swoodle was uncertain about its place in this world and the feeling was reciprocated. I did not want you to think me ungrateful, so I smothered you with kisses.

I know Lady P expected Parker back in one piece, after all. God knows what she'd think of you if she knew you'd stolen his fur and made it into a love token for me.

I reached toward the swoodle but you leapt forward to grab my hand as if I were an infant reaching for fire.

"Careful, Scarlett. It's a bit unbalanced."

"How do you mean?"

"I haven't decided how to make it free-standing."

I stopped myself from laughing. You would think I was laughing at you. I would never laugh at you. You put so much thought into it and would be affronted if I showed nothing but respect. And, besides, it was all for me.

"I didn't have time to attach the wings." You held one up to show me the expanse, stretching it full breadth as if it could soar to the heavens on its own.

"They're magnificent." I took it, stroking it with the back of my hand, realizing I had never touched a swan's wing before; I had only touched a single feather. The swans were a common sight, and yet they remained elusive and regal in their stark contrast to the peat-packed land where they nested. The feathers were magical, and I had made some into quills, dipped their sharpened shaft into indigo ink and watched the hollow retain the dark liquid. I scratched archaic letters onto a card, made up symbols, and mimicked the movement of the birds with the nib. But even the large feathers were scarce compared to how many swans actually populated the marshes.

"Imagine having wings," I said.

You clasped me about my waist and lifted me effortlessly as if I were a child. You were always sweeping me off my feet one way or another. You set me down. I felt breathless but exhilarated by your strength.

"I must be the only woman alive to own a swoodle!" With my arms looped around your neck, still clinging to the swan's wing as if it were my own, I could feel the warmth of your body, yet I felt a chill run up and down my spine.

You had worked so hard that week and also completed your taxidermy of Parker. He looked so life-like, and the missing fur was negligible. Penny said she'd collect him as soon as you told her he was ready. Until then, he was positioned silently in the corner of your workshop.

<hr />

The shelves were filled with jars of objects, eyes, feathers, driftwood and moss as if you were a witchdoctor ready to dispense cures to the sick. Pebbles and fossils from the beach were dotted around the edge as if the tide had washed up and left them like flotsam. I pulled a mound of wood wool from a bulging sack and inhaled its herbal fragrance. Various shapes of wire were hanging from the ceiling, some shaped like limbs of animals, some shaped like heads. Solid mounts of deer heads positioned facing left and right were stacked up against one wall. You kept your brushes in jars and your tools hung by nails. Piles of newspapers and textbooks of your craft were scattered on the remaining surfaces. Sketches of animals were pinned up haphazardly. Cans of toxic spray with skull and crossbones labels, bottles and plastic tubs were lined up. Nearly all the space was used. I was amazed at how you could create anything from so much chaos.

I caught a glimpse of something behind the clutter on the shelf: a glass jar filled with liquid and something floating inside. Beside it, a label with my name written clearly in your handwriting.

I turned to find you watching me. I smiled at you and held out my hand so you could kiss my palm. A gesture I had come to expect as if I could collect and carry your kisses.

"Will you do something for me, Scarlett?" You licked at the corners of your moustache and took both my hands in yours.

"Anything," I replied without hesitation and as I looked into your eyes and promised, a pact was made with that look. The purest spell of all. Intent combined with sincerity. A little part of me slipped away.

"Will you stay with me—ever after—I mean, will you be my soul mate for all eternity?"

"Are you proposing to me, Mr. Pepper?" You didn't get down on one knee but looked deadly serious. Your vulnerability was intoxicating; it made you seem more animal than human.

"More than a proposal. I'm not talking *til death us do part*. I'm talking eternity—love after death." That was the biggest ask of anyone, but I'd already decided. You didn't even need to ask. Love transcends all. Doesn't it? Even death.

You drew me toward you and planted your mouth upon mine with such force it was suffocating at first. I kissed you back with more passion. Then our breaths grew fast and urgent as you reached beneath my skirt, pushing your fingers inside me while I grappled with the belt on your trousers. I gripped your workshop bench where the swoodle was balanced precariously, its swan's heads rocking together in rhythm with your thrusts as if nodding encouragement to your proposal.

I later found out that swans have a violent mythology. Zeus and Leda. A woman and a swan—how terrific! Something extraordinary and far more erotic than a man and woman. I imagined his feathery wings beating around her fleshy body. All that phantasmagorical weird-ness thrusting into the minds of great artists, encouraging them for millennia to replicate such myths through paintings and sculpture. And taxidermy perhaps?

We seek what is familiar, don't we? But we cannot resist that which is not—the intrigue, the mystery, the sheer horror of the unusual. *The great swan with its terrible look.* Yet we baulk from it, shy away and titter, ridicule and fear it. More often than not, we kill it. Those swans you used, positioned in the shape of a heart, were an omen. And Parker the poodle never asked to be paired with such brutal mythology. He was only Penny's dog, after all, who happened to die at the right time, in the right place. Or the wrong time, in the wrong place.

I thought I heard a hiss and a growl as I left the workshop, or it could have been the door hinge or our dogs grumbling for their dinner. I didn't think much of it at the time because I was so wrapped up in you.

<hr/>

There were few people in this world I would trust with my life, but you were one of them. I'm not saying that in a needy way, more of a statement of truth, for posterity. You had a way of holding the space around me with such delicacy, unabashed and confident. We would never be afraid of silence, being present with one another was conversation enough, a veritable feast flavored by your rough edges and my sharp quirks. Creatures come alive if they are noticed. Is it not love that fuels the spirit? When we name something, we create it, allow it to materialize.

I often wondered if we would have met at another place and time had we not met how we did. It seemed fated, but don't most lovers say it was fate that brought them together? Love at first sight is overrated and condescending; there is no love without connection, and how can you connect to someone so instantly, like a battery clicking into a plastic casement? No matter how much technology we use, plugging up our orifices with wires and noise, data repetitively infiltrating our senses through the jittering pads of our opposable thumbs, tap—tap—tap, the truth is, we have souls.

We met by the edge, you and I. I remember it like this because you always said the sea was the last great unknown, an undiscovered part of our world. That roguish day I was searching for meaning by the shore and you were searching for items that could serve as a backdrop to your taxidermy mounts.

The beach was bleak and littered with spoils from the tide's regurgitated breakfast. A mutated plastic bottle top fused with a shell, a red Connect Four token glaring like a spilled drop of blood on the rocks, and polished blue and green glass sieved clean like jewels among the grit. Twigs and branches were tangled up with seaweed and driftwood on the pale pebbles. The licked stone-smooth texture rolled onto the rocks like alien limbs spewed up from another planet. What is it about driftwood that evokes romance? It was little wonder I was drawn to you—transformer of dead things, creator of curiosities—my beautiful, big-boned taxidermist extraordinaire.

That day could not have been coincidence. Even in my darkest hours, when my faith was seemingly whittled away, I still believed in fate. Was it at this time, when my headaches began to gnaw so frequently, that others' thoughts infiltrated my own? Or was it that I was weakened by the headaches, less able to control the endless chattering noise that seemed to come from being around other restless souls?

You carried a huge tub of fossils as if you were merely carrying an empty cup. Mainly ammonites, those curly whirlpools of delight exhibited Fibonacci's sequence on slabs of slate like an old-fashioned teacher's board. The ambitious patterns seemed to have humility even in extinction, but what do we ever learn? We are absorbed by the past, drowned by sentimentalism, yet somehow we still aspire to timeless values like faith, hope, love. Of course we do, but to prove what? That we are above it all, that we are human, entitled to act like God. As you can tell, I have been mulling this over for some time now. I was intrigued by a mass on the shoreline, so moved closer. We first met looking down at a large creature washed up by the tide. There were smatterings of dark fur over a decaying and deformed animal the size of a small horse; an exposed elongated skull grinned to show oddly shaped teeth.

"What is it?" I asked you.

"Dead," you said.

That is when I looked up and saw you gazing not at the creature, but at my face.

"I'm Henry." You offered your hand and I noticed one shortened finger as I reached to shake it, a hand scarred and strong.

"Scarlett." I smiled.

"Scarlett? That's my favorite name." I felt the warmth from your hand on mine, so when you released your grip, I plunged it into my pocket to retain the heat. You towered over me. The wind had started to thrash the waves onto the pebbles and roll them back and forth like a hypnotic lullaby.

Suddenly, thoughts of my father surfaced like flashes of sunlight on the waves, unreachable and fleeting. He was not a big man like you, but he was tall and made me feel protected. I yearned for that void inside myself to be filled with a man. A solid, vital being surging with life. Protector, fighter, creator. And there you were. I wanted to become something else even then, to be noticed, to be transformed by a higher will. There was an ocean inside both of us, huge and helpless, so was it any wonder we sought solace in one another?

I remember you commenting that it was possible nowadays to find almost anything on a beach. Did you find me? Or did I find you? Or perhaps we both followed some innate homing device? But back then I would never have believed that I could feel a connection that intense to anyone but Rhett.

⁕

I don't know why I didn't tell you at first that my brother was my twin. You never seemed that interested in my family. Rhett and I had an unspoken bond, the kind you find with twins, a connection that excludes anyone else. Like a well-guarded secret we kept from anyone else. Even from you. When we were children, we would roll about together and pretend we were conjoined, wrapping ourselves in a sheet so our bodies were tightly pressed together and breathless. Sometimes I felt a burning inside me to reach Rhett. He was never far from my thoughts.

On Valentine's Day, the day you presented me with the swoodle, I decided that I needed to speak with my brother in person. That was easier said than done, seeing as I didn't know where he was in the world half the time. I tried his mobile but it just kept ringing. There was no answering service. I checked on Facebook, but he'd not posted anything since last July when he was traveling around Spain. I had sent him an email and hoped he would answer it. I even tried some telepathy, the way us twins do, sat in front of the mirror and concentrated really hard, visualized him calling me. But whenever I opened my mind I seemed to tap into some other frequency where spirits seemed to reside. They wanted me to notice them, to contact them, instead of Rhett. The voices emerged as a soft buzzing at first, then a low thrum like the sound you get in theatres, hundreds of people chattering and whispering before the start of a performance. Then the sounds seemed to infiltrate my head, not actual words but background noise. And the only way to get rid of them was to keep my body moving, to get outside and away from all the interference.

I took the dogs out onto the moor. It was cold but bright, and I needed the fresh air. As I moved, the voices and sounds seemed to swarm behind me like angry hornets. I walked faster and faster and nearly broke into a run, a hurried pace between walking and jogging. The wintery wind was making my eyes water. The dogs were ahead of me on the pathway and I knew it would be dark soon.

I stumbled a little on the ground, which was quite ridged and rocky, uneven in patches. Then out of nowhere a buzzard swooped so low I felt its wings brush my head. It made me shriek out in surprise; I'd never heard of a buzzard doing this to a human. Gulls I would expect to take their chances with a human in broad daylight, especially if there was food, but buzzards were wild. They kept apart from man on the periphery of civilization, in fields and woods. Had it simply flown off, I would've thought it was an error of judgment, that it had mistaken my woolly hat for a rabbit or even a newborn lamb. But it did it again, swooping low with talons outstretched in a position of attack. I stooped low and raised my arms above my head to ward it off.

It startled me so much that I wondered if it was trying somehow to communicate with me, to get my attention. With its final brush of feathers against my cheek and outstretched arm I realized in my panic that the voices in my head had stopped abruptly. The animal sounds that were following me had ceased. The dogs came crashing back through the undergrowth, panting hot steam into the darkening February chill, tongues lolling and tails moving at speed. I kept them close by me and we headed back toward home.

When I was nearly back to our house, I saw a field full of swans, too many to count but I estimated well over forty, all sitting or wading across the sodden ground on their wide black feet. Some regally dipped their heads to feed. Others rested with necks curved toward their backs, beaks burrowed in their feathers. I thought of the swoodle and had images of you bearing down on me in your workshop, the swans' heads butting together. What you had said about us being together for eternity made me walk faster to tell you what had just happened. You would have an explanation.

Then my phone rang. I didn't normally answer calls when the number was withheld, but I was yearning for human contact.

"Scarlett?"

"Who's this?" The line was scratchy and sounded distant.

"It's me—Rhett. Listen I haven't got many minutes left. Can you call me straight back on this number if it cuts off?"

"Where are you? I've been trying to contact you for months."

"Is everything ok?"

"Yes, why shouldn't it be?"

"You said you'd been trying to contact me. You're not knocked up, are you?"

"No, Rhett, I'm not. Why are you calling me anyway? I'm walking the dogs."

"Dogs? I didn't know you had any dogs."

"Henry's dogs." Then I realized Rhett had never met you. It had been such a whirlwind romance, and I'd moved in with you soon after we met. He'd gone off traveling long before. And we had not even seen each other at Christmas.

"Did you get my Christmas card? I'm hoping to come back sometime in June." I hadn't received a card, and I'd redirected all my post from the flat where I'd been living before I moved. It was just like Rhett to expect me to sit around waiting for him to return.

"Where are you now?"

"I'm just about to leave Romania. There's a guy I met who has some work for me."

"Work? What kind of work?" But the line went dead. I wasn't even sure what he did to earn money, and something prevented me asking, even though he was my brother. It was probably illegal or immoral. He had never had a problem exploiting others. I was nearly home so I thrust my frozen hands in my pockets and hurried up as I neared the house.

After letting the dogs back in their pen, I kicked off my boots and stripped off my gloves so I could redial Rhett's number and give him my full attention. It rang a few times before a woman answered.

"Rhett?" It clearly wasn't Rhett but I said his name anyway. The sound of a phone being passed from hand to hand scratched at my ear.

"Yeah, I'm here, sis." He sounded a bit breathless this time.

"I didn't know how to contact you. To tell you I'd moved."

"Text me your new address—to this phone."

"Okay, but where are you?"

"I won't be here much longer."

"Who are you with? What's that moaning sound?" A muffled giggle and whispering in the background made me press the phone closer to my ear. "Rhett? Whose phone is this? Who are you with?"

"Just promise me you'll text me your address—soon yeah?" His distraction was even more noticeable. He said something in another language the words muffled as if he were holding the phone against his skin—I couldn't catch what he said and didn't even know what language he was speaking. He could pick up languages without much effort, a gift I did not possess. "Sis, you still there?"

"Who are you talking to? Rhett, what are you doing?"

"You don't want to know—Christ! Got to go, Scarlett. Text me . . ." A louder giggle and some fumbling. Then it cut off with some short beeps. At least I knew he was alive. That was a relief. So that's why I totally forgot to tell you about the buzzard; Rhett had upstaged it and it was him that played on my mind all evening. Whenever Rhett and I got together, we seemed to create some sort of chemical implosion, and his visits were always preceded by a phone call.

"Do you think he was having sex?" I asked you.

"Who?"

"Rhett. Do you think he was having sex while he was on the phone to me?"

"Possibly? How should I know what he was doing?"

"He sounded breathless."

"Maybe he was walking. Briskly." You raised one eyebrow and winked at me.

"He shouldn't talk to me while he's having sex."

"You phoned him—what was he supposed to do?"

"This is my brother you're talking about. My twin brother. Whom you have never met. He just—well—he wouldn't do that to me." Would he?

"Scarlett, my darling. This is the same brother who hasn't contacted you for months. Who disappears without a trace not telling you where he's going or who he's with? And you think he'd have the foresight to pull out before answering the phone?"

I scowled at you. But I knew Rhett. We were close once. Closer than you'd ever imagine. He'd share everything with me. I felt it all unraveling even then but pushed it away as if ignorance were the best strategy. Snatched conversations with him were not enough. I needed something more substantial, time to really open up and talk about our past. Just Rhett and me. Not you and I. But I'd have to wait until June. If he was true to his word.

You lit the fire and I watched the flames lick and spit. Whenever I thought of fire, I thought of Rhett. You know about how he got those scars don't you? A sort of shared reminder of consequences and our lingering past. Perhaps if he'd returned sooner, things would have turned out differently.

"Bitch!" I spat the word into the air as I lay in bed that night. Whoever he was with, I decided to hate her. I had never liked any of his girlfriends. The other voices landed on me as if they had latched onto the venom in my remark, whispers at first, followed by howling and cackling, like the rasping burn of an unreachable itch.

CHRISTMAS DAY / TODAY

Morning

The sun has come up, but it is still dimpsy as we say here on the moor; the night never really gives way to the day at this time of year. We are only just past the shortest day when we begin to beckon the light back, as if we have any say in the matter. The world turns and we turn with it.

I am listening to Christmas music. Carols, of course. Traditional. Once in Royal David's City, Away in a Manger, Hark the Herald Angels Sing, and— the inspiration for many a taxidermist—The Twelve Days of Christmas, featuring no fewer than twenty-three stuffable birds. (Sorry. I know how you hate that misnomer.) "Taxidermy has evolved into an applied science and art that does not involve the process of stuffing," you frequently remind me. I'm a little disappointed that you didn't put the car sticker I bought you on the back of the truck—World's Greatest Stuffer.

You are showering. I hear the water upstairs and think of the water that has crept toward us out here. It has risen up and up, forcing houses to be evacuated as the rivers overflowed and crept up upon fields and farms and homes. We are slightly elevated here on our small mound, our magic island. At least the rain has stopped, but the water has not subsided, saturating the ground to its limit then freezing over. It smells of retribution—leach dank and vengeful.

Everything is grey; the sky, the silhouettes of trees, the water. I am sick of grey now, yearning for the colors of spring again—daffodil-yellow and crocus-violet. The world stands still, but today I push away the darkness and let in the light. This is Christmas Day after all. You will soon light all the candles and we can celebrate properly, invite the color back into our home.

In the early days we used to shower together, letting the water ricochet from our bodies, lathering the gel onto each other's skin, reaching into crevices with our fingers, wanting to claim every inch like conquistadors. You'd hold the loofah between both your hands, and pull me toward you, rolling the rough fibers against my back while kissing me gently on my forehead, cheeks and eyelids as the water cascaded between us. I sank into you then. But today there is dryness between us where familiarity has drained away the immediacy of union. We no longer share those moments of cleansing.

I hear the drains gurgle as you step out onto the bathmat, squeaky fresh and dripping. The cockerel crows outside and a robin lands on the windowsill looking directly at me, his eyes like shining black beads. I watch for a moment. Then he is gone, as if an invisible hand has erased him from a sketch.

The music is on repeat and Bing Crosby starts singing again about his dreams. "Where the tree tops glisten and children listen . . ." It won't snow today; it is too still and cold. Besides, the ground is a lake of ice. We may as well be the lonely cherry on the top of all that grey icing.

". . . just like the ones we used to know . . ." Your voice echoes down the hallway as you appear for the final verse of the song dressed in jeans and a thick fisherman's sweater. You rub your hair with a towel and smile at me and I feel safe. I sense your warmth and know that as long as you are near, I will be complete.

"This is going to be a wonderful Christmas." You kneel beside me and stroke my knee. "I love you so much."

You set about lighting the fire. There is a pile of dry logs against the wall, enough to last for several days if it is kept alight. First you kneel down and clear the ash, place a fire starter and some kindling on top of a few rolled up scraps of newspaper. Then, lighting a match with one strike against the brick fireplace, you hold it there and I watch as the flames appear. Magic. You load more wood and I watch as the flames grow and channel up the flue.

But as the fire takes hold and roars, so too do the stuffed animals in our home. The mammals, wary of fire, try to bolt, but remain stationed in their bodies. I can taste their emotions like charred wood. Then the birds attempt to fly away from the flames. And those creatures more suited to an aqueous environment attempt to hop or crawl from the heat radiating toward them. It is a struggle that tugs and stretches me in all directions. Fire does not unite; it cleanses and absolves. What do they fear? I know. But do you?

All you do is gaze at the fire as you would a painting. And then you gaze at me and all your creations lined up like odd spectators in a Christmas nativity gone wrong.

$\mathscr{M}$ARCH

March became roadkill month. It was a bountiful free supermarket out there if you got up in time and other road users had already done the deed. Badgers, foxes, pheasants, buzzards, rabbits, squirrels—most of the rural wildlife ventured out at night only to be taken clean out by a vehicle. Sometimes the driver didn't even notice they'd killed an animal or bird, oblivious, unless of course they felt the impact or their vehicle was damaged. You told me a stag could total a car; sometimes the stag would right itself, shudder and carry on running, leaving behind the wreckage.

Mornings were not my favorite time of day, but for the sake of art I would rise earlier than usual. Well, for your art I suppose. Raw material is key when practicing an art, you said. Practice makes perfect. It's like cooking. If you have the best raw ingredients, you will produce a tastier dish than if you have inferior ones. The same with taxidermy—the more perfectly preserved the specimen, the more lifelike its representation. And the fresher, the better.

So, 5am at the beginning of March, I was dressed and waiting in the truck. It was one of those frosty, slow mornings so we didn't anticipate many people on the roads. The light was gaining but the darkness still held on with obsidian fingers. I loved the smell of those mornings when we ventured out early, as if the earth were defrosting, giving up its layers of scent one by one. I enjoyed watching the dogs wag their whole back ends with excitement when I took them out in the fields. They couldn't even contain themselves, orgiastic delight spilling from their pink tongues as they panted and foraged with wet noses in the undergrowth.

Our lawn slopes down to the hawthorn hedge then further to the pond where it levels out with the surrounding land. The house was elevated from the surrounding moor, our own personal island. On those March days, we could see the mist delineating where the water once lay before the land was filtered and drained. I half expected a fleet of silent boats to emerge carrying ghost merchants from the Far East, stuck in a time loop, still searching for precious metals in what had once been a valuable trading destination.

Some say Jesus came here once—to Somerset. He sailed with his uncle, Joseph of Arimathea, and visited Glastonbury. The stories appear all over the place like objects placed behind glass cases and labeled in a scrolling font. Just like the glass cases you sometimes used to display your creatures, traditional fishing or countryside scenes where a fox is carrying a pheasant in its mouth. Those images infused this land of apples, Summerland, although it seemed so far from summer during those short, bitter winter days.

The windscreen is scraped clear of the cold white layer and the heater put on full blast to clear the glass. You got your gun in case there were any creatures that needed a final dispatching (this did happen, and I learned quickly that it was kinder to put them out of their misery—you would not hesitate to shoot an injured deer).

The dogs jumped in the back of the truck and we were off, bumping down the drive. "We'll go the back way," you said. Soon we slipped down a side road and headed off toward the flat, narrow lanes of the moor, the truck clattering and the dogs whining with half-contained excitement.

We'd not gone far when I saw it, the dark shadow of a badger lying on its side as if sleeping. It was probably killed only a few hours before, as the bloat hadn't set in. Top of the food chain, not many creatures eat badgers in the wild. They tend to have a tough outer layer too hard for the birds or other mammals to penetrate. I wondered what they tasted like; they had once been eaten in times when food was scarce. They could not have been a first choice. Not even the carrion seemed to have a taste for their tough flesh; some badgers remained intact for days at the side of a road.

One day when traveling to the Dorset coast, I counted fourteen of varying sizes and states of decay. Those badgers followed me all day, dragging behind at a distance in the back of my mind, as if wanting to keep moving toward a death that had already happened. I shook them off when I dived into the sea and let the waves crash over my ears, drowning out their grunts and snuffles. It was my attention that had allowed them to latch onto my thoughts.

"He'll do," you said, and jumped out to retrieve the carcass. It was a big old dog badger with hardly a mark on him. Probably a car had clipped him and he'd died at the side of the road. I noticed that most of them seemed to make it to the side of the road as if one final burst of adrenaline launched them to the verge before their journey to the underworld.

We carried on across the North Drain and I saw a heron rise up out of the mist. It appeared prehistoric, a reincarnated pterodactyl with an angular, thin head and wings, a mechanical wind-up bird that looked as if it didn't belong in this time. I enjoyed the serenity of those birds when I came across them undisturbed at the edge of a rhyne, gazing into the water. They seemed pared back to the bones as they stood on spindly legs, in-between worlds, balanced between the space of reality and legend. With their beaks they pierced the water, yet they remained on land and swept up in slow motion on wide wings as if fighting through something denser than air. I had a lot to learn from herons. Their stoic patience made them looked stuffed even while alive, as if they had already been taxidermied and put among the reeds to outstare the fish.

Later that morning we found a hare with blood up its hind quarters, angled like a sleeping dancer across the road. I felt my heart sink. You killed the engine of the truck and we sat in silence looking through the windscreen. Distinctively larger than a rabbit, these magnificent creatures were a rare sight. To see a hare run wild was to witness a miracle; they flew on land like a witch riding low on her broomstick. The pagan folk used to say they were shape-shifters, the embodiment of magic, their elusiveness giving rise to their mystery. Yet they were difficult to catch sight of, experts at hiding, although the diminished shelter offered in the low fields kept clean by machinery seemed to make them all the more distant, as if they were removed from this world and faded beyond the veil into the Avalonian past.

There is a legend out here on the moor that to see a hare portends a tempest. The hare was symbolic of a grief-stricken woman who had returned to haunt her unfaithful lover. That hare was a message to the both of us and I know you felt it too.

We continued to look through the windscreen of the truck until our breath started to steam the glass and obscure the view. Then simultaneously we both got out and walked toward where the hare lay, and, reverently, we stood before it. Its eyes were open just as they would've been when it was born. Hares, unlike rabbits, are fully furred at birth, you once told me—bright eyed as a hare—glimpsing the world as soon as they entered it. This was an adult Brown Hare, still sporting the grey of its winter coat. These lunar creatures were said to be crazy, moon-struck, exhibiting wild displays at night-time that gave rise to the legend of the mad march hare.

"Will you use it?" I broke the silence first.

"I have to," was all you replied, and crouched down to lift the limp body. You carried it in both your hands as if carrying a tiny sleeping infant. We went home after that. Neither of us uttered a word. Even the dogs had quieted down by then. I felt glad you would resurrect it, even knowing it would never live as it had, racing wild across the fields at dusk.

When we returned and drove up the driveway, I could hear the ducks noisily initiating pairings, ready for spring. Their busy bodies were upturned in the pond, ripples radiating outwards like an old LP. The sun felt hot and sharp behind the glass of the truck window, but I knew it was still chilly.

March was on the cusp of change, plants tentatively poking through hardened winter soil, sap rising and buds bulging with promise. The birds knew the score. They were a barometric signifier, tuned to the slightest dip or rise in air pressure. They knew when to gather in and take shelter from impending storms.

The rooks reached a crescendo of white noise from the trees, then subsided into background nasal tones with an uneven tempo. And the sun emerged from behind a hook-shaped cloud. Stillness, but not silence. Even in the space between the rooks cawing, the trees still spoke in watery hushed tones and the earth pulsed beneath us. I wanted you more than ever then. I wanted each cell of yours to merge with mine. I wanted us to create something together through passionate union. My body ached for you even when you were inside me. The more you wanted me, the more I succumbed. *My darling Pepper, you know how I will always ache for you. I remember our Valentine's Day pact. Will you honor it, too?*

◆——◇——◆

March was about the time I dispensed with cutlery and ate with my bare hands. Even the messy, intractable foodstuffs like fiddly peas and beans. I ripped steak between my incisors then chewed meditatively, the juices still running down my palms until I licked them clean. I even scooped up cream with my fingers. Yes, it was disgusting! How could it not be? But strangely it excited me as you watched me ingest with such relish the things you had prepared for our dinner, such primal delight. You'd make these small grunts too, almost imperceptible as if emerging from beneath your beard. Then when you finished your meal, satiated, you'd sigh and wipe your mouth on a napkin like some Lord of the Manor and toss it onto the table. I, on the other hand, would suck each one of my fingers clean as if taunting you to taste me.

"Is this some kind of protest toward cutlery?" you asked.

But I couldn't explain it to you then. It was as if I needed to literally get my hands dirty. You must've understood this; you were always burrowing yours into the afterlives of animals.

Since I had been living with you, I had less and less compassion for the human race, preferring the complexities of our animal neighbors. You were my one exception. Although at times you behaved like the animals you were working with: a wily old fox, a watchful egret. I could measure the colors of your mood by your responses—morning orange or midnight blue. I read once that most of human communication is nonverbal and wondered why we bothered to speak at all. Most of the time when I turned on the radio, I turned it off again almost immediately.

You were in the kitchen searching for something but would not let me help you. So you continued to open cupboards, at first just tentatively fingering jars and tins aside, but then removing some larger objects and shoving them blindly up onto the worktop: a glass bowl, a metal grater, an electric whisk. Then the drawers were pried open like a dentist would stretch a patient's jaw to its limits, reaching to the very back to discover if decay had set in. You pushed your hand to the back of the drawer, a thick, hairy arm with your rucked-up sleeve straining at the lip of the counter. I heard the utensils swish like stones in a basket under your probing digits. You were like one of the badgers that ransacked our garden foraging for food, trampling the plants and knocking over anything that stood in its path.

"Can I help you, Mr. Pepper? What are you looking for?" I posed the questions as a test of your mood, a gauge for the start of a guessing game. Another device of mine to incite you. But I wasn't even sure you were listening. The furrows on your forehead were stationed like sand on a beach at low-tide, rigid and shadowed, waiting for the next wash of lunar movements to push them flat and malleable again.

You knelt on the floor, looking into the corner cupboard, the one whose door opened like a pop-out greeting card, a false hinge concealing more space behind. More space to fill with needless things. I don't even remember buying most of my belongings; they seemed to collect over time but I'd left nearly all of them at my flat when I moved in with you, as if shedding my old life like a skin. I even forgot the sketches I had drawn and framed, and all my old photographs.

I stood behind you, watching. You looked heavy on your hands and knees, like a piece of ancient stone planted firm on the earth. Your head was halfway in the cupboard, inquisitively searching in an unknown territory, when you reached forward with one arm and retrieved something. I could not see immediately, but without retracting your head, you slid it back past your kneeling body and placed it behind you—a colander. The one we would use to strain elderflower and blackberries later in the year. We had not made elderflower cordial together, but you promised me that when it bloomed in May or June, we would pick it together and make our own. The colander trailed a neglectful thread of an old cobweb; a relic of your life before I moved in with you, shoved to the back of a cupboard. Where do all these things come from? I continued watching you search for whatever it was you wanted. Then as if all the effort was worth it, you casually pulled a pack of brown luggage labels from the cupboard, stood up awkwardly and left me to tidy the mess you had left behind.

Your moods could test me to the limit. It was the silence within you that viciously penetrated me. I endured those lingering days when you pretended I did not exist, not responding to my voice or moving away when I tried to touch you. You turned me into a ghost. Each time I heard the door close and your footsteps recede to your workshop, you took a thread within me and uncoiled it. When I tempted you with my warm body on yours, you would lie motionless like a cold corpse until I sighed and moved off you. It was only when I was close to breaking that you'd switch back to being my sweet love, an ember within you flaring to give back to me the warmth I had expended.

◆―◇―◆

You had lived in this house with a whole host of other women whom I tried not to think about. I imagined their footsteps echoing on the slate tiles and the house filling up with more and more belongings. Where there is space, it will be filled. I had filled that space, hadn't I? You reassured me it was my home as well as yours.

I could see that neither you, nor previous residents, enjoyed gardening; the weeds had spread like wild fire. Even after I started clearing them, I swear they waited until I turned my back and spurted like triffids from the cracks, as if playing a childhood game.

Tendrils pushed up through the paving slabs and along the stone wall. Ivy twined its flat, shiny hearts across any surface it could find. I ripped at its suckered ropes held fast like a captain's oath, great ribbons of emerald green suffocating the tree trunks as if the ground had birthed a monster with ravenous veins. A climbing ladder like Jack's beanstalk would burst to the sky-giants if I didn't stop it, and once I started ripping and clearing the neverending tangle of weeds, it became a meditative obsession that I could not contain; I needed to strip back to the bare bones of the garden.

Bindweed, goose grass, nettle, all rampant and verdant, fought back spitefully, sticking thorns in my fingers as I tried to wrench the stubborn roots. When I paused, I saw the futility of my efforts. No matter how much I tore at it, it would renew and re-grow. I may as well have been a mere lone insect in this vast jungle. So I retreated, cutting the lawn up to the edges and leaving the wildness to dip down to the rhynes and woodland and fields that surrounded our home.

"*Land—it's the only thing that lasts, Miss Scarlett!*" you faked a mock Irish accent like Scarlett O'Hara's father and waved a branch at me. But was it? What if we could last forever too, you and I? What if we could stave off the ravages of time to become our own legends? That was when I began feeling sick in the mornings and my belly felt rock hard. I thought of what Rhett had said on the phone. *Knocked up.* Just like him to be so crass and so correct at the same time.

I didn't normally disturb you in your workshop, but I couldn't wait until the evening. You were stretching the skin of a zebra over a head mount, its black and white markings looked out of place without its eyes, but I could tell what it was from its thin layer of short, coarse hair and the color of its markings. You looked up and smiled. The smell met me more strongly than usual in your workshop with the doors shut, but I swallowed and tried to hold my breath.

"I couldn't wait to tell you . . ." I beamed at you with a smile probably too wide for my true feelings.

"Scarlett. Just a moment." You finished positioning the hide, then turned and faced me.

"I've done three tests already this morning." I waved the last of the pregnancy wands at you, its blue line stating the result in more than words.

"Tests?—Oh! Scarlett. Come here . . ." You looked around for a cloth and not finding one, wiped your sticky hands on your apron and held out your arms to me. I fell into them and cried, unable to hold it in any longer.

"You are happy, aren't you?" I wanted you to be happy so that perhaps I could ride on your bliss.

"Of course, of course." You were smiling but I saw a flicker of doubt in your jaw. Was it because you felt you were too old to be a father? Or that you doubted us being parents so early in our relationship? My tears continued hot and wet even as you wiped them away. I cannot tell you if I felt happiness or fear. The bond between us was thickening.

Memories of my parents are hazy. Rhett and I were only ten when they died, and there was no one else to fill in the gaps of family history after they were gone. There was a time when I saw my mother's face almost everywhere. Clouds formed into the shape of her eyes or the soft curve of her neck; her face would look down on me from the sky before dissipating into cloud again. The back of her head materialized as I followed strangers through crowded streets, making me rush and push so as not to lose sight of her, in case it really was her, miraculously reanimated. Reflections from glass bottles and windows, even puddles, mimicked her smile. I'd even catch my own reflection and think it was her looking back for a split second.

And for all the visitations I used to get from other dead things, my mother never, ever returned. Not even in my dreams. I liked to think this was because she was happy and had no need to revisit, but I also wondered in my darker hours if it was because she had never been good at goodbyes and simply chose not to look back.

The last day I saw her was not exceptional. We'd not planned any great event; it was a weekend and my father was due home after working away. With just Rhett and me to entertain, Mother had left the washing on the line, given us both a talking to because we'd left chewing-gum on the windowsill and it had become a stringy, sticky mess that the cat had trodden in and stretched from his paw to the carpet. Then to make matters worse, Rhett decided to iron the carpet, as if to remove a stain. This was a ten-year-old boy's understanding of domestic science. Not wanting to get into more trouble, we tried to clean it up ourselves. The burning chewing-gum smelled sweet yet acrid as it was sizzling and spreading out on the plate of the hot iron.

"It's part of the process," Rhett had said, laying on the carpet and peering at the bottom of the iron. "It will melt then evaporate." I watched him with a sinking feeling in my stomach, knowing he was blagging, but half hoping he might be right.

It not only wrecked the carpet and the iron but the curtains as well. We were not popular even when we explained that we had both tried our best to clean it up.

Butch, that's what our cat was called. He was long-haired and grey with the squashed, disgruntled face of a reincarnated mafia boss. He was not too impressed by the chewing gum episode either; we had to shave a chunk of his fur off his leg, which left a bald patch.

We didn't really expect any treats that day, seeing as our parents needed a new iron, a new carpet and new curtains. But my father was home after working away for several weeks and Mother wanted to make the most of it, as a family.

"Let's enjoy family time," he said amicably when Mother explained what had happened. He was due to fly out to the Middle East after the weekend so she wanted us to have our family picnic together, and afterwards Rhett and I would go stay over at a friend's house.

Mother had made egg sandwiches and they stank. Rhett called them fartwiches and scrunched his face. We had all sorts of party food in Tupperware: crisps, sausage rolls, pork pies, scotch eggs, tomatoes and celery, those chocolate teacakes with the marshmallow on the top. It was the only food she was really good at. In fact, it was no different than our normal meals at home, only this was outside, all laid out on the picnic rug at the edge of a wood, near a stream.

After we'd eaten, Rhett had gone off to explore down the shallow stream with an empty plastic pot and a spoon to catch tadpoles or minnows or some unsuspecting creature minding its own business. Mother and Father sat together side by side, legs outstretched, his arm protectively at her back. We looked like a normal family.

I was looking up at the trees, wondering why the sparrows used so much energy hopping when they could just walk, when out from the edge of the woods a wolf came loping toward us. I screamed and leapt up from the blanket with visions of Little Red Riding Hood being tricked and eaten, just like her grandmother. The wolf headed straight for me, and I saw my father scramble to his feet shouting, "Scarlett," and Mother retreating on her hands and knees, although I couldn't see her as I was running really fast. Or so I thought.

The wolf sank its teeth into my leg. It pulled me backwards and pushed me down at the same time. I was waving my arms and still screaming when my father whacked it on its jaw with the bat we'd used to play cricket earlier. I heard it crack as the bat came into contact with the wolf's massive head. The wolf just slumped down on my leg as I lay screaming. I blacked out but then felt its cruel, hot weight on me so couldn't have fainted for long.

When I woke, a fat man was stumbling toward us and Father was pulling me out from underneath the limp creature, his hands hooked under my arms. I glimpsed nervously toward the wolf, which lay heavy on the grass as if it had just decided to go to sleep. Only it wasn't an actual wolf but one of those dogs that looked like a wolf, a Siberian husky or a Tamaskan? My eyes drank in its now-docile expression, tongue protruding from its bloody muzzle.

"Sorry—sorry." The fat man was breathless as he came toward the grizzly scene. "He slipped his collar."

Father looked up at him and down at the unconscious dog.

"Bruno—Bruno boy?" the man wheezed as he knelt down by his dog, the dog's lead swinging round his neck like a stethoscope. "What happened?"

I had buried my head into my mother's jumper but quickly looked down at my leg to see I had only been scratched by the dog's paw as he had jumped at my back. There were no bite marks as I had imagined. There wasn't even any blood, just a long pink scratch.

"What happened?" the man kept asking the question and wheezed as he moved his weight from one knee to another. He was holding the dog's head in his lap, the blood seeped from the side of its jaw discoloring its teeth. The man lifted the dog's eyelids like you would an unconscious patient. "What have you done?" He looked up at my father, then toward the cricket bat that now lay conspicuously on the grass, then back up at my father. So many emotions flickered across that man's chubby face that I began to feel confused. His eyes seemed to flicker about like midges over a stagnant pond.

"You shouldn't let a dangerous animal off its lead." Father moved me and Mother away from the man and his dog.

"Bruno's not dangerous—what h-have you done? You've hit him, h-haven't you? With that bat?" The man waved his hand to the pale wood slightly smeared with red.

"He attacked my daughter." Father sounded calm, so I hid behind him looking down at the dog; my heart was racing. I was responsible for the death of an innocent creature. It made me feel sick and excited all at once.

"You've f-fucking killed my dog!" I'd never heard that swear word before and it was the word that made me jump, not the volume of the man's voice. He said it with such vehemence I actually felt it penetrate me. And I thought he was going to punch my father but he just puffed and stooped and struggled to lift Bruno over his shoulder. Then he carried him off in the direction he had come. And then he was gone.

"Is the dog really dead?" I asked my mother forgetting the sore scratch on my leg.

"No, I think he's just concussed."

"What's concussed?"

"He'll be fine."

"So he's not dead?"

"Scarlett." My father turned to me. "Enough!"

I sat down on the blanket and twisted my leg to look at the scratch on my calf. Mother held me in her arms, and I could not stop the tears. Not because my leg stung and pulsed at the same time, but for Bruno the wolf-dog. I knew he was dead. My father had murdered him with Rhett's cricket bat.

As we drove home, Mother and Father were talking in hushed tones. I tried to catch what they were saying, but Rhett was being loud and boisterous, indignant that he had missed the whole drama while he'd foraged in the woods and splashed in the stream.

"There aren't any wolves here anymore, stupid," he said to me, holding his helicopter toy and swooping it about in front of him, bashing it into Father's headrest and making crashing noises.

"It looked like a wolf to me," I told him.

"No bears either—we've killed them all off."

"It attacked me," I said, reinforcing my father's flaky story.

"Can't believe I missed it. Did Dad whack it like he was playing cricket?"

"That's enough, Rhett." Mother stuck her hand back between the car seats to squeeze Rhett's leg.

"Dad killed a dog," Rhett taunted me, "and it's all your fault."

⬥

We celebrated the night of the three pregnancy tests with a bottle of homemade wine. A small glass won't hurt, you'd said, and we curled up by the fire.

"What shall we call her?"

"How do you know it's a "her"?" I said.

"Him then? What shall we call him?"

"Do you think it's too early to talk names?" I felt superstitious. Not wanting to plan anything. This wasn't planned.

"We could call her Halo if she's born on October 31st?"

"What? As in Halloween?" I screwed up my nose at you. "God, imagine all four of us having the same birthday."

"Four?"

"You, me, Rhett and *it*, of course."

"Oh, I forget you're a twin sometimes. So how about Halo?"

"Isn't that a Beyoncé song?"

You laughed and said, "I've no idea!" and slurped your wine as I readjusted to get comfortable on the sofa. "How about Bruno?"

As you said the name, I felt a jolt of pain through my abdomen and flinched.

"Scarlett—what's wrong?"

I sat up and breathed deeply to ease the pain. "Nothing, just sat awkwardly."

"Was it something I said?"

"No, it's fine," I lied.

Visions of my father pulling me out from under the dead dog danced before my eyes.

"I'm going for a lie down."

<hr/>

I woke in a hot sweat later that night with my nightdress all screwed up behind my back. You were snoring. As I pulled it back down over my body, the sheet felt sticky and cooler somehow. There was a slipperiness between my legs, and when I reached down I felt the warm wet. It was dark in our room, so I held my fingers up to my face and sniffed but I already knew that this was blood, lots of it, from my own body. I swung my feet round onto the floor and paced to the bathroom, flicking on the light to reveal a bright red patch all over the white cotton of my nightdress. Scarlett, I thought, just like my name.

I froze, looking down, not sure what to do. It was on my hands and smudged on my arms, between my thighs, down my legs. Should I pee first? Or wake you? Did I need to go to hospital?

I felt sick and woozy but there was no significant pain, just a dull ache like the start of a period. I knew what had happened and, for a moment, a surge of relief kicked in. I turned the shower on and stepped into the bath tub watching the blood wash away down the plughole, and then I saw it. As I sat underneath the shower stream with the water rushing over my head and down my body, I watched the clots of blood slide down the tub toward the plug hole where they rested being cleansed by the currents.

I shuffled forward to clear the plughole with my forefinger. And there was what looked like a tiny amphibious creature with head and knobbly limbs curled up, as if resting. It stuck to my finger, not wanting to be washed away. I wanted to show you so I placed it carefully on the edge of the bath tub and turned off the shower. All the while, as I dried my skin and wrapped myself up in a dressing gown and put on clean underwear, I came back to look at the edge of the bathtub feeling numb. That's when you came in.

"I want to keep him," I said. You understood what had happened and nodded.

You didn't speak but looked at the tiny creature on the edge of the bathtub. You knew what to do. You could preserve animals, so why not our own flesh and blood? He could just as easily have been washed away down the plughole or in the toilet. But I caught him and kept him here. With us. You understood my need, didn't you? He was made from the both of us.

CHRISTMAS DAY / TODAY

Mid-morning

We are lost songs in the morning mist.

I can hear them fighting one another. The crow is cack-cacking at the rabbit. Trapped inside one body, stitched together for eternity, these creatures fight with all their might for freedom. Survival of the fittest. Indignant crow, grounded by the rabbit's mammalian traits, his wings replaced with what? A furry back and paws. He tries to launch into the air but finds he only flops forward on all fours. Mopsy, flopsy, cotton-tailed humiliation.

Crow, once harbinger of death, carrier of souls, now a lowly half-breed, emasculated into a doe rabbit's body—at least he still has his head. I feel frustration spike from him in sharp jabs; he does not know who he is. How is he defined now his wings have been stitched to another species? And what of poor rabbit, demoted to a headless ball of fluff doctored with a beak and wings? The crow's head watches, but the rabbit is blinded by decapitation—she can only sense with her body, a tail still twitching, a paw lifting tentatively to taste the air without a tongue.

They are agitated. Something is coming, they say. Listen. The waves are breaking in the distance. The ice is being cut.

April

I noticed the first butterfly appearing like a small flake of fire over the hedge. It always lifted my spirits to see one, especially the first one of spring, an awakening, a transformation occurring before my eyes. This was a Red Admiral, living up to its name, commanding attention. I stopped and followed its jagged flight across the garden and out of sight, and as I stood marveling at the warm sunshine on my face another signifier of spring cut an arc across the sky—two diving swallows.

April—yet some bare trees still silhouetted the skyline behind the freshness of new growth. I tentatively exposed my skin as the sun strengthened. I wondered at the way the color green lifted my mood. On those spring days it was as if the earth started sighing again in content-ment. I breathed in deeply.

There is a certain faith in the cycles of life, and you had instilled that kind of faith in me. Natural cycles and patterns swam between us, defined us.

"How does it hurt you?" you asked as I curled up in a ball on the sofa that time of the month, cradling my belly.

"It feels like my insides are being tied into knots," I answered, grateful that you were not flippant, but curious and tender. "Then the ache spreads through me. It's better when the flow starts."

"Like a release?"

"Yes, a release and a mourning too."

Then you rubbed the small of my back while perched on the arm of the sofa, your touch sending messages to my core. In those moments of intimacy we were so in tune like the rhythms of nature. We were destined to mutate into something else. Only we didn't know it then, when the buds were protruding like sweet tight cotyledons.

You watched the wilderness creep up on our home as you watched all things, letting it absorb your identity with a quiet playfulness. I think that was how you recreated those specimens with such accuracy. You observed and absorbed. Then, as if by magic, they became something new while their essence remained. It was more than sculpture; they looked as if they could come back to life at any moment, launch into action and scamper or leap or launch into flight.

"The fox does not run like the badger," you said. I assumed at the time you meant this literally, but there was always another layer of meaning brushing amongst your words. "It scurries, stops, sniffs, darts. Whereas the badger lopes, slinks and sways." Did you mean that no matter how we were changed, we never could escape ourselves?

"You need to show its true character," you said. "It's no good placing a fallow on a mount with his ears up, looking about. He should look dopey, like a clown."

"But I've seen a deer look alert . . ."

"Yes, sika deer—now there's a different character. On that type I would position the mount with its head looking up."

You saw beauty in all those creatures who revealed their essence to you. With careful study you would resurrect them as they were in life.

Did you know then that you could stitch parts of their soul back to their spent body? Some days I wished I could have a new body. I felt so fragile at certain times of the month, bruised and tender.

I remember watching three feral pigeons on our broken fence like musical notes on a staff, each staccato head a restless note. A whisper of breeze lifted their feathers and their silent crisp movement softened. Two faced inwards, one away—a dance of mimicry. This was a ménage-a-trois staged grey on brown, intuitive, magnetic, heads facing east then west. They looked oversized, filled with seed, and I envied them. I was jealous of the common feral pigeon. Why? They belonged. They were so completely in the moment like all the other creatures, they merely seemed to react on instinct.

Dandelions and grasses, sycamore and clover, seeded and planted themselves everywhere. In April the growth accelerated as if launching a stealthy attack of foliage on our garden. Did you want it to consume you? Or were you too absorbed in your work to even notice?

Tidiness and completion, in-its-place-ness, all corresponded with my internal landscape, the molding of my new home. After the miscarriage I needed to make our surroundings more like our home. First, the clearing by hand of the blocked, stagnant pond at the side of the house. Then removal and disposal of other detritus, after the felling of split willows and shrubs grown woody and gnarled. We burned up the debris, letting the smoke anoint us like incense. After the flames had died down and a smoldering pile of ash remained, I witnessed the light enter the front windows of the house like a long-lost friend; there was space again, as if in that clearing we had also made way for our own new growth. The moldings of our new life together began.

One morning I woke to find the windows of our home coated with the fine particles of another continent, as if a golden ghost had walked around and brushed against them. As I rested in bed, I looked out and imagined a sandstorm in the Arabian Desert traveling like a magic carpet across the ocean, raining gold dust as it reached land. I blinked, thinking something was in my eyes, until I realized it was not my eyesight but a filmy layer coating almost everything. The outer world had shifted, a subtle but marked change like the blurring of edges, not worth commenting on at the time. I heard about the sandstorm on the news, but it was passed over as if unremarkable compared to celebrity gossip. To me, it was a miracle. Dust had traveled for thousands of miles, and it was ignored like the passing clouds of moisture above us. Did we ignore the subtle erosions of our partnership? Would honesty have saved us?

You saw the miracle in life, didn't you? You would still marvel at the sheer beauty presented at our feet as if you were the ruler of a magical kingdom. An unfurling crest of bracken. The silent flight of a barn owl. The murmuration of starlings at dusk. The rawness of bark where a deer had rubbed its velvet antlers. All your observations were worth more to me than your physical presence. And in your work, you tried to preserve some of it, uncompromising and self-effacing. A cruel master to your art, you craved perfection in a world of beautiful imperfection. Yet, all the while, I witnessed your obsession, as if mimicking Orpheus descending to the underworld, and I did nothing but encourage you. You couldn't help but look back at me. Perhaps I was past saving, even then.

Do you remember how you taught me to mimic a deer when we first met? You said I was lucky, as you could only attract a doe with mimicry in the short window of a few weeks. You held the edge of a beech leaf between your forefinger and thumb and blew a short *pheep*—once, twice. Then we waited. I started to fidget, but you placed your hand on my arm with a look that told me to be patient. Then, emerging from the thicket, a doe. Her nose twitched; her head tilted from side to side, testing the vibrations. In that moment I felt her heart as if it were my own; I tasted her fear. I was amazed how a cautious creature like that could be lured so subtly by your simple tricks. No buck followed, so you did not shoot. Was there peace in your eyes as you watched it leap back into the undergrowth?

You held power in those moments. I wondered if you felt anything, wondered what it was like to take a life. Was the impact instantaneous as the shot pierced the hide, or did it affect you later as you washed the day from your skin? Perhaps that was why it was important for you to ingest the deer. That time I went stalking with you, I understood your relationship to your work. You did not use your bare hands like a savage to kill the deer; you were removed like a god from the physical act of death. Although I have no doubt you were prepared to use your hands if you needed to. Yet when you killed a deer you showed respect and reverence. I understood the need to cull a creature that swelled in numbers. They were damaging to the environment when no other predator hunted them. This insight could not deaden the spike of sadness each time you dispatched one and brought it home in the back of your truck, limp and lifeless as a wilted plant.

As I watched, I had not even considered the striking similarities between myself and those deer. But now I see it. You lured me with a silent, powerful instinct. The pain of not keeping your child within me hit me and I wept, not for our loss, but for my failure. It crept up like indigestion from the pit of my stomach to my throat, and once the tears started, I just couldn't stop crying.

I sought out natural water to cleanse myself, the barrierless rhynes that marked the division of worlds, each side looking to the other, above and below the waterline. There, the marsh marigold adorned the intimate passing place between water and earth. Arrowhead pushed to the light from its liquid foundation. I sat on the edge of the rhyne, soaking the hem of my dress with the fields' juices, and let my bare feet slide slowly down the soft margin where the bank meets the waterline. It was here, in this liminal space, that I felt freedom. The world seemed unfinished, like your experimental creatures. Frogbit and duckweed pretended to offer support with dense green blankets coating the surface of the water, yet the rhyne was deep. I felt the cold water deaden the sensation in my skin as my ankles were enveloped. Then came the point of no return as my calves, then knees, sank deeper below the water. I slid down, hoping my feet would reach the peaty bottom of the rhyne, but I kept sinking. Beneath me lay the silt-laden layer of nutrient-rich liquid that would spill up and over onto the land like the dark, deliberate pouring of gravy on a pie.

My waist reached the water level and deliciously caressed my groin, heavily sticking the fabric of my clothes to my legs. I kept sinking and slipping as my feet tried to find some footing below. Something wide and ribbon-like touched my leg but I raised my arms above the surface so I was half-floating, half-treading water. The willow trunks on the far side had grown tall and lean, split down vertically like flipped up diver's legs. I dunked the upper half of my body beneath the waterline, once, twice, then completely submerged my head for only a few seconds before emerging, plastered in duckweed and dead reeds.

Shivers took hold of me even with the sun directly on the exposed parts of my body. I tried to swim, but my clothes were hindering me. Pulling my dress up and over my head, I was nearly naked in the water. I rolled it into a sodden ball and threw it toward the bank, where it landed with a liquid kiss. Even though the water was cold and dark I found solace there among the sedges. Then it began to rain, and all became water. I was born again, baptized.

◦─◦─◦

I knew my tears would soon dry up because I had you, the love of my life. And even though I had no idea we would get married so quickly, I am happy we did. It was another bond forged between us. We are both impulsive, I know. Yet this memory still remains one of the most vivid days of my life. I only wish Rhett had been there to give me away. I know you thought him selfish but, really, he is a simple soul; he is not in the slightest bit interested in others' pleasures unless they directly involve him.

It was so easy, just the two of us. No guest list to worry about, effortless. All we did was book the register office and ask a passer-by to be a witness. A bit like a lucky dip, selecting a stranger from the crowd who hesitantly signed her name as if signing a death warrant. Do you think she dined out on our story or let us drip from her memory like blood off a knife?

I wasn't going to miss dressing up though, even if we were the only participants at our wedding. I had never fantasized about my wedding day like some girls seemed to do, planning every detail even before they'd met their potential spouse. But I loved to have the excuse to spruce up. The frills and lace of my mother's wedding dress were perfect, if a bit dated. The flowers I had picked from the garden—red and white roses with ivy trailing like an emerald ribbon—were gorgeous. I couldn't stop touching you in your tweeds; you looked so smart.

"Do you, Henry Royston Pepper, take this woman to be your lawful wedded wife?"

I can still hear her lisp as she said your name. But I became Mrs. Scarlett Pepper—sounds like something sprinkled on your steak to hot it up. Sssscarlet Pepper.

You chose a Bob Dylan song and it still rings in my ears—*I want you.* How I wanted you then—*So bad.* You held me close, and we walked in step toward the truck to go to our honeymoon destination.

It wasn't far from home, but for one night we pretended we were miles away. It might as well have been anywhere, as we hardly left the room apart from a short walk about the grounds of the house. It was a medieval house hotel, something private and decadent. The peacocks strutted about looking for mates and let out high-pitched shrieks that seemed to reverberate through the thick stone walls. I think the receptionist was a bit shocked when we turned up, as if she had overlooked a wedding reception taking place. But you laughed and reassured her.

"Don't worry dear," you said, "we're only passing through."

"Are there any other guests in your party?"

"No."

"Would you like to book a reservation for dinner this evening?"

"I think we'll have it in our room." You looked at me. I know you were thinking of me eating with my hands in front of other diners; it would have raised quite a few eyebrows.

The receptionist looked at the both of us, probably wondering how we could make such an unlikely pairing. What did she see? A young woman and a man twice her age, a typical father/daughter scene. However, we were clearly bride and groom. Age didn't seem too much of a taboo, but I remember once I was mistaken for your daughter. Did that make you feel old? Perhaps it was because I looked so young for my age, so the gap seemed to widen in the eyes of those who inquisitively judged us.

You kissed me on my neck, lingering, while still facing the reception desk. The poor girl looked down, an uncomfortable rash of red spreading up her neck. How were you able to cast such spells, so quickly? Was it something about your aura pushing forwards and enveloping everything in intoxicating smoke?

The girl gave a nervous cough as she passed us the key, then blushed even more as you winked at her.

"The peacocks are very loud," you growled at her.

"I'm so sorry, sir," she blushed again.

I pulled you away and we ascended the stairs, side by side, arm in arm.

Once in the room you took no time to set about consummating our marriage.

"Keep your dress on," you grunted as I sat on the edge of the four poster and kicked up my legs so you could glimpse under my dress. You unclasped your belt and slipped off your jacket, then popped the buttons one by one on your waistcoat so it hung open.

I leaned back and kicked off my shoes. You faced me, loosened your belt and whipped it off with one movement. I could see you bulging to release from your trousers so I lay back. The bed was harder than I anticipated, and the room was dark. Dark wood, dark burgundy brocade curtains that hung tied back from the bed, dark walls and dark polished wooden floor.

You stalked toward me with the front of your trousers unzipped, your shirt tails loose. I felt like prey you were about to play with. My blood quickened.

"Well, Mrs. Pepper—what do you propose we do about this situation in which we find ourselves?"

I had reapplied the reddest lip gloss so it shined pornographically. You reached beneath the hem of my wedding dress and stroked your hand up my leg to my inner thigh. I parted my legs, and we were surrounded by a furrowing balloon of lace and silk, layers of petticoat billowing like a cloud between your body and mine. Yet, beneath, the heat was rising as you felt round my suspenders, hooked your fingers around my silk underwear and stripped it all down my legs with the same care you took in your work. I fidgeted on my back and slid further up the bed, and you disappeared in a flourish under the layers of my dress. I gazed up at the ceiling of the four-poster bed, ornate carved figurines of angels and naked women entwined with fruit between their breasts and thighs. You were waiting, not touching me, so I edged my body closer to your face.

Then came the sweet, wet pleasure of your tongue dancing as you swept your lips over me. I could feel your beard grazing and tickling my thighs and tried to imagine each expression playing across your features. I wanted to tell you how it felt, to try to put it into words but the words didn't matter anymore. I could not define how you made me feel.

From beneath the covers of my dress, you emerged and pressed your body into mine. We found each other instantly, pushing deep and rhythmic as my body convulsed in waves.

You grabbed my waist, lifting me up onto you, me still inside you. I pushed my weight down as the material of our clothes concealed our bodies.

"Oh, Mrs. Pepper—you are so hungry today."

I wanted you to lose yourself, to be so removed you could not speak, so thrusted faster and deeper with my pelvis, contracting my muscles to suffocate you and suck you inside.

"Fill yourself my darling. Fill yourself up." You kept taunting me as if I were the needy one. None of my movements seemed to make you speechless.

"Just fuck me harder, Rhett!"

I don't know where the words came from but you looked startled, then the shock turned to brute force. You pushed me roughly against the hard mattress, turned me round so I was facing down on the bed. You fumbled with my dress, pushing it up and over my backside, and crushed against me, your thick cock pushed hard inside. In and in and in, your hand hard against my back crushing the air out of me.

"I'll fuck you if you want—is this what you want?" You drilled me harder and harder, panting and grunting. I couldn't speak. I couldn't move.

"Please—" I tried to move but your weight pinned me and I felt hot tears sting my eyes as you kept crushing me as if a mallet were driving me into the hard mattress. "Please."

"Hard enough, you bitch!" You shuddered then collapsed onto me. We lay breathless. My face was pressed into the sheets. My body felt split, wet and filthy. La petite mort.

Moments before, my body had felt soft, clean and gloriously open. This was my wedding day, our wedding day. But after I had spoken another's name, you turned from lover to beast as if a door were slamming shut between us. My world darkened; the heat dissipated from our bodies. Everything felt fake and undone.

Knocks at the door broke the silence, like a little pecking bird. It roused me out of my stupor. It was nearly eight o'clock.

I must have fallen asleep. I felt you ease off the edge of the bed before getting up to answer the door. With the door opened just a crack, you said, "That's fine, just leave it there—I'll fetch it in a moment." Then the awkward fumbling of keeping the door open as you pushed the trolley inside.

"Scarlett?" you sat back on the edge of the bed and touched my back with your fingertips. I know I must've flinched because you lifted it away. "Are you hungry?"

I turned around to face you, my make-up smudged and my hair disheveled. Was it something in my expression that told you our love had changed, shifted into a matrix of power?

"You hurt me," I said.

"I didn't mean to. You made me do it."

"Made you . . . ? I don't know why I said his name . . ."

"Hush, it's ok, it's ok." You placed your finger to my lips silencing me. Sitting before me was a different man—a reflective, calm, gentle man. The one I had married earlier that day. But I was left puzzling over who was right and who was wrong.

"Shall we eat?" You lifted the domed metal lids off the plates to reveal what looked more like a piece of modern art than our dinner. You picked up the menu and read: "Spliced sea-bream enrobed in mustard seed jus, set on a bed of steamed purple-sprouted broccoli."

I sat up, hugging my legs, and looked toward the food.

"Scarlett. Let's not fight. This is our wedding day—be happy." You patted me on my leg.

"I am happy." I was. You made me happy.

You lifted another cover from the dishes on the second tier of the trolley.

"Look—strawberries and meringue with chocolate sauce and berries."

You held the plate between us, and I dipped my fingers in to retrieve a strawberry. It was sweet and firm. The meringue fizzed as I crushed it between my teeth. I liked you watching me, consuming me with your eyes.

Of course, we forgave each other for our little ways, our strange quirks. We were destined to share everything. I wanted to share it all with you. The whole fucked-up mess that I was.

◆━━━◆

I woke later that night and for a moment didn't recall we were in the hotel. It was so dark, but it wasn't the dark that bothered me. There was something in the room other than the two of us. I tried to listen between your snores but there was no sound I could discern, not a footstep or the rustle of clothes. But I could sense a presence. There was a disturbance in the atmosphere, like a ghost or the echo of a ghost. As if something had been reflected into this world and was testing the environment, much like a reptile tests its surroundings by flicking its tongue. It was the space in between the space that I could sense.

The peacocks' cries had lessened as darkness fell, but this was closer. I thought of the frieze above us carved on the ceiling of the four-poster. I pictured the birds flitting among the women, bulbous fruit draped around the cornices. I attuned my senses to the window. It had turned chilly later in the evening and now, out of my wedding dress, I felt cooler under the sheets.

I pulled the heavy covers back over my body from where they had shifted over toward your side of the bed. Then I felt as if something small but weighty leapt upon our bed.

At first, I thought a cat had entered our room unnoticed and now wanted to claim its place on the bedding. But as I strained my eyes, I could see it was not cat-shaped. I tapped you on your arm but you carried on sleeping.

Frozen, I watched as the creature, the size of a small dog but with giant outstretched wings, wobbled toward me, growling and hissing. It sounded similar to the guttural echoes from your throat as you snored. A scream got stuck and I strained to emit it; only a breathy exhalation came from my mouth. The thing was getting closer to my head, now rolling slowly up my body—it had huge wide wings. And in front of that appeared two giant snakes, until I realized they were not snakes' but swans' heads swaying with wide-open beaks. A mad gorgon unleashed in the form of the—oh my god, I thought—it looked like the swoodle. I couldn't move. Both swans' heads were arched back as if to strike out my eyes. Sssssssssssss, the creature hissed. Ssscarlett. Releasssse ussss.

"Scarlett!" You were leaning over me. "Scarlett, what's wrong?"

I opened my eyes and sat bolt upright. A shaft of morning light burst through the heavy curtains of the room. You looked alarmed. There was nothing in the room except for us and the ornate furniture. The trolley of food looked too metallic and out of place in such a medieval room, as if a futuristic aircraft had landed in the middle of a period drama.

"Did you have a bad dream?" You were looking at my face, stroking my damp hair.

"It wasn't a dream."

"You were mumbling, trying to say something."

"The swoodle was here."

"The swoodle?" I could tell you thought it amusing how I named all the hybrid sculptures.

"You have to stop making those things—those mixed up creatures."

"Scarlett, what are you talking about?"

"The show, the Spring Show. You can't do it. It's not right. You need to go back to stuffing creatures the way you used to. As they were in life. True replicas."

"But I've got so many specimens ready now. I can't just pull out at the last minute. Besides it was *your* idea. You talked me into it, remember? Why the sudden change?"

"It's not right."

"You keep saying that. What's not right? They are already dead. This is exactly the kind of outdated attitude that people have about taxidermy. I thought you were different."

"No, I don't mean—"

"I'm doing the show, Scarlett. You can come or not. I've made all those exhibits and I'm going to be there."

So that was your final answer and, like being swept along by a strong current, I could do nothing but hang on and hope we didn't drown.

CHRISTMAS DAY / TODAY

Around Midday

It occurs to me that I am bound to you by nothing but a verbal promise. But promises have strength greater than the breath from which they are born. You are doing up the back of my wedding dress with nimble fingers, tying the cords of silk gently so the bodice compresses my naked breasts. I have not worn the dress since that impulsive day in April and I wonder if you feel a tug of passion as you see me in it again.

You hold a sprig of mistletoe above us and kiss my forehead then my cheeks one after the other, then whisper, "Merry Christmas my darling." Your lips are so close to my ear, but I would've heard you through the thick walls of our house.

"I sometimes forget how sweet you taste, Scarlett."

You toast us, clinking your wine glass against mine. Red wine. And the food is laid out on the table. You at one end, I at the other. There are no beasts in the dining room. They are all in the lounge by the fire. Before us, on the table you have placed red napkins in silver napkin rings. The candelabra sits in the center and all around are plates of delicious food. The three-bird roast is glistening and steaming, the sprouts healthily vibrant in glowing green suits, buttered and hot. The cranberry sauce is piled high in a silver dish, red and juicy. It is a feast. I watch you take a bite of turkey coated with gravy and crushed against the sage stuffing. I want to sink my hands into your meal and feel the wet flavors ooze between my fingers, the sweet cranberry sauce like innards on my skin.

It is nearly midday but the light has hardly gained outside. The mists have settled in one dense mass, making it feel colder than it is. We could be living on a cloud. A patch of blue, shaped like a dragonfly's wing, appears for a moment in the sky, then the white mist resumes its dominance like the smoke from your pipe. I am too interested in what happens outside myself. I am diffused like those clouds.

After lunch we move back to the lounge where the creatures are waiting. I am on the chair but you sit away from me, your legs up on the sofa looking at the fire, puffing on your pipe in silence. You doze off. I sit with my face toward the window, casting my thoughts toward Rhett, wondering if he will arrive before nightfall.

M A Y

May was a month of up-and-down days. It was sunny, sit-in-the-garden weather one day, then grey and clouded over the next. I'm not just talking about the weather. When the day of the exhibition arrived, I was all over the place. My emotions had become more tempestuous; you were my knight in shining armor one minute, then confined to the dungeons of my mind. I couldn't explain this to you at the time, but you must have had some indication of my rampant highs and turgid lows.

You were a purist, I guess. I can see you shaking your head at my assumptions. You learned taxidermy the traditional way, preserving the creature in its most lifelike form. Would you have considered anything else without me prompting you to make something different? Circumstances force us to change, adapt to our environment, like a species that evolves and sheds its tail to escape a predator. People can get lost and left behind too. Living things can make themselves extinct by a refusal to adapt, allowing the cruelty of time to eradicate them. Take the dodo for example; all the paintings make it look senseless. Early specimens of the stuffed bird show a stupefied expression, as if it were surprised it had been caught. It was big and cumbersome with tiny wings and, having adapted to life on the ground, perhaps too trusting. It was easy pickings for the rats or pigs brought onto the island of Mauritius by overambitious sailors. *Dead as a dodo.* Should we feel sorry for creatures that have not had the foresight to change, or do we start blaming the one species that seemingly has control over all of them—humans?

What about the platypus? Once, it was thought to be a made-up creature, an invention like the hybrids you have stitched back to life. Only this was not a man-made invention, it sprung from creation itself. Perceptions change, as do fashions, and you were on the edge of a fashion that intrigued and repulsed. You were no more accepted than the platypus in its early discovery. You must have known you didn't fit into that glitzy art world that Felix so easily domineered. Did it matter?

Don't think I'd not noticed how you avoided others of your own species (apart from me of course)—you were private but it didn't make you unaware. So, when I met Felix at the show, I had already anticipated friction. Even with the common interest of hybridization, I knew the gap between the both of you was too far to bridge.

"That idiot is *not* a taxidermist," you said. But there was no doubt he had a remarkable following. We only bypassed the queues because you were exhibiting there too. But I knew who they were queuing for, and so did you. Felix—king of the taxidermy jungle. Top of the tree. #DyingToBeStuffedByFelix.

I felt conspicuous but exhilarated as we arrived and parked the truck in a designated space in the private parking lot, your name written on the wall—Mr. H. R. Pepper / Exhibitor. You seemed unfazed by the queues of people snaking around the building, clogging up the sidewalk. The spectacle of the exhibition had attracted couples and groups, young and old, casually dressed like tourists huddled together untidily with their backpacks and bottled water, picnics and umbrellas. It looked like some of them had camped outside overnight just to claim their place in the queue. People were laughing and taking selfies, chatting and eagerly waiting for the exhibition to open its doors. I breathed in their vibrant colors as you tightly held my hand and we marched into the building without speaking to one another. Taxidermy was back in fashion, just like I had told you.

For you, it was a prestigious honor to be exhibiting in the place you had trained, the Museum of Cultural Studies. But also a sting in the tail, as the old was replaced with the new—this was modern art, not the precise representation of a living specimen you had been taught to replicate. Had you been compelled to adapt against your will? I often wondered about this. Those animals were telling me something was wrong, and I turned a blind eye to it.

I looked about the gallery and saw exhibits right up to the ceiling: wings and tails, beaks and claws, feathers, fur, scales and eyes. It was a carnival of organic matter reformed and staged under spotlights. I learned that the hanging crocodile was a tribute to the oldest known piece of taxidermy, found squatting in the roof of an Italian church some five hundred years after its demise. It is odd to think that a ruthless, unemotional creature such as a crocodile would be suspended from the ceiling of a religious building as a sacred relic, but you told me many specimens had survived in churches, probably due to their tough skin.

Now, high above the main auditorium of the exhibition space was a redeemed crocodile given pride of place, sporting the ominous switchblade wings of an albatross. It looked as if it could glide away at any moment if the metal wires that held it in place were to snap. It had a mission, a buoyancy about its pose, capable of sinking its teeth into the spectators below and rolling them to the depths or launching itself up into the air and out the glass roof—a perfect killing machine manufactured by sewing together bird and reptile. With more sufficient legs than God intended, gone were the prehistoric flaps that caused it to waddle ungainly on land.

Attached to its hips were the long legs of a large rattite, possibly of an emu or ostrich; the clawed toes looked muscular and lean compared to the hard, scaled exterior of the croc's body. Those huge striding legs primed with power, its wings strong and proud, and solid unbreachable body, witnessed individually, were impressive parts from a butchered whole.

As I observed it up there, in suspended animation, I witnessed a cool, slow tear squeeze from its eye and roll slowly down its preserved cheek. It had been paired with creatures that would impair its true nature, and no doubt those other creatures felt affected by its essence too. The crocodile knows what it is; it thrives in swamp not savannah, it waits beside hollows and dips, not the wide-open space of the desert plain or the vast depths of an ocean. How could it be persuaded to share a body (join ranks) with a species it could crush easily in its jaws? Why should it? I felt its pure frustration festering. "Release me," it screamed. "I need to be what I am," it said. It seemed to plead with me, begging for help to sort out the confusion. The croc dominated, but the other creatures fought with all the might of their will. The sailing craft of albatross wings stretched out and sought freedom in the suffocating auditorium; the bounding muscle of the ostrich legs poised to kick back with sharpened toes. It was a troubled mess.

Of course, I admired the artwork, the precision, and the time it had taken to make the creature appear as if it would come alive at any moment. This was your lifelong obsession. And here was an exquisite piece of work, created by Felix De Souza, which rivaled your talents. It was a demonic invention, a brutish fiend with the charcoaled wings of a fallen angel.

The museum was packed by now with milling visitors and I felt a surge of pride that you were a part of it, yet Felix's creations were magnificent. You had worked on almost all species over the years ranging from birds, reptiles and large mammals. "Fish are mostly replicated and remodeled," you told me. "True taxidermy only uses the outer layer of the animal, its skin." I remembered when you applied your craft to the fallow deer, muntjack and tufted ducks that were delivered to you in frozen packages. Their effigies were so lifelike I needed to touch them to make sure they were dead. There was no confusion of their souls like the chaos I witnessed in the hybrid creatures.

My eyes flicked toward a winged, web-footed beast with fangs. Its monkey face was cute but, combined as it was with two protruding fangs and spread wings, the menace was palpable. A pseudo nativity display created a bottleneck of spectators who craned their necks to take in the busy scene: the baby Jesus replaced by a lamb with a dog's head (the lamb of dog) and life-size woolly pigs with antlers peered into the crib. Mary and Joseph were nowhere to be seen, but a looming yeti with three phalluses offered gold, frankincense and myrrh from its groin. A few people shrieked with laughter, others held their hands to their mouths. Most simply stared or took photos. I thought about our next Christmas, although it was many months away, and wondered what gifts it would bring.

A hush descended over the gallery as the squeal of a microphone was switched on.

"The seeds of dreaming are formed. Creative energy exchanged."

Felix's voice was silky soft, even when delivered through the amplifiers. It looked like he was about to fellate the microphone; he held it to his lips like an indie singer, caressing it, so his breath was heard between each word.

"We create because the impulse is within us."

His long brown hair curled onto his shoulders; his smooth tanned skin looked like hot caramel against his off-white linen suit. He was even more attractive in real life. Standing next to me, two girls giggled and nudged each other, holding their phones up to record every word. He was one of those men whose persona created enough enigma to attract interest, but there was something incongruent about him. He was like one of those creatures in the gallery and you knew it: a manufactured fake.

I don't remember his words, but I felt hot while watching him move, the muscles in his arms flexing as he gestured toward the exhibits. His beautiful neck and jawline, his lips. It was not until his gaze met mine that I realized how enchantment worked. He looked inside me as he spoke. I felt as if he were speaking directly to me while addressing the enthralled crowd. It was not a fleeting glance but a penetrating look of longing and wonder. I felt my cheeks flush with blood, then he looked away and stopped mid-sentence. I followed his gaze to see you standing at the other side of the balcony scowling at him, shoulders back, arms crossed, chest puffed out. I shrank back against the wall as you turned your head slowly to see me looking at you. I offered a nervous smile, but your features hardened. In that moment, there was no one but us three in that crowded space. Felix, you and I, a triangle of differences. The heat from my cheeks was replaced with an icy film of sweat down my back.

What was that look that passed between you and Felix like a flint-hard spark of recognition? Had you seen how he looked at me? Or was it just professional rivalry?

Apparently, all his art was formed by sourcing already-dead specimens—he prided himself on never killing a living thing. Somehow, this did not endear him to me. If you are going to enter this kind of world, surely you need to enter it fully. And that means you need to look death in the face. You were never afraid to kill, but you never killed out of malice. Nor did you ever kill just for your art. No, you just had the gift. Some men, like Felix, like to talk about things they have never really experienced themselves. On a visceral level. There was a rumor going around that he never actually got his hands dirty (those sensuous, sinewy artist's hands), but instead employed a workforce to stitch and glue his creations together, guided by his pristine, computerized designs.

He finished his presentation by gesturing to the display of bizarre hybrid creatures that littered the gallery and invited people to buy his book. Once more, his eyes met mine, but when my eyes flicked around to find you, you were gone.

The noise was escalating in the room, hot and dense like the volume of people swarming about in a sludge of anticipation and intrigue. There was timed entry to the building due to the crowds who were lingering in the sunshine outside and loitering around the exhibits. Some were taking photos on their mobile phones even though the signs everywhere stated this wasn't permitted. Security guards in their dark, synthetic uniforms looked dull among the natural skins of the animals and high art set on plinths and behind glass screens.

Birds wings were attached to mammals, scales and feathers were stitched to fur. There was even a mermaid with a grotesque human face—a bit like a full-size parody of a child's doll. A water feature trickled behind it so the tail was immersed in a turquoise pool full of enormous fish bones. A trio of zebra with cows' heads rode on a moving carousel. The zebras' bodies had what looked like udders attached to the underside of their monochrome bodies. I had to look away when I realized the udders were actually bags of eyeballs suspended in viscous fluid.

I took a breath and stared up at the crocodile with outspread black wings, hung from the ceiling. Its mouth was open in a toothy grin showing a row of dazzling gold teeth.

"Doesn't he make you want to cry?" a smooth voice curled behind my ear as if a cool breeze were caressing my neck. Patchouli and hints of some delicious musky scent enveloped me and momentarily eased my headache. Felix was behind me, having prowled his way through the crowd. Where were you? In one of the side rooms, where your exhibits were shown?

"How long did it take you?" A short, round woman butted in and pointed up at the hybrid croc. I noticed her rounded fleshy hands so unlike my own. She seemed to be made from concentric circles. I was trapped between the wall, Felix and the heft of the other woman.

Felix stared upwards at his creation as if puzzled by the magnificence. "It comes to me in such floods, I think I might wake drowned one day."

The woman greedily eyed his soft, parted lips as he basked in confidence and flashed a grin at me. She mopped her brow with a crumpled tissue and continued staring up at him as if *he* were the artwork to be admired. He was good-looking in a film star crossed with a pirate sort of way, but it wasn't his looks alone that fixated me. You would have described him as a self-obsessed wanker, yet it was as if an intoxicating drug oozed out of him. I was as hooked as this other woman.

The woman rummaged in her large floppy bag for a hand-held fan; she switched it on and moved it about in front of her face as if she was scanning with a mini searchlight. "I love your work, Mr. Felix. Could I have your autograph, please?"

He looked sideways to check who else was lurking to attract his attention, then pulled out his own pen from the breast pocket of his jacket (a quill pen with a biro nib), and scribbled his name on the curled-up postcard she held in her free hand. She kept it within her grasp as if it were a valuable heirloom. Then, when he finished signing, she clutched it to her chest as if she'd been anointed by a holy man. "Thank you so much," she huffed, still circling her fan with the other hand, and disappeared into the crowd like an embarrassed schoolgirl.

I needed air, but all those animals were vying for my attention in their mortal struggle against suffocation. They knew when I sensed them; their ears twitched or their hackles rose. I felt their souls trying to make sense of their misassembled body parts in some sort of cohesive way. I felt better, almost free, if I kept moving rather than standing still, so I prepared to escape from Felix, but he blocked my way.

"So, you are a fan of taxidermy?" He smiled revealing his perfect teeth. I flinched as he reached toward my neck as you so often did. He slowly ran the back of his hand over the mink stole I had draped over my shoulder, lightly skimming my breast.

"I'm hot," I said.

"Yes," he said, "yes, you are."

We stared at each other a moment longer and I felt sure he was leaning in to kiss me when a woman wearing a dress that revealed ample but artificial cleavage tapped him on the shoulder. Her symmetrical rounded bosoms were engineered by another form of surgical art. Her dress was the sort of red that oozed confidence.

"Duty calls," Felix sighed and winked at me. I know I shouldn't really be telling you this now, but it was that wink that totally transformed how I saw him. To me it said he knew he was riding on some bubble and even though every cell in my body hated him for usurping *your* rightful place in the taxidermy world, I couldn't help but smile back at him.

He slipped me what at first I thought was a piece of giraffe hide, but it was his business card. His details were stylishly pyrographed onto the smooth tanned leather—his name, mobile number and website. I wanted to sniff the skin. But that would have looked like I was kissing it, so I slipped it in the pocket of your coat that I had draped over my arm.

Copies of his latest book *Wolpertinger Dreams* were stacked up on a table near the stage, waiting for his flamboyant signature. Curiosity overtook me. What if we could use him to further your career—network a little, do a bit of schmoozing with the loveys? Not that you needed to ride on some false kudos devised by a—what did you call him—a cockadoodle dandyfucker?

I reached the front of the book-signing table and stroked the fur stole around my neck. The softness seemed to calm me. It seemed pure and peaceful among the hashed-up hybrid creatures.

"We meet again, so soon." His cheeky wink hooked me as he took my book and turned the pages ready to sign. "Who would you like this dedicated to?"

"Scarlett," I said.

His pen hovered over the page for a moment. Then he wrote my name and did an elaborate illegible scrawl of his own.

"Miss Scarlett? I could be your Rhett, y'know."

"You could," I replied before I knew what I had said. "But I'm Mrs. Scarlett Pepper actually."

"Is that so?" His twinkle dulled for a split second.

"Yes, Henry Pepper is my husband," I said.

"Interesting," he said, and nodded his head, slowly raising his eyebrows. "He is a very lucky man."

Although you had both chosen the same profession, he was so unlike you. He was glamorous, stylish, modern. I admit I fantasized about our names combined: Felix De Souza and Scarlett Pepper. But it was a recipe not fit for the same plate, like too many strong flavors vying for the top note.

The woman in red appeared and leaned over him in a way that reminded me of Penny fawning over you, but this woman was young and beautiful. She gestured to her watch and looked up at the long snake of queue forming behind me. Felix waved her away impatiently and rolled his eyes at me as if to say he was so in demand, what could he do? The customer behind me was already pushing two copies of *Wolpertinger Dreams* toward his erect pen.

I slipped away and heard a cackle from the corner of the room and saw a crowd of young girls laughing at a particularly phallic snake sculpture gripped by a disembodied hand, painted lurid pink. I wanted to scream; there were too many people around me now.

I knew if I didn't get outside, the creatures would hound me. Their souls would launch upon me like locusts devouring a field clean of its crop. The pestering sound of creatures wanting their souls to be freed grew louder and louder. Was no one else aware of it? How did they expect me to help them when they were already dead and unanimated? Just because I could hear them didn't mean I knew how to help them be free.

I hadn't drunk enough water all day, and the combination of dehydration and the heat from all those living bodies seemed to tire me out. I felt like a mermaid that had been on land too long. I looked at my hands, all shriveled up and dried out between the webs of my fingers, scaly like a bird's feet. A chicken or crow, I thought. I could feel the pulsing in my head and looked around for some reprieve, but everywhere I tried to focus I saw the eyes of the exhibits on me. There was the croco-bird looming down, swaying slightly on his metal harness from the ceiling; the wolpertinger was leering with cold eyes; the two headed doe-fish pleaded with me to rip it apart and return its body parts to the river or fields. I wasn't sure what reality was anymore. This world or the next. Both placed demands on me of equal magnitude. My failing physical body surged with guilt; my fragile fractured mind was attacked by their lingering presence. I needed to get away.

Every way I turned, people pressed against me, nudging and muttering, shooting me odd looks, their breath vinegary near my nostrils, a woman's hair flicking my face, a shriek, a backpack swung and bashed against my arm, the hot dense mumble of the swarming crowd, no way out, no direct route to the exit, no direction, heart thumping, shallow breaths, limbs like stone, animal eyes staring at me, pleading with me to rip them free, my ears thick with pulsing blood, nausea washing upwards to my throat, sweat trickling down my spine as the crowd swarmed, bustled, heaved like an undercurrent, spinning, tripping, stumbling. I couldn't breathe. Couldn't breathe. Where were you? What was happening to me? I was falling. Falling. Darkness.

"Scarlett?" A voice greeted me in the dark.

Rhett? Felix?

"Scarlett? What happened?"

I forced my heavy eyelids to open and you were there looming over me, smoothing your hand across my brow like a concerned parent. A semi-circle of legs was around me but you waved everyone away with your arm.

"Let's go home," you said, lifting me effortlessly to carry me away from the madness like a rag doll over your shoulder. I raised my weary head to see Felix watching your back as you parted the crowd like a beast crashing through the jungle.

⟵———•——➤

In the following days we did not speak about the exhibition, but I could not forget the way you looked at Felix and the way he looked at you. Those endearments that once drew me to you, like the way you chewed the edge of your moustache, seemed to irritate me and enflame me, but sometimes just a look from you evoked a sexual pull that I couldn't control. The way I would devour my food with my hands like a wild thing seemed to arouse you too. All these emotions surfaced, I am sure, because of that meeting with Felix. My mood swings seemed to fuel them all the more. How much further could I push you until you broke? That was a reason to loathe myself, over and over again.

I felt that you had been overlooked, so I was resentful of Felix's seemingly easy path to recognition while you slogged away with such determination and precision. It was self-inflicted loneliness. Pride was always your biggest enemy. But there was a synergy between his artwork and your own. I noticed it even then. I didn't question it, though, because I was infatuated with you. Please believe me, my darling Peppercorn, I can tell you only the truth.

I never told you, but later that month I visited Felix. He said I had good boundaries, but I don't believe I managed them at all well. His behaviour was outrageous, touching me on my lower back, steering me to his sofa, trying to feed me fresh cherries by dangling them near my lips. I wanted to devour them, but his incessant questioning about your work made me suspicious. He reminded me of a leech, I guess, drinking on its host's blood, until gorged, it fell off, and slept. I saw a look on his face when we parted that repelled me; it was a look of weakness. When he closed the door, I wiped away the residue of his goodbye kiss that he had planted on both my cheeks.

I stomped away from his door treading on the snails crossing the wet path. Each footstep finding a sticky, filled shell that exploded ceremoniously between my shoe and the paving slabs. The soft innards bubbled up through the cracked, broken shards like foaming mouths of saliva. Felix said I was his muse. But all I ever wanted was to be *your* muse. Was I attracted to Felix or his creations?

Nevertheless, as this was happening, I could not help but notice the birds were procreating in the hedgerows and my urgency to create also fired up the will to be close to you; you were my steady one, my fortress and safety net. You were my generous, attentive, self-assured, confident husband. Yet there we were after the exhibition, bickering, picking at faults with each other. Our moods, responses, attitudes, manners—all were scrutinized, both of us finding it impossible to reflect or accept one another for who we truly were.

Doesn't every life have major cracks in it? Some are easy to plaster over depending on who's looking; some are just too obvious to be concealed by superficiality. I tried to mask my true feelings so I didn't affect your creative flow. Did you notice me reassuring you when all I wanted to do was explore the gold deep within my shadow? You said I went too deep, as if this were a bad, harmful thing to do. Yet you were the one tinkering with the dark side. I judged you in an attempt to deflect from my own failings, and then I hated myself, over and over again. I even asked those pestering creatures for some clarification on what I should do. But they just confused me all the more, adding to my feelings of inadequacy and self-loathing. Felix made no effort unless it profited him in some way. What did he want with me? He pretended to be attracted to me, but I knew he didn't understand me.

Did you?

One night I woke you as I clawed frantically at the covers. I told you I had dreamt of riding a bicycle, gripping handles which seemed too loose and unsteady. The handles detached and floated in mid-air like some cartoon sketch. I told you I was traveling too fast down a steep concrete slope and knew the brakes would not work. And the moment I woke was the moment I grabbed at the covers as if breaking my fall.

This was a lie. What I really dreamt was this:

I was a crocodile caught in a trap set by you. My hind quarters were being crushed by jaws of gold, and every movement I made to escape the pain and restriction bound me ever more tightly to the spot. So I clawed at the ground in front of me to drag myself free, only to find my feet could not grip. They were soft, floppy paws that would not react to my brain's commands. I could not break free. I started crying out of frustration. I was going nowhere.

Among these darker days I found my mood and energy lift as the clouds cleared and the temperature rose. I felt angry and resentful for even suggesting you should change the way you work, and part of me knows you only did it for me, not yourself. I know you said you were tired of the usual deer and game birds unceremoniously presented to you, but that was what you were good at. You could make a dead creature come alive. The rest was my idea.

One day, when a bird flew at the window, I thought at first it was an accident, a misjudgment due to the heavy mist, but the third and fourth time was not something I could ignore. It was a hawk trying to break the glass. I was not used to such violence and it froze me for a moment, shocked by the recognition that something usually so silent and elusive should be in the foreground vying for my attention. If that's what its intention was. I assume so, as I was the only one there to witness it. I remember thinking, *It is anger, not fear, that drives the bird toward the glass with such ferocity.* I felt it the way I heard the essence of creature's moods infiltrating my head. It was a physical sensation starting with the pulsing at my temples.

"What do you want?" I shouted at it, worried it would kill itself or break the window. For a moment it actually stopped, alighted on a nearby branch, and looked at me, panting heavily, its feathers fluffed up and its beak open. "Why are you hurting yourself?"

But it flew off and left me asking my reflection the same questions. I had no answers either. I did not recognize my own image. My hair had grown long and wild, way past my shoulders. I looked so thin that my eye sockets seemed to sink further into my skull. And my cheeks were sharp like carved ice.

CHRISTMAS DAY / TODAY

After lunch

Eggnog flavored with bourbon, you say, to satiate our need for warmth. Gardens, hills, fields, trees enshrouded with un-melted snow. The Big Freeze they keep saying, after the Big Flood. They tempt us with temperatures such as one degree centigrade, a tropical figure. Not the minus-fifteen that it has been. Rail, road and air stand still. Passengers wanting to reach their families are stuck fast, in limbo, advised to stay indoors, not to travel.

The milky liquid in my cup cools, and a skin forms on its surface.

A rabbit fur hat, wrapping paper, crackers, holly and ivy, a log fire, music to sidetrack our frozen minds. A dull, grey, uncertain block of a day hangs around us. Did I believe that I had any control over my destiny? Like a hidden relic in a junk shop, I feel undiscovered. Am I your treasure? Do you intend to show me off like an exhibit?

JUNE

It was pretty obvious that he'd turn up around June. Glastonbury Festival drew the crowds, and Rhett was a seasoned festival goer. He'd like to think he was a free spirit, but really, he was just no good at settling in one place. But I guess even wanderers have to settle somewhere eventually. You knew I was Rhett's only family.

He stood with his backpack resting on his feet—his worldly possessions in a beat-up, dirty bag. He had grown a gingery beard that didn't match his thin face; it was too bristly and unevenly spread. It looked pubic. But he was my brother and I loved him.

"Forgot how fucking dreary this country is!" These were his first words as I walked up to greet him at the coach station. A scrawny woman was draped over him like an unsavory rash. Both of them badly needed to wash their hair. A stale smell wafted off them like the insoles of a well-worn pair of trainers.

"This is Andreea," he pronounced it *Andraaaya* as if she were made of liquid. Andreea did one of those smiles that seemed restricted to her jaw. She revealed boxy, uneven teeth. There was a hardness about her even

though she was painfully thin. Thinner than me. "She's from Romania."
Romaaneea.

Why did he do that? He picked up girls as if they were offered to him
as part of a universal buffet. His girlfriends always had the same worn,
aimless look. Rhett was not handsome, but I'd say he had striking features,
like myself. He was better looking as a child, with strawberry blonde hair
and fresh ruddy cheeks from running about a lot. He smoked too much,
but had taken a liking to hot yoga, which made his frame wiry and lithe. I
couldn't get used to his beard so kept trying to touch it to see if it was just
stuck on like a bad collage. Andreea–*Andraaaya*–didn't say much but kept
sucking the ends of her hair in a way that made me feel queasy.

⟵•─➤

"I take it you're going to the festival?" I felt the warmth from his body, his
gangly arm wrapped around my waist as we walked to the car. It had been
ages since we'd spent any time together. For all his faults, I loved having
him near.

"Yeah, we've got volunteer passes," he said, "which means free
tickets to the festival for a few shifts, holding the space in the dome of
transcendental masters."

"The what?"

"It doesn't matter," he grinned at me. "Have you got any grub, sis?
We're starving."

He couldn't believe where I lived. The last time I saw him, he'd crashed
on the sofa at my studio. It must've been just before he left for Spain,
and shortly after dumping some other girl by text. I don't remember her
name, but she kept phoning him incessantly, weeping and howling like
a banshee. I think she was French. Anyway, he said that was why he'd
ditched his old number. He thought he had let me know his new one.
All that mattered was that we were back together. I just wish he hadn't

brought anyone with him; there was never much chance to talk about old times when someone was lingering.

"Landed on your feet here, sis," he said, as he saw the expanse of garden on our drive up toward the house, your workshop nestled beneath the trees. He was always quite impressed by size, even though he pretended he liked to live a simple life with only a backpack to store his belongings.

As he entered the lounge, Rhett saw the crabbit and the swoodle among the later creations that had spilled over from your workshop to our home. We'd not had much chance to sort them after the exhibition, and you liked to keep them on display so they didn't go musty. I knew I had to do something about them sooner rather than later; the house looked like a natural history museum of specimens discarded by evolution. They looked like the rejects from *The Island of Dr. Moreau*, stitched-together legs and bodies from disparate species. Having them in such close proximity was affecting my physical health too. I was finding it difficult to breathe most days.

Rhett looked about the room and gasped, then looked at me with something resembling awe, disgust and puzzlement.

"What is this? Some kind of fucking freaky zoo? Oh my god! What is that?" he moved toward the crabbit as Andreea stayed frozen to the spot, just staring. Her face looked as if she'd seen a turd come to life and wink at her from the carpet.

"They're not real," I said. "I mean they're dead but real. What I mean is . . ."

"I can see that," he moved toward the cowstrich, his hands held stiffly by his sides, but he leaned forward so he could examine it close up. "But are you sure they're actually dead?"

I didn't reply.

"When you said your boyfriend was a taxidermist, I thought you meant stag's heads and stuffed foxes in glass cases biting off a chicken's head?" This made me laugh, not least because he called you my boyfriend but it made me think back to the days when you happily recreated the trophies brought to you—ducks, geese, deer—all perfectly represented and restored as they would have been in life. But now, as I looked at what Rhett was seeing for the very first time, I felt a bit sick. Had I made you do this? I wanted to defend you.

"It's actually very sought-after artwork."

"It's mad, fucking mad, that's what it is." He looked back at Andreea, "Babe, have you ever seen anything like this before?"

"It's cutting edge," I continued. "We're going to have some exhibits in a gallery in New York."

"God, sis. You really think people will buy this stuff?"

"They already have. We've had orders—well, Henry's had orders. He's got a huge backlog. He'll join us after he's tidied up. I didn't think you'd arrive until tomorrow."

Rhett put his arm heavily around Andreea's shoulders and whispered something in her ear. I couldn't hear what he said but she shook her head and hugged her skinny arms about her loose cotton dress.

I think she was shivering. I looked out the window at the sky. It was going to rain again. June was not a very warm month, was it? I made some tea and I sat in the kitchen with our guests, nursing our mugs and catching up.

"Henry exhibited in this big show last month—it was quite exciting really." I don't know why I said this, but something compelled me to show how proud of you I was.

"What? A circus freak show?" Rhett was only teasing but the anger welled up inside me.

"You always have to put others down, don't you?" I stormed off and left him open-mouthed. It was like the old days when we used to fight like weasels. He got up quickly and followed me.

"Sis, I didn't mean it was crap—that's not what I meant—it's just a bit weird," he tried to console me, but all I could focus on was Andreea's expression as she stared out the window, trying to avoid the glass eyes of the stuffed animals. She reminded me of the crabbit and the swoodle, the way she sat really still, almost uncomfortably so; I thought of frozen wings and tails.

I was so glad you put aside your usual contempt for strangers and made my brother feel welcome. I watched Andreea prod a mushroom around her plate with her fork and began to doubt my ability to rustle up a meal. I'd fried up some venison sausages and black pudding accompanied by some left-over potatoes and asparagus. Rhett and Andreea arrived so suddenly I'd not had time to prepare. We were so used to picking at whatever we fancied—a venison fillet, a bowl of peas, bread and cheese or some broad beans from the garden. It was nice to actually sit down and eat at the table, even if it was prompted by their arrival. It made me feel like we were a family, like the time when my parents and Rhett were all together.

"So where did you two meet?" You looked directly at Andreea as you bit noisily into a sausage, but Rhett answered for her.

"Andreea's a singer. Totally awesome, aren't you babe? We met on the Camino."

"The Camino?" you said.

"Well, it was at the party in Santiago. We didn't actually meet walking the route."

"That's quite some way, isn't it?"

Rhett started spouting anecdotes about the people he'd met on his pilgrimage who were totally awesome and had these awesome lives and awesome transformations. You squeezed my thigh under the table as he preached on about how vital he felt, how his body felt more opened up. I know you were wondering how this person could be my brother, my twin brother. He was so loud and rolled his words together. I didn't see the point in speaking half the time. I sensed what most people were thinking, so I found speaking a waste of energy. People were more interested in talking about themselves anyway, so I just let them. Rhett had not inherited the same damned psychic gifts I had and seemed totally unaffected by any sensitive shifts in the atmosphere. He liked to say he was in alignment with the gurus, but he loved the blatant physicality of life. He loved the excesses of smoking, eating, drinking and shagging. At least you knew where you stood with him.

"What's your style of music, Andreea?" I felt protective of my brother even though we were the same age.

"I play *balls* and chanting."

"Balls?"

"She means bowls, Scarlett," Rhett scowled at me, but I saw a little smirk form at the corners of his mouth.

"Sausage anyone?" I thrust the frying pan toward the table, and Andreea flinched.

"Actually, Andreea's a vegan," Rhett looked sheepishly at her. "Sorry honey—forgot to mention."

I wondered why she hadn't said anything. Perhaps she was being polite, or maybe she felt a little uncomfortable being around her lover's twin sister. That was if he'd actually told her we were twins; no one would make the assumption unless they knew.

"God, I'm so sorry." I actually meant it. Poor girl looked like she needed more than a few meaty sausages to build up her iron content. I could see you eyeing her up. She was a bit younger than me I guessed, and when you stood next to her in the kitchen while she washed up and you dried the dishes, it was like looking at a bear towering over a flamingo. You could have snapped her like a twig. I wondered if that was how people viewed us, too. I wasn't much bigger than her, but about a head shorter. Did people wonder how we fit together, how we made our bodies merge so seamlessly when we made love? I could sense them measuring up our torsos as we stood side by side and wondering how it all worked. Perhaps they saw *us* as bear and flamingo, an unlikely duo. A bemingo or a flabear? Thankfully that was a hybrid you hadn't considered.

"Henry seems quite . . . mature," Rhett whispered to me while you finished in the kitchen and we sat on the sofa nursing glasses of wine. "I mean that in a good way. He's very earthy—and looks like he's not short of a bit of money, sis."

His eyes swept around the room, taking in the antique dresser housing some heirlooms, porcelain dating back to the seventeenth century and those ugly Staffordshire figurines of King Charles spaniels. There were a few modern additions of sculpture, some black Labradors cast in bronze and a painting by an artist I couldn't recall at the time but came back to me later as I lay in bed thinking about the colors and texture and what made a piece of artwork come alive.

"Yeah, he is good for me." I meant it. You and I, we complemented each other, didn't we? But with that thought I couldn't help letting Felix penetrate my mind. What had he said—*I could be your Rhett?* He was nothing like my brother to look at, but there was a similar sort of energy I felt in his presence. Like we were two charged particles bouncing off one another, unsure how to react.

Of course, Felix couldn't have known about my brother, about this Rhett to my Scarlett. And yet, I couldn't help merging you all. In no time I was blurting out to Rhett how you and Felix made similar things.

"Felix De Souza? That's actually his name?" Rhett spluttered.

"You can talk, Rhett."

"Yes, thank you, Scarlett—no need to remind me of that particular legacy." Then he launched into one of his Rhett Butler impressions. "*Tell* me, *Scarlett, do you never shrink from loving men you do not love?*" He fell to the floor in front of me and held his arms up pleading, "*Would you be more convinced if I fell to my knees?*" We used to do this as kids, play-act the parts of Rhett Butler and Scarlett O'Hara—the two tempestuous lovers—which is a bit odd for a brother and sister, now I think of it.

"*Turn me loose, you varmint, and get out of here.*" He clung to my legs; his arms wrapped around the back of my knees so I nearly toppled over. I slapped him across his head, but he buried his face into my crotch and growled like a dog. Sometimes I think he never really grew up, that he was still the ten-year-old that lost his mother and father. The therapist used to get us to talk to each other about the happy times before it happened, but I didn't see the point. It wasn't going to bring them back, was it?

"Rhett, get off me," I hit him repeatedly with the palm of my hand, but he made me lose my balance and tackled me to the floor. Before I could scramble free, he squeezed me tight in his arms and whispered in my ear. "I'd do anything for you Scarlett, never forget that." It was an awkward moment, as if he were confessing a secret. He was deadly serious. I shook him free and stood up just as you and Andreea appeared through the doorway with four glasses of brandy. Was there anyone in that room that didn't feel uncomfortable, I wonder? Even the stuffed creatures seemed to shrink back in embarrassment. If they'd had eyelids, they would've squeezed them shut over their glassy eyes.

❦

On Midsummers Day, Rhett thought it was a good idea to climb Glastonbury Tor with the masses and watch the sunrise. We could've gone to Stonehenge, but when I told him we'd probably just get stuck in traffic, he settled on going to the Tor.

"We could give Andreea a taste of the local traditions," he said, although I felt like I was the odd one out, dressed in my tweed jacket and riding boots. Most people looked too summery, all floaty scarves and flip-flops as we tramped up the rain-moistened steps to the top of the hill. The sun had yet to rise but it was still quite light. There was an expectant stillness among the crowds. I wish you could've been there with us. I can't remember why you weren't now.

When we got to the top, Rhett lit a cigarette and blew a smoke ring into the air. He always did that when he was nervous, letting his mouth form an "o" and his tongue pierce the middle so the smoke quivered upwards like an imbalanced flimsy hoop.

A boy with a rainbow-colored ribbon tied to a stick ran around the legs of a woman who was talking to a man who held a dog, a mixed breed with wiry short brown hair and spindly legs. There was a smooching couple leaning against the tower holding hands and tasting each other in noisy slurps. The dog raised its head and sniffed the air. We all faced east, waiting for the sun to rise behind the clouds. The sun crept quickly up over the horizon. Its rays were soon glinting on the metallic fence that surrounded the festival site in the distance. The clouds parted to offer a warmer day than we had experienced for some time. After such a cold winter I don't think we quite believed it could ever be warm again.

A grey-haired woman lifted her arms to the sky and revealed hairy armpits. I felt quite uncomfortable being among all these strangers and realized I had been used to my own company, or just the two of us, for some time now. I looked at my brother and felt a pang of regret that I had not tried harder to stay in touch with him. He hugged Andreea from behind, drawing her close, and I felt an emptiness seep into me as I listened to the murmurs of others around us. He used to hold me like that when we were growing up. We'd moved to a few foster homes after our parents died, but Rhett was always close, even when he wasn't physically near me. I know he meant what he said, that he'd do anything for me. His words pressed against me like he was pressed against her and what should have been a celebration of light and perfect balance, the Summer Solstice, became clouded by my memories.

<hr />

"Rhett, we never get a chance to talk properly." I sounded whiny and hated myself for it as I offered him a drink in the kitchen.

"What is there to talk about?" he said.

"Just things—family things."

"What sort of family things?"

"About the day—you know—it happened."

"Are you talking about . . ."

I nodded.

"You have to put it behind you, Scarlett." He stroked my arm and I felt a tingle of excitement. I loved having him close to me.

"Don't you ever feel—well, like it *wasn't* an accident?"

"What are you saying? Of course it was an accident. Why are you getting like this?"

Andreea sauntered in the room with wet hair and no make-up, her face creased with anxiety. She stood beside Rhett and offered one of her half-faced smiles toward me.

"Thank you for letting us stay," Rhett said sincerely, once again swerving off subject and leaving me floundering.

"Where else would you have stayed?" I snapped, and walked out to feed the dogs.

That night I felt ravenously hungry and crept down to get a snack from the fridge. I heard music in the lounge so thought I wouldn't be disturbing them if they were still up, but as I opened the door, I was met by Rhett's bobbing ass on top of Andreea's contorted frame. They looked like a pair of insects locked together. He was holding her right leg up by her ear, her left leg was entwined around his back. Rhett's scars were shiny on his backside and down his right hamstrings like polished pink marble. They were so enraptured in their coitus that they didn't hear me. I reached forward to touch Rhett's scars, marveling at how, even after all this time, they still marked him so clearly. My fingers were millimeters from his skin when Andreea's eyes sprung open and spotted me leaning over them. She shrieked.

"What? What?" Rhett turned to see what had startled her and didn't notice me at first, then relaxed as he saw me standing behind him.

"Christ, Scarlett! Don't you bloody knock?" Rhett sat back on his haunches, cupping his genitals with both hands.

"It's my house. I don't have to knock." I noticed Andreea's feet were exceptionally large, like smooth hobbit's feet. She pulled her long flimsy dress back down over her naked lower half, tucking her feet underneath. I glimpsed her toenails, painted alternate black and red.

They started mumbling while I was in the kitchen. I nibbled a few pieces of cheese from the fridge and found a pack of cashew nuts and tipped them into my mouth, then I ran the tap and lapped from the stream of water like a thirsty cat. You normally would make my bedtime drink but must have forgotten with the disruption of visitors. I had to walk back past Rhett and Andreea to go upstairs.

"Don't mark the upholstery," I snapped at them and closed the door behind me, wondering how long it would be before he got bored of her and passed her up for another. He was a man addicted to variety. As far as I knew, he'd gone through women from at least three continents and seventeen countries. God knows how he hadn't contracted something deadly. Maybe he had. However, he seemed to have inherited a strong constitution. It was just as well one of us had.

The next morning Rhett was still laid out on our sofa as if it had become some extension of him. I'm not even sure they ever used the bed in the guest room. He was eating olives out of a jar with his fingers and leaving the stones in a pile on the coffee table, like a neatly arranged pyramid of rabbit droppings. I noticed all the taxidermied creatures were rotated so their eyes faced the wall or out the window. With their backs to the center of the room, they looked even more real to me.

"You've sold out, sis," he put the olives down and pressed the recline button on the sofa so the footrest lifted with his outstretched legs on it.

"What do you mean?"

"Look at it—middle-class sofa, middle-class log burner, a lawn."

"A lawn?"

"If you were proper bohemian, you'd dig up the lawn and plant parsnips or beetroot. Use your green fingers." He waggled his long, oily fingers at me.

"You don't seem to mind eating my food sourced from the supermarket, or shagging on my comfortable middle-class sofa."

"Scarlett, I'll be out of your hair in a few days." He was never out of my hair. We had the same thin, flat hair, mine darker but only because I'd started dyeing it. Flecks of grey had appeared at my temples and even in my eyebrows and after initially extracting the culprits with some tweezers, I decided the most effective way of tackling the effects of age was to paint over the cracks, so I colored it nutmeg brown.

You, my darling Peppercorn, on the other hand, liked to let the ravages of time greet you as an old buddy, positively welcoming any changes to your physique as if you'd discovered a new element, "My word! A silver hair." Your splayed fingers parted the mat of dark chest hair as if examining the pelt of one of your specimens. I loved how your body resembled my fantasy of Neolithic man, a kind of capable brutishness combined with intelligent passion. It pleased me how you rarely felt pain; it seemed to bounce off you. My protector. My King Kong. Your strength seemed to come from within, an untouchable force residing like a latent volcano. You radiated power. Beneath that craggy surface was molten lava, and I was the recipient of your pyroclastic surges. Even if I wanted to, I could never leave you.

Rhett and Andreea stayed for a few more days, then set off to the festival. That was one good thing about Rhett—he never outstayed his welcome. It was just that he never really announced he was coming. But I was grateful for your flexibility and you were quite absorbed with your work anyway, so maybe you didn't even notice them come and go or lounge about the house and garden.

I didn't want a tense goodbye with my brother, but I ended up sabotaging it with my flippancy and swings of mood. Rhett was my twin. How could he not sense things as I did? Was he affected by those creatures as I was? However, I think it was Andreea, and not him, who had turned the crabbit and swoodle to face the wall, along with the other creatures that seemed to stare at anyone entering the room. He seemed to be able to accept change much better than I. We had talked about the day our parents died, but it was all disjointed, as if memory had already distorted the facts: the picnic, the dog attack, the cricket bat, the car, the fire.

"I meant what I said, sis," he squeezed me hard then turned to you and shook your hand vigorously. "Henry, look after my Scarlett." His voice took on a manly, gruff tone and you both locked eyes until you nodded your goodbye and he nodded back. Andreea pecked us both on our cheeks and skipped away toward their hired campervan in flipflops, her toes like black and red scurrying beetles. She seemed more enlivened now she was leaving, or it might have just been the excitement of going to the festival. It started to rain again.

"I hope you've got rubber boots," I called after them, hoping for Rhett to look back. "Looks like it's going to be a mudfest." But their van disappeared off the driveway past the dogs barking in their pen, the ducks giving them a noisy send-off too, and we were left alone once again.

"We should go next year," I snuggled up to you as we watched them go. You said I could if I wanted to, but you didn't fancy all those crowds. Neither would I, come to think of it—others' thoughts and feelings bombarding me. It would've been like an avalanche hitting me full on.

"There's never enough time to say what you really mean, is there," I stroked your beard and you kissed my ear then my hand and looked at my wedding ring, then kissed that too. "Why do we wait to say the important things?"

"What important things?"

"The things that matter, Henry—the reasons why we love or hate, stay or leave."

"I don't understand what this is about. You didn't fall out with your brother, did you?"

"No, we never really fall out. He just walks away whenever I want to discuss the past with him."

"Maybe that's because he understands you can't change the past."

"You're so bloody wise, aren't you?" You knew I was only teasing. And that you were probably right. But I knew that the past had a way of creeping back into the present, especially if it sensed unfinished business.

When Rhett had gone, I felt the heaviness seep back into my bones like damp slowly working its way up a wall. I hated to admit it but, for all his failings, Rhett seemed to blaze some cleansing fire through me, as if he could banish my demons by being near me. There was nothing I could do to change his wandering ways though. He would probably just keep moving around the world until his legs gave up. We joked about his ability to keep walking even when he was asleep. His sleep-walking used to wake everyone but himself. We'd have to steer him back toward his bed, and he'd get back in without even waking up or remembering he had even moved. Our parents had even put up a stair gate to prevent him falling at night. I was more of a sleep talker—or mumbler. But you already knew that about me, didn't you?

⟵—▸—▸⟶

We took advantage of the long days and went out onto the moor with the dogs.

"We could pick some elderflower," you said.

"In the rain?"

"It'll be romantic. We could get wet together." What you really meant was that we could strip each other when we got home and warm up in the bath, my legs entwined around you.

Elderflower, that sweet splayed mass of stars that opened out like an explosion in the hedgerows. I inhaled the sweet pollen as we picked the heads of flowers, piling them in a bag still attached to green stalks. A few insects clung to the scented sprays. We moved slowly along the hedge in the field on the way back to our house and picked enough to fill a big plastic bag. The dogs patrolled back and forth across the long grass, sniffing and wandering, then racing back to us. The rain never came to anything, just a short sharp shower, which soon passed over, but the ground was already quite damp underfoot. The evening felt hushed and clammy as we returned home and shook out the elderflower heads to free the bugs and bits of unneeded foliage. We left them in the kitchen overnight, as the tiredness left by Rhett and Andreea's visit hit us both head on.

The next day I found a recipe and set about boiling the water to infuse the flowers. There was plenty of sugar and lemons in the house but no citric acid.

"Where can I buy citric acid?"

"The chemist," you offered, "or the supermarket? Supermarkets sell anything these days."

When I asked the lady at the pharmacy counter, she said they don't stock it anymore. I was surprised, as everyone seemed to be making elderflower cordial these days but later found out that citric acid was used for more unsavory purposes.

"Drugs?" You said it like you'd never heard of them.

"She said people use it to mix with heroin or cocaine or something like that."

"What, in cordial?"

"No, not in cordial—in the drugs, silly."

"The things people do to their bodies." You shook your head and got up to fetch another glass of whisky.

What about the things we did to our bodies? I mean the visceral, probing things. Delicate explorations with fingers and tongues. There was not an inch of you I did not know, and I know you had mapped all of me too. If only my body would work more effectively; I felt cursed by my headaches and tiredness.

"It doesn't make you any less of a woman," you said to me as you held me in bed one night. "I love you for you, not for your body."

Maybe we couldn't create another being together, but I wanted you to admire me for being something different. I wanted you to recraft me, to somehow replace those parts of me that didn't work with new vital organs, or fantastical designs like the ones you had crafted out of mismatched animals. Wings would allow me to fly and be free, and a tail could be my weapon, fast and strong, so I could flick it at those demons trying to claw their way into my mind.

You do understand what I'm talking about don't you, Peppercorn? Even though I fought against those hybrid creations and changed my mind from one day to the next, what I really wanted was to become one of them, by your hand. I had thought that Felix was the one to change my world, but he could never fulfil me the way you did.

I wanted to enter a new world. I knew it must be possible, as the voices had told me so. Once we were free of this physical body, we could inhabit others. The only condition was that we relinquished the body we were currently using. Of course, this isn't as easy as it sounds. You know what I mean, don't you? The cells of our bodies hold memory and until they have decayed, the spirit lingers. Death is not enough. It is not complete like we are led to believe. There are fragments of people scattered all over the place, all over the world. Why do you think ghosts are seen in graveyards and cemeteries or the sites of bloody battles? They are trying to move on. They are asking for help. The attachment to the physical world is keeping them there. There was still a lot I did not understand but I was going to find out. We all were.

CHRISTMAS DAY / TODAY

1 p.m.

A mystical menagerie. Did I really suggest that to you?

Mynah bird with lizard tail and feet–a mynizard? It mimics all the other animals' patterns and calls with a precision I admire greatly. The most adaptable of all your hybrids, made up of a chameleon and a mynah bird. Chameleons adapt visually to their surroundings; mynah birds are auditory. The perfect match. But no, no. There should be no match at all.

It stinks in here. You don't seem to notice how it has infused the walls, the carpet, the paintwork and even the furniture. I feel as if I have been marinated too, like the pickled specimens you first introduced to me in the museum. The two-headed lizards, the frilly fetus of a bovine calf swimming in mock-amniotic fluid. It is a sense that brings back strong memories. The stronger the smell, the stronger the memory. Cows–walking through the fields where I grew up. A bucketful of eels slipping and sucking like sex on a hot afternoon. Cockatoo–the shake of exotic feathers dusts the insides of my nostrils, precursor to a sneeze. Giraffe–warm toffee-colored hide, like caramel straw with a long, black liquorice slug of a tongue.

But the creatures you have stuffed are not of one species. They have been bastardized by your masterful craftwork. The wallopea is indignant with its showy peacock tail on display like an oriental fan, and muscular short-haired body of a wallaby complete with a large meaty tail to counterbalance its weight, then the legs of an ostrich that seem to slip down from the body in strong, straight trunks of sinew.

We have our family, our menagerie of strange and wonderful creatures. The room is crowded with them, some in glass cases, some set upon wooden plinths or slabs of slate. Others hang from the ceiling among the paper chains and glittery, metallic decorations. Still, I wish for more. The fur on the crabbit has faded slightly where its left side has been facing the south windows all year.

You have left the room and before me appears the last person I expect to see. She is holding something in her hand as if she has scooped a froglet from the grass. She is moving toward me and I feel torn between staring at her face and what she holds in her hand. From the fire my mother emerges. My mother stands in front of me holding my fetus in her hand. The miniscule blob of red jelly that you buried under the buddleia, so the butterflies would visit and carry its soul away on their wings, is here with her.

"What are you doing here?" I ask her.

"You called me," she says.

"I call you many times but you never answer."

"I always answer. You don't hear me, Scarlett."

"I miss you."

She smiles.

"I was angry with you."

"Yes."

"I was angry with father for what he did to the dog."

"Yes."

"Mother, do you forgive me?"

"Yes."

"I've made some mistakes," I say.

She holds out her hand, and the fetus becomes a butterfly, flaps its wings and flies away. I watch it disappear into the flames.

"You look—different," I say. Her hair is long and wavy, nearly to her shoulders. She is slim and wearing an orange and brown maxi dress, beads jangling about her neck. Her face seems calmer and glows like sunlight off harvested apples.

"You too," she says, and we laugh. Each peal of laughter scrapes over me like flint sharpening a bone.

Then you reappear, and she is gone with the flash of fire from the grate. Without saying goodbye. Again.

J U L Y

When it rains out here on the Levels, the water from the ground rises up to meet the water falling from the sky. As if we hadn't been saturated enough by Rhett's visit, shortly after their departure, Penny arrived in a cloud of Dior. Her short frame did not detract from the huge aura that extended at least three times beyond her body. I knew she was nearby, not only by her expensive perfumed arrival but by a powdery odor that diffused from her like mold spores off an old piece of fruit. It caught in my throat when she moved. Her hair fluffed up and out like a seeding dandelion head. She wore gold hooped earrings and rouge dashed up her cheekbones.

A woman with romantic tendencies, she must've been nearing seventy yet wore the most inappropriate shoes for the countryside, high heels with stiff leather bows on the back. The visible backs of her ankles were creased like folded towels.

I was in the lounge watching the highlights from the festival on TV, trying to spot Rhett among the crowds, but it was like searching for a poppy seed in a tin full of black pepper. The camera shots swept over heads, obscuring any facial details, and even when I paused the screen it looked blurred, and most faces were shrouded by ponchos against the sheeting rain. There was not a patch of green grass anywhere in the vast expanse of fields. It had been trampled by the masses of moving feet into large peaks of mud and brown pools of slurry.

Yet the atmosphere rose up from the site like steam from a freshly baked pie, and the festival goers doffed their plastic beakers full of booze to the cameras or danced as if they were not in a sodden field laced with human effluent. This was the awesome fun that Rhett was craving, although he was probably keeping dry in a tent with Andreea's limbs wrapped around him.

I popped open a new jar of gherkins and plucked one from the watery vinegar; my cravings for salt had increased over the past few weeks. The taste reminded me of your fingers after you had thrust them inside me, then shoved them into my mouth. I sucked at the firm, ridged surface then bit it in half.

"Darling—only a flying visit," Penny was clutching Virgil, one of her startled-looking poodles under one arm. Today he was sporting a blue bow, not dissimilar to the bows on her shoes, and I'm sure he sneered in distaste as he took in his surroundings. I thought of Parker and the little heart-shaped patch missing from his fur.

"Henry's in his workshop," I told her, "would you like a cup of coffee?"

"Given it up, darling—St. John's raving about green tea. It's got antioxidants. He says it makes you live longer."

St. John—it sounded like 'singe-on" when she pronounced it, as if her latest beau had charred himself. I wondered how old she really was; I'd seen her around the village with a manicured young man, arm in arm, like they owned the place. He was almost half her age but with the placid, compliant look of a man-servant who knows how to service an ageing woman.

I had no idea where he'd materialized from, but at least it kept her away from you. Or so I hoped.

"Ooh cornichons! How very continental." She was staring at the jar of gherkins, so I twisted off the lid and offered it to her, but she waved her hand away as if I'd presented her with a gangrenous finger. I bit another and crunched it loudly in her face. She looked away from me, out the window toward your workshop.

"A little proposition I'd like to discuss." She petted Virgil as she spoke, whose lip curled in a snooty expression. In a stage whisper she said, "It's about my bitches." She feigned a sickly smile and I wasn't entirely sure if she was making a joke. Her face always seemed to swim about as if it were made of boiling gravy.

"Want them stuffed as well, do you?" I couldn't help myself.

"Scarlett, please! You know how sensitive poochie poo is." Penny didn't know how right she was. She may have been more attuned to life and death than most, especially as a breeder, but *after* life and *after* death was another matter entirely.

"Actually, it's something Henry might be interested in," she sniffed as if inventing a story.

"Go on."

"All these *things* Henry's created. You know the mixed-up creatures with wings and fur and horns in the wrong places . . ."

"What about them?"

"It's sparked off an idea."

"What sort of idea?"

"Just a little business venture. By the way, I wanted to congratulate Henry on such a spectacular show." Oh, I bet she did. I saw her stroking your arm and simpering whenever she managed to position herself near you: the village shop, the wassail ceremony, any given moment when she happened to be within flirting distance.

She peered toward the lounge where I had left the TV blaring—a band at the festival was playing loud tribal beats, and a woman sounded like she was giving birth on stage.

"He does *so* inspire me . . ." She was harping on about how she'd visited your exhibition with St. John, who apparently dabbled in contemporary art. "That crocodile was magnificent . . ."

"The crocodile was made by Felix," I said flippantly.

"Of course, yes—I mean—those cows on a merry-go-round."

"Those were Felix too." As I said his name, I felt my belly flip, the way he looked at me, the way he looked at you.

"Of course, silly old me." She cast me a probing glance, as if she'd been testing me. Or my loyalty, perhaps?

"Well—it's all wonderful art. Wonderful!" She went on to say how lucky I was to have such a creative man at my fingertips. I wondered how she'd known about you exhibiting. Did you mention it to her? She seemed to know a lot about it.

"We didn't see you there," I said. Not that I was looking, but Penny was not a woman who faded into the background at any event. I can't see how I could have missed her.

"We popped by later, after the crowds," she exhaled loudly from her nose as if a bad smell had reached her nostrils and she was trying to expel it. "I do need to speak to Henry—it is quite urgent."

"Well, I'll give him a message."

"I'm not sure—well—no, it can wait. When can I catch him?"

"I thought you said it was urgent?"

"No, no. It's fine. I'll pop back later." She pursed her lips and flared her nostrils. More boiling gravy.

"We might be busy later."

"Then I'll call him. Remind me of his mobile number?"

"He never turns his mobile on."

"Email?"

"He doesn't even use the computer."

"Oh dear—still the same old Henry," she hoisted Virgil up onto her hip and he started growling. "Poochie Poo, darling, whatever's the matter. It's only little Scarlett."

But I could tell he wasn't growling at me. He had spotted the stuffed creatures in the lounge and was looking directly at the swoodle. Penny peered through the kitchen door into the lounge to see what he was craning to have a look at. "Gosh," she said, "is that a two-headed swan?"

"Yes," I moved across her line of vision, not wanting her to look any closer at its orb-like body; the same body that had a swatch of Parker's fur on it. We had decided not to exhibit the swoodle; it felt too personal, as if we were reading our love letters in public.

Virgil leapt from her arms and scampered toward the lounge, his hard claws tapping like stilettos on the kitchen floor. I knew what he was sensing. I had felt it myself. Parker was trying to communicate with his brother, pleading for his soul to be released from the swans. He needed to get free of the flapping and honking. The swans too, were not enjoying the confinements of their limbo state.

"Poochie! Virgil! Come here this minute." Penny was after him like a shot, her arms outstretched.

But Virgil had reached the swoodle and stood growling in front of its glass case. He pawed at the glass and the swan's heads nodded in unison. I was reminded of Valentine's Day when you had presented it to me in your workshop; they'd been bobbing in rhythm back then, too.

"He's not normally like this," Penny stooped to pick him up but he turned on her and snarled. "That's enough," she said firmly and held his muzzle with one hand and lifted him with the other, teetering on her heels and sweeping out of the lounge. I followed her and shut the door.

"Apologies for that intrusion. I don't know what's got into him. Don't forget to tell Henry I need him." And she was gone, but her scent remained in the house for ages afterwards. I had to open the windows before it gave me another of my headaches.

Penny was one of those people who seemed to rule the village in a matriarchal capacity. She had power from knowing almost everyone's business before they even knew it. She was a voracious committee member: Women's Guild, the Flower Arranging Club, Harvest Festival Committee, Crafting for Couples, Baking for Beginners, Book Group—you name it, she was in it or on it, or had been at some time in the past. I admired her boundless energy but also wondered when she stopped to consider the purpose of all her involvements. She just loved being busy. You did, too. Why did you have to be busy together?

The rain started pattering again. I could still hear the ghost of Parker whimpering from the curls of his fur patched onto the swoodle. Now I knew I was not the only one to sense something unnatural and sinister in those stuffed creatures. The echoes of Virgil snarling and pawing at the case compelled me to act. I needed to help them, or I'd never get any peace.

Back in the lounge I faced the swoodle and lifted off the lid of the case. When I reached forward to touch the fur, I felt the familiar pulsing at my temples and breathed deeply, hoping it would subside. The heart shape had been sewn so neatly there was hardly a seam but I probed my fingers to the edge where it met the feathers and pulled at the soft, white dog fur. It resisted and the swoodle's whole frame shifted, the swan's heads rocked together as if kissing. I eased my other hand into the case to steady it by holding one of the swan's necks and continued to increase my pressure and tighten my grip on the poodle fur. I needed to remove that part and return it to Parker's original taxidermied body—which was now stationed somewhere in Penny's house. Only I had no idea how I could get it there unnoticed. The thought of removing the fur was all I could put into action at that stage.

Your stitching was strong, I'll admit that, and you had used some strong adhesive to fix it to the mount. I looked around the room, trying to scan for a sharp tool or some scissors. My nails were not strong enough to pull it free; your hold was that powerful. I found an old letter opener among the litter of newspapers and envelopes on the coffee table and jabbed it under the fur to lever it up and away from the mount. A corner came free as the stitches gave a little so I could see the thread. I picked at it with my fingers and even tried to lean in and bite through the thread like a seamstress or a dressmaker might. But I couldn't fit my head and arms into the case. I know this sounds crazy and you must be wondering why I would go to such extremes instead of just telling you how it was affecting me, but the truth was I wanted to beat this. I wanted to prove to myself that it was all in my head and if I removed the fur, and it still affected me, I would know it was not your creations that were the problem. I would need to face facts and ask for help.

As I tugged and strained to remove the fur, I realized I could not do it without damaging your artwork, so I sat back, a little breathless from my exertions. What was I doing, destroying something you had taken time and effort to create? A loving gift, a unique creation. For me. I had no right to destroy something just because I felt it was existentially wrong. I had planted the seeds when I insisted you branch out like Felix. Who was I to change my mind and expect you to change yours, too? You were my one constant in this changeable world, and I needed to hang on to you. Everything else seemed to crumble or disappear. I smoothed Parker's fur back over the swoodle's body and re-positioned it in its case, replaced the lid and walked away.

I reluctantly told you about Penny's visit. "You're far too busy to get involved," I said, knowing that you had a backlog of work to complete.

It seemed to be never-ending, especially since the exhibition. I wasn't complaining. It was good money, but we seemed to be letting it take over our lives. I sometimes wished I'd never said anything to you, never given you the idea to tinker with your tried and tested methods. You were not inundated before, but you had a steady flow of trophies to mount for your regulars who'd been out hunting. The freezers were bursting full of specimens waiting to be dissected and mounted.

In summer, the Levels are a moveable feast, eat or be eaten, where close up the cruel survival of the fittest reigns above and below the water line. Is there a more natural way to live? Those creatures knew the order of life; they had their place within it and acceptance was key in the instinctive flow and order of prey and predator. It was the old story of bird and worm, pike and stickleback, otter and trout. You knew which one would capture the other in its jaws. I wasn't so sure. The hunters brought you deer heads to stuff and mount. I will remind you, the deer seemed to say, of what you have taken, yet I will outlive you.

I had let my hair grow wild under my armpits and on my legs. My ankles and calves were scratched from walking along the hedgerows, and my feet were stained and hardened by the mud. You still indulged in my body the way you always had, filling every part of me with every part of you. Whatever the time of day or night, you would satiate your desire in short, sharp bursts of passion. But instead of feeling liberated, I felt empty and hungry most of the time.

We were driving home and stopped at the traffic lights in town. Three magpies hopped by the side of the road, *pica pica*, flashing their metallic blue-black wings, like men dressed up in evening suits. "We live and die," they said. "You are not meant to enter our world." That was when I vomited into my hands and you had to pull over so I could slop it onto the verge. You handed me tissues to mop up the splatters. Everything seemed bright and hysterical after that. I could hear the voices much more clearly then. The crabbit and swoodle had missed me, I could tell by their excited tones. I was the only one to listen to them after all.

"Perhaps it was something you ate," you said as you prepared me a bedtime drink.

Perhaps it was, but I knew the only way to fix these symptoms was to release those souls. I waited for you to go to bed and I took a pair of sharp scissors and a knife to cut Parker's fur from the swoodle. It became my mission to release those damned souls. Was there another path I could've taken? Was I left with any other choice?

On the days I used to watch you work, I admired you stitch the skin of a roebuck onto its mount—a measured piercing with the point of your needle and a long withdrawal of thread high up in the air like a seamstress darning clothes. You gave it an affirmative tug to tighten the pieces of hide together in an invisible seam where the fur tufted up and concealed the join. All the while, you intently gazed at your creation, concentrating on the detail, turning it this way and that, observing its form and dimensions. You resurrected it so it would be recognized as in the wild. A miracle.

The blackbird, robin and woodpigeon were starting up the morning chorus. A song thrush joined in and the volume grew. Each day our alarm call rang out from the trees and hedgerows, a wake-up siren. The cockerel's long call cut across the morning like a butter knife.

My parents have been dead for more years than the years they knew me. When I add up the time in numbers it clarifies how slippery it is; how the minutes, hours, days, months, and years are like soap on our skin, easily washed away. In all that time, my memories are worn thin like a threadbare blanket. Some are so lacy that they have become see-through and unreliable. A strand of visual here, a cord of conversation there, like cobwebs revealed by the morning dew.

But it shifts and floats away like the memory itself. It is personal. Senses are in the moment; you might be able to capture the essence of a perfume, its smell or taste, like one of those scratch-and-sniff stickers I used to collect and attach to my tin pencil case. But they still smelled fake; they were a poor replica of the original. I even had a sticker that was supposed to smell of gravy, colored brown, a spilled gravy stain, but all it smelt like was furry paper and yesterday's rubbish. The strawberry sticker smelt too sweet, a synthetic red drawing of a strawberry with a spiky green hull. Even in their gaudy reality, these were just ghosts of smells. But you can't properly express scent in drawings or in sculpture. You can't act it out or deliver it on a stage. You can't replicate it in pictures or in visual form. It is only implied on the faces of the perceiver. You can describe it and speak about it: acrid smoke, tarry, choking, black and billowing, dense and putrid, strong and sweet or meaty like a piece of barbequed pork.

But a memory of what you have witnessed can never be undone. It is etched onto your mind in a way that transports you back to when it happened. It can creep up like a stalker and shoot you back to that moment.

The day my parents died is still in vivid technicolor, a piece of moving art. Rhett's green t-shirt and black shorts, my pink dress with the white polka dots, Mother and Father's blue car, the fireman's yellow helmet. All these things could have been in one of my story books or re-drawn in outline in a coloring book for me to fill in with chunky wax crayons; the pink line like someone tried to strike a giant match down my leg; the dark red of the blood on the dog's jaw as he lay on his side in the green grass.

<hr />

I watched as you inserted the glass eyes on to the mount.

"You need the correct eye, or the rest just won't look right at all," you said. "An alligator has thin vertical pupils, like a downward slit; a deer has a large black horizontal pupil—he is the prey, ever-cautious of his predator, so he needs to see around his body." You swiveled the eye left and right. "The eyes of the predators are branded with a round pupil so they can focus directly on their target. The wrong eye could mean the wrong creature."

I knew what you meant. Rhett had a phase of wearing fashion contact lenses to make his eyes look like those of a cat; they were like emeralds with an elongated pupil. It made him look like a lagoon creature. Did he think by changing his appearance he could alter the way he viewed the world?

Glass eyes were never meant to be functional. But doesn't it make you wonder how difficult to preserve are the parts we most value? The outer parts—the skin, fur, feathers, claws, teeth and bones—were what you worked with, discarding the rest. Yet the skeletons were not used, just the skulls of stags sometimes boiled in peroxide to clean the flesh away to display impressive antlers.

I thought of the relics I had seen in an old Greek church once: the finger of a saint, complete with gnarled fingernail, positioned on a velvet cushion in a glass case so visitors and worshippers could parade past and gaze upon it. It had been removed from its owner, long dead, but even so, those pilgrims still sought tangible proof. They needed to see the miracle with their own eyes.

You turned the glass eye around in your fingers and polished it with a small cloth so it gleamed. I half expected you to roll it on its edge across the floor like a boy playing marbles and recalled a school friend saying how she opened the drawer in her grandfather's bureau while looking for chocolate, and his glass eye rolled toward her. I always wondered if her grandfather had placed it there on purpose to teach her a lesson or just stored it in a space where he knew it would not be lost. The eye would slip and move about his eye socket, she said, and sometimes he would not even know that his own eye had turned the wrong way; instead of facing the world, the fake pupil observed the inside of his head. The white of the glass stared at her like a zombie.

The eyes you used were fixed in place, concave, yet they looked as if they might blink or flicker with consciousness at any moment. You stood back, and the creature was complete. It had been born again and opened its new eyes to a new world. A world where nothing was as it seemed. But its destiny would outlive us. Some exhibits housed in museum collections were older than the lifespan of humans or animals. They were immortal, and their afterlives were played out by their longevity and the shuffling spectators that viewed them. A celebrity gorilla who lived most of his life at a zoo was preserved and stationed in a nearby museum, now a static resident of another institution. There were specimens collected by the Victorian explorers who extensively shot, trapped and skinned endless species for research and curiosity. Stately homes adorned their walls with rhino and elk, bears and beavers. Objects were made out of animal hides and bones and horns. It was a ransacking that allowed species to live ironically past their extinction.

◆━━━◆━━◆

I faced the mirror on the antique dressing table in our bedroom and studied my face. When I first met you, I was slim, not thin, but now I was actually bony. My cheeks had sunk and, although I wasn't old, I could see the beginnings of gravity taking its toll. There were dark rings under my eyes, from the headaches I guessed, and my eyebrows had grown thick where I had not plucked them for many months. My hair was wild and long but not unclean. It stretched down past my waist. When I was about twelve, I left my hair to grow and grow until I could sit on it, stretching it taut between the back of my head and my bottom like a frozen waterfall.

My eyelashes were pale but long and, as I leaned in closer to the mirror, I realized how hairy my face actually was. On my cheeks and lips a fine furry down like that of a baby animal was growing. Just inside my lips was a slightly paler color, a fleshy pink that matched the color to the entrance of my vagina. The pores on my nose reminded me of the skin of a pear. And lines on my forehead I had not noticed before had appeared like the ridges left on sand by the moving tide. It was more pronounced when I lifted my eyes in puzzlement.

I studied my eyes and thought of the glass ones you handled. Mine were shiny, as if they could conjure up a tear and let it drip down my cheek with no effort. There were tiny bloodshot capillaries, more so in my left than my right eye, and it added to my tired look. My pupils contracted and expanded as I moved closer to the mirror, like a camera's aperture controlling the light. Around the rim of my iris was a dark black that complemented the hazel. It reminded me of oak trees when they are felled, not only in concentric circles but in the lines radiating out from the center as if reaching for something unspoken, something unseen. I realized as I studied myself so intently, that I was holding my breath.

"Scarlett?" Your gruff voice from downstairs tore the hazy veil that surrounded me. I went to find you. "Scarlett?"

"What is it?" I called as I came down the stairs.

You held something small and square between finger and thumb. A piece of animal hide pressed flat. Giraffe markings.

"You tell me." There was a hint of accusation in your tone.

"Henry? Why are you so mad?"

You thrust the furry square toward me and I took it. I knew immediately what it was. I saw that flamboyant pyrographed name on the back and choked back my reply.

"How?—I mean? Why are you giving me this?"

"You've been with him, haven't you?"

"I—I don't know—" Your rage met me head on.

"Answer me, Scarlett!"

"I met him at the exhibition. That's all." *The sweet scent of patchouli. His breath like a cool breeze on my neck. His fingers brushing against mine as he passed me his business card. I could be your Rhett, y'know.*

"So, he's not pestering you?"

"Henry, why are you so jealous?" *Cherries dangling before my welcoming lips.*

"I don't want you having anything to do with that—man!"

You had no need to be angry with me. I had already decided. I was devoted to you and you only.

You pulled me close and buried your face in my hair, breathing heavily and clutching me so I thought I'd never be released.

"You are mine, Scarlett." You softened a little as I tried to remain still in your embrace, afraid that any movement would break the spell, and me, in half.

I had forgotten about putting Felix's card in the pocket of your coat. We had been so busy when we returned that I didn't think to retrieve it. But I was startled by your reaction. Perhaps I had been talking in my sleep. Felix's presence was as potent as the creatures, always in the back of my mind.

Later that evening, we sat outside until the sun had sunk low behind the hedge and midges were biting my ankles. That was a rare balmy evening in a summer of showers and lower-than-average temperatures. I can't remember when I last bared my arms and legs outside. I wanted to curl up on the sofa with you beneath me, my man-sized cushion, so we retired to the lounge and fell asleep together, my head resting on your chest, listening to the thud-thud of your heartbeat.

I closed my eyes to dream but all I saw were colors dancing on a knife edge and Felix winking at me.

CHRISTMAS DAY / TODAY

Around 2 p.m.

All I ever need is here and now. I have you, and you have me. It is as if the land has weaved a magic spell and kept us bound together.

Some mistletoe berries drop to the floor like fallen kisses. The holly and ivy weave their healing shapes around the hearth, protecting us from demons and ghosts.

The clock strikes two and I become more aware of how empty this house is. We have no guests. Penny has not even phoned. No one has. The fire dies down while you doze after our Christmas lunch. Then I remember the flooded village is empty too. But still no sign of Rhett? It is past lunchtime and I vaguely remember him saying he would join me this year for Christmas. Or did I imagine it? My memory shifts like the light on the wall. It is shadowy and plays tricks on me.

Look. It is silver, bravely piercing the velvet dark that threatens to envelop us. It rises royally over sheets of hardened soil and, myrrh-heavy, it creeps past the empty homes. Starlight seems to emerge from the darkening day, or is it just reflection?

Cross your heart, my beloved. Cross mine too. Let's make a wish together, then you can open your gift from me.

 AUGUST

"Penny asked if I'd like to breed Jinx and Rudy with her poodle bitches."

"So that was the big secret she wouldn't tell me?"

"What big secret?"

"When she came round with her business proposition last month." You didn't pick up on my sarcasm.

"It's just money, Scarlett," you said, "easy money, if they produce a good litter."

"But Jinx and Rudy are labradors."

"They'll produce labradoodles."

"That's been done," I said. Everyone had heard of a labrador crossed with a poodle.

"I know, which is why she wants to do it. People love them; they look pretty and don't molt. Aren't you always telling me to keep up with the times?"

"Can we keep one?"

"We've not really discussed that far ahead."

"So you've been discussing with her already." I felt a pang of jealousy although I didn't know why. She was old enough to be my grandmother.

It was the fact that you were creating something with her, I think, and not with me.

"To be honest, I thought you could sort the breeding with her," you said. "I'm up to my eyeballs with this backlog for the gallery, and I got two more commissions last week."

"Two more? You didn't tell me."

"It was through some of the other clients I've worked for. Nothing too difficult, but I'll have to source some unusual specimens for one of them. The laws are tight even using existing material. There are ways around it, but I like to keep things as genuine as possible. Especially for the ones who like to pay the big bucks." You were rambling on.

"So when was Penny thinking of doing it?"

"Soon, I think. She has her bitches coming into season, so we just have to drop Jinx and Rudy over."

"Won't they have to meet beforehand? What if they don't like each other?"

"Oh, they've met often enough," you said.

"What? When?" My mind started to backtrack over the days when you walked them or took them out in your truck to go shooting. Were you with her then? I left that thought alone, not wanting it to spoil our evening.

The next day, after I had dropped the dogs at Penny's, I made my excuses to leave and said I'd be back later. I felt an urge to plan for Christmas even though it was four months away so went in search of inspiration.

I had seen two women enter the book shop and let their inhibitions drop as a girl exited with an umbrella and yellow coat, letting the wind catch the door and bang shut. The shop assistant had disappeared to the store room and I knew those women did not sense me there, so I loitered behind a tall bookshelf and carried on studying the spines of books. The tone of their voices indicated an intimacy kept for those private moments. I thought perhaps I should rustle my jacket or cough politely to alert them of my presence, but instead I found myself holding my breath, poised like a camouflaged leopard, spying on them.

"You could feel sorry for them out there in the sticks," the taller woman picked up a book on Japanese Flower Art from the low table, not seeming to take much notice of the title as she flicked through and paused at pages with illustrations of lurid bouquets.

The other woman snorted her reply, fingering the edges of books as if testing they were real. "Right in the middle of the flood plain. You'd think they'd have more sense after the floods we've had."

"A friend of Sonya's said they have wild parties, dance naked when it's a full moon and swap partners," the first woman exclaimed, seeming to enjoy the gossip, "You never really know what goes on just under your nose, do you?" She sniffed and I heard her turn the page of a book. "You know who I mean, don't you. That odd bloke, big fella on that island in the middle of the moor, stuffs animals for a living?"

"The taxidermist? What about him?"

My ears pricked up at the mention of you.

"They say he's got a new woman. Gets through them, doesn't he? This one's at least half his age apparently. Pale—like one of them—what d'you call them?"

"Goths?"

"Yeah—goths. Always wearing black and looking miserable."

"I don't know, though," said the smaller woman, "I bet he's good with his hands!"

They really laughed at this, great snorting guffaws. Then the shorter woman with the mousy hair loudly blew her nose and made me jump. It was harsh, listening to strangers mock us just because we were different. I wanted to tell them how good it felt when your hands smoothed over my skin and delved into the crevices of my body. I wanted to tell them how they would never know the depth of our passion. I wanted to tell them how you stoked me like a furnace and that they'd be lucky to feel this heat in their lifetimes. I wanted to dare them to sink to the depths we had. What did they know, with their sensible shoes and buttoned up coats?

I looked down at my clothes. Perhaps I didn't pay enough attention to my appearance. That day, my colors coincided with the dreary weather. Maybe I did wear too much black. I did not have the energy to confront them, so I silently opened a book in case they moved around the corner and somehow recognized me. I pretended I was engrossed in the intricacies of needlepoint techniques used on Victorian bodices but really my mind was ticking over what they had said about us.

The shorter woman blew her nose again, breaking the silence like a trumpeter tuning up for a concert, then screwed up her used tissue with one hand, sniffed and said, "Come on, I'll treat you to a coffee. You'll never guess what I heard . . ."

I realized my fingers had gone numb. I felt like I'd not breathed for those few minutes. Had I even blinked? My fingers were cold, and pins and needles prickled up my arm as if the subject of the book fused with real life. I thrust it back on the shelf and it met with resistance, not quite fitting into the gap. Pulling it back out I saw a small paper manual was lodged at the back of the shelf so squeezing my hand between the two books I teased it out with the tips of my fingers. It looked old and foxed with age. The title was in dark red ink:

Taxidermic Suppression:
Exploring the mystical through the preserved specimen.
by R. H. Wensley.

A cold flush traveled through my veins. I flicked through the wispy pages, thin as tracing paper. They were almost see-through and the type-face looked as if it had been handwritten with a quill. I don't know what made me do it, but I slipped it inside my coat and left the shop with my stolen treasure rustling against my body. Who else would have use for such a thing?

The clouds were gathering, and a breeze flicked the back of my head so my hair fell forward in front of my face. As I started the truck, the radio tuned in on the presenter's voice mid-sentence—". . . only one hundred and thirty-three days until Christmas!" The first recognizable notes of Wham's Last Christmas made me feel instantly nostalgic. It seemed out of place to hear such a Christmassy tune in the height of summer, like eating Christmas pudding on a beach. *"Last Christmas I gave you my heart . . ."* I was looking forward to spending Christmas with you. *"This year, to save me from tears, I'll give it to someone special . . ."*

With the taxidermy booklet on the passenger seat beside me, I found myself turning left, not right, and continued out of town. There was a new estate of houses crushed together on one of the fields where I used to pick cornflowers and cowslips as a child, yet the tarmac was potholed and rough on the main road. I slowed down as I reached the bend by the pub and pulled up on the verge by the row of old willow trees. I remembered those willows; they had been there for years, eternal, woeful, hardened trees that grew straight branches like spikes from their nugget-like trunks.

The pub sign swung a lonely, creaking lament in the breeze, waving a faded painting of a man ploughing a field the old-fashioned way with a horse, furrowing up the soil in straight, deep lines. Letters promoting The Plough Inn were faded and ghostly. Its windows were boarded up with pale chipboard, making the dark walls stand out as if pieces of a jigsaw puzzle were missing. A family of house martins had used the eaves of the roof to build their nest, and droppings spread down the wall into a thick white mound below. It must have been uninhabited for some time, as the paint on the door was peeling and the "To Let" sign had been cracked in half. It hung from the wall like two broken wings of a bird. Someone had spray-painted an "i" between the two words so it read, "Toilet," and a badly sketched outline of an ejaculating penis angled across the wall.

A jackdaw landed on the roof tiles and hopped up onto the chimney stack. It disappeared headfirst then, like a rabbit from a magician's hat, it reappeared and flew off. A few cars passed me by, splashing the summer puddles onto the verge. On the other side of the pub was a field left for pasture. A few new farmhouses were built on the land here, as if competing with the old rambling houses that had stood for centuries, passed down through the generations. Most of the people who lived in the area wouldn't remember my family now. Nor would they remember me. Rhett and I had been buffeted from foster home to foster home when our parents died, and all the old folk we had known had passed on. The towns and villages seemed to merge together like spreading ivy.

I turned down by the pub and followed the narrow dirt track to the end of the lane, stopping the truck in a layby. I killed the engine and waited, looking in my wing mirrors and rear-view mirror, but all I could see were hedges and the occasional sparrow alighting then flying off. As I stepped out of the truck, a sheep let out a noise like an old man complaining and then continued ripping the grass noisily, its jaw rotating and grinding in circles. The rain had stopped and the smell of fresh earth greeted me like an old friend. I breathed in deeply and leaned on the rusted metal gate to look out over the fields toward the blue house.

The rain had dampened down the grain, ripe and ready, with heads of corn dipping heavily with water like they were woefully ashamed. A pair of swallows dived over the field, and the blue sky was dotted with puffball white clouds. A cloud passed over the blue house, and for a moment it was in shadow while the fields all around were lit up. This was the last house where Rhett and I and our mother and father lived as a family. It was the house where I felt most at home, where the badger came to visit me in my sleep and the slow worms meandered silently in the compost heap. It was also the place where I met death head on.

Rhett and I had therapy sessions after the death of our parents, a relatively new concept offered to us as bereaved children. I think they sort of used us as guinea pigs. I remember one particular session when the therapist was perched informally on the edge of her table as Rhett and I sat on the floor on beanbag cushions. We were talking about our feelings—all part of the process to explore our reaction to our parents' death. It was quite revolutionary back then.

Normally people swallowed death down like a piece of gristle with a pat on the back and a sympathetic smile. Then it was a case of count your blessings and get on with it.

"If your feelings were a color, what would they be?" Tina the Therapist asked. This was not her actual name but she had quite shiny cheeks like my Tiny Tina doll with eyes that rarely blinked and synthetic spiky blonde hair, so I remember her as Tina.

"Red," Rhett answered without hesitation and I nodded in agreement.

"Scarlett, how about you," she said.

"Yes, mine are red too."

"And do they have a shape?"

"They are blob-like," Rhett again answered first, keen to grab her attention.

"Liquid," I said, "like skin that's just been burnt off." Rhett looked at me and sort of winced.

"How do you mean, Scarlett?" She was getting interested in me now. Rhett was fidgeting with his Rubik's Cube, trying to beat his personal best time. He was really good at lining up all the colored squares. I could only ever complete one side and that took me ages.

"Well, one moment I feel fine and I think they are ok and that they'll be alive again. Then some days I feel like I'm drowning."

"You said something about skin being burnt," I knew what she was getting at. Rhett had a history of setting fire to things, and no one actually found out how the fire had started that night.

"It gets better but it doesn't actually disappear," I looked at Rhett, who had completed the blue and the yellow sides and had his tongue poking out while he considered the next moves to complete the whole cube.

"Yeah, like my scar," he said. I thought about Rhett's leg, where the smooth skin arced like someone had tried to remold him. He didn't seem to worry about it. Or if he did, he had buried it so deep, his feelings no longer showed.

"And how can we heal scars?" The therapist leaned forwards with her elbows on her knees as if I was about to prophecy an answer to all the world's suffering.

Rhett tossed the toy up in the air and caught it, "Ta da! Done!" He grinned. I grinned back at him and the therapist sighed. He always did that. Swerved off course when we were getting to the nitty gritty. But I had heard him screaming when they changed his dressings. I'd smelled his wounds healing from the inside out as the sticky, gelatinous mess that was his leg formed new skin. Our scars were a permanent reminder of our inevitable pursuit of renewal.

◆—◦——◦—◆

Back in the truck, I reached in my pocket for a tissue but instead pulled out the taxidermy booklet and the swatch of Parker's fur I'd managed to cut off the swoodle. I had to try and redeploy it without Penny noticing.

I flicked through the pages. Wensley said that if the body parts of hybridized creatures were reunited, then soul harmony would be easier to promote. There were hand-etched drawings of the specimens he had researched, including strange mythical hybrids that had been the result of experimentation in soul diversification. It was the distribution of parts that made the transition to the afterlife more difficult. Wensley had described in detail the assimilation of the material and the spiritual in the case of disparate body parts. There was a process whereby the initial reintroduction may be troublesome, even though it came from the original. The separation would have tainted it somehow, but I would try anything to get these damn hybrids to stop harassing me. I knew I was rushing it, but there was no other way without Penny knowing about Parker's missing fur.

I left the blue house without a backward glance and headed toward Penny's to pick up our dogs. This was an ideal chance to try.

When I arrived at Penny's, the door was wide open and I could hear her talking. I stepped into her porch and listened. She was on the phone.

". . . no darling, I won't mention a thing . . ."

I strained to hear without her registering my presence. She was speaking in this hushed, secretive tone, and prickles ran up the back of my neck.

". . . it's for the best . . . no need for her to know . . ."

I'm not normally the snooping type, but something in her voice made me think she was talking about me. You can imagine the jealousy rising up in me like acidic sap in a volcanic tree. What did I not need to know?

I walked down her hallway and stood at the living room door. Penny was perched on the edge of her orange chaise longue holding the phone, letting its curly cord stretch from the large, Bakelite handset that rested on a mahogany side table. The phone cable sort of crossed over her chest like a thin, coiled sash. She saw me and held up her finger in acknowledgement, but she didn't bat an eyelid or act in any way as if I'd caught her out. A practiced liar, a true deceiver, I thought.

". . . no problem, darling. Got to go. Scarlett's just arrived . . ." and she replaced the ancient handset back on to the phone and smoothed down her skirt.

"It's all gone well," she said with no reference to the caller on the phone. I knew it was you.

"Great," I stuck my hands in my pocket and fumbled around for the piece of Parker's fur. And as if in answer to my question of his whereabouts, there he was, pride of place, sitting erect as if waiting for instructions to stand or lie down.

His perfect little stuffed body was positioned near the patio doors, head slightly tilted with an expression of distaste much like Virgil's when Penny visited and encountered the swoodle. I had no idea how I would attach the missing fur without Penny seeing me. I certainly didn't have a plan, but some things just work out better without a plan. You'd know about that, wouldn't you?

"Would it be possible to have a drink?" I asked Penny, moving closer to the patio doors, closer to Parker.

"Of course, darling, would you like to try some jasmine green tea with goji berries?"

I didn't want to try it but said yes to get her out of the room for a while. She left me standing in the crowded room bulging with trinkets and cushions and chairs and piles of *Country House* magazines and paintings in mismatched ornate gilt frames all jostling for space; it was like an antique furniture emporium mixed with plastic tat.

Parker was waiting patiently in the corner. As soon as I heard Penny rattling spoons and cups in the kitchen, I kneeled down next to him and began to inspect his fur.

You had made a good job of making the fur complete, but as I tilted his stiff little body I could see a patch just underneath his rear leg that didn't quite match the other side; it had a slight curve from where you must have stenciled the heart shape. I retrieved the missing fur from my pocket, dabbed it with some superglue and pressed it firmly underneath his leg.

"Lost something?" A man's voice startled me and I dropped the tube of glue onto the thick cream carpet. I was on all fours and had to crane my neck to see a man about my age wearing a black silk kimono.

"Oh, hi. I'm Scarlett." Blushes spread up my neck and face as I shuffled round onto my bottom and blindly reached behind me to grab the glue.

"You certainly are!" he laughed and moved toward me. "Admiring the taxidermy, are you?"

"My husband did it actually." I could feel the leaked glue start to stiffen my fingers together and tried to prize them apart.

"Oh yes, Penny mentioned he was a stuffer." A *stuffer!* The jumped-up twat had nerve. His lips were moist as if he'd just applied lip gloss, and he had shoulder-length damp brown hair that looked freshly washed.

"You must be Singe-on," I said and held out my left hand (the one without the glue) and he took it awkwardly with his right and shook it, a puzzled expression on his face. The glue was well and truly hardened, so two of my fingers were stuck fast. Penny arrived with a tray of rattling floral tea cups on bone china saucers and a matching tea pot, steam curling out of its spout.

"St. John, darling, I see you've had the pleasure of meeting our Scarlett." *Our Scarlett*—I didn't know when I became hers. I was yours and yours alone.

He puffed himself up, more peacock than cobra, as Penny came in the room. His feet were encased in flat black espadrilles and I couldn't help noticing a large tattoo of oriental writing stationed up and around his calf. He saw me looking so I pretended I was admiring the vile upholstered chair whose pattern made it look as if someone had been sick on it several times, then sat on it and smeared it with feces. It was too much to be in their company.

"I've just remembered I'm late for an appointment." I had accomplished what I had come for and quickly squeezed past Penny, keeping my glued fingers behind my back. I bundled Rudy and Jinx in the car. Later, I told you I glued my fingers while mending an old picture frame, but that was actually how I came to have superglued fingers that day. I had been reconstructing Parker. Only it wasn't as simple as putting it all back together again. He wasn't Humpty Dumpty. It was more like mending a china cup where miniature gaps could still let the liquid seep through. Parker's soul was not going to be released so easily.

After my fingers had been unstuck by your special glue-dissolving liquid, I found my copy of Wensley's booklet wedged down the side of the sofa and retrieved it. One of the pages had been creased. Slightly annoyed, I turned to the section entitled, "The Transition of the Soul." I was trying to work out if the sketched image of the mermaid had a real human head when you came crashing through the door, loud enough to wake the dead.

"What are you reading?"

"Just an old book . . ."

"What's it about?"

"Souls and stuff . . ." I didn't want you to know I was unnerved by your taxidermy when you had become so inspired.

"Souls? What about them?" You came nearer so I covered the book and averted you with the offer of my lips.

"I meant what I said about us." You looked intently at me and pressed your lips against mine.

"What?" I slid Wensley's book beneath me and enfolded my arms around your neck.

"The ever after. Us together, Scarlett."

I knew what you were saying, but how could we promise something when we had no evidence it could even be achieved?

"What *is* ever after, Henry?" I wanted you to be clearer, irritated at your assumptions that we could just float off together like happy spirits.

"Us—we'll be together forever. Ever after."

"But where and how and what will it be like?"

You sat beside me and touched my leg. "Scarlett, you think too much. It's just a promise. That's all we need to remember." *Just a promise.* It was never just this or just that, there was always something more, something hidden.

"But what if consent taints free will. Souls can be tainted by other souls in the transition from this life to the next if their material, or physical, bodies are polluted in the process." I was quoting from Wensley at this point.

"Polluted? By what?"

"Don't you see, Henry? These things, these weird hybrids," I swept my hand around the room to further highlight my point. "They're not right. There's a reason they aren't real creatures. Because once you start messing with nature—it, well, it starts messing with you."

"Scarlett, what has got into you? They. Are. Dead. Animals!"

"No, no, that's where you're wrong," I pushed myself away from you and you watched me with a puzzled, slightly concerned expression. "You haven't let them die. Can't you see? You keep them alive."

"I assure you, Scarlett, they are very much dead. Even the ones that look like they are alive. It's not like us humans who can live eternally. They are dumb beasts." You patted me on my leg and got up. I felt like a child again, consoled for having wild fantasies, but I knew I was right and you were wrong. Those dumb beasts, as you called them, were more alive than you could imagine. Wensley confirmed all the feelings and suspicions that had haunted me over the years. Death was just as important as life. And while all living things were not equal, it seemed all dead things were. You went to have a shower.

The floorboards above creaked as you walked about, stripping off your clothes and stepping into the bathroom. I peered behind me at the hybrids. Their glass eyes peered back. "Glue us and stitch us and harness us to this world," they said, "but we will always be yearning for the great beyond. The time will come. For all of us."

I turned my back on them and wondered what Rhett was doing and where he was now while I was trying to survive. He could've been camping in a desert or hiking up a mountain or building an igloo for all I knew. I heard the water from the shower splash against you in synchronized beats with the raindrops on the window ledge.

There should be different words for rain, because the rain here is not uniform. It can be cruel and hammering, lashing down in sheets like a waterfall, or it can be light and misty, almost as if someone were spraying an aerosol over your head. There is the type of rain that soaks, rain that bounces, rain that trickles or floats or ripples like tears down a cheek. We have seen and felt all types of rain since living here on the moor, but the rain at the end of August was not just unwelcome; it was intrusive and hindering. This was biblical rain. The rain Noah had been warned of, that prompted him to build an Ark for his family and all the creatures of the earth.

Out here we knew the risks of water sinking and meandering through the landscape. It was pumped and managed from our rivers and ditches so we could live in dry, clean homes. But when the rain kept falling, the noises from the villagers rose up above the pitter pattering of raindrops. We all knew that water found the easiest route. It didn't discriminate between those who had built a home and the vulnerable farm fields absorbing the excess.

Yet we continued to mop up the water that dripped into our lives, onto the floors as we discarded our saturated clothing, down our necks, between our toes. Muddy smudges were all over the kitchen floor, and the dogs in their pen shrank back into their kennel and looked out with low, gloomy expressions.

"This is not a proper summer." I felt depressed as I looked out at the grey sky and darkened ground. "When will it ever stop?"

I still walked the dogs every day in the rain, and even they seemed reluctant to go out, lowering their muzzles and shaking their coats to spray droplets of water in wide arcs. "It's good for the plants," you said and kissed me on the top of my head. "I thought you liked living out here."

I said nothing but stared outside at the rain lashing down.

CHRISTMAS DAY / TODAY

3 p.m.

I see him limping with a delicate hop on one white paw, like a ballet dancer protecting an injury. I turn away but cannot avert my gaze for long. He whimpers, and I feel a slow ache leak from my heart area. Then I sense eyes behind me and lurch from sympathy to survival. The head of a hawk on the body of a sloth edges closer, a slow-motion parody of predator matched with placid tree-dweller. A laugh surfaces from within like a hic hic hic and the thing turns its head away, as if it were an adult disgusted with the presence of a child with a dirty nose. My soul dips to the soles of my feet and spreads out in a viscous puddle like black treacle.

I take a mental note of the hybrids in the room:

Swoodle

Wallopea

Mynizard

Cockapussy

Cowstrich

Slo-hawk

A collection of jackalopes

If I catalogue them like this I can be prepared for their shifts in activity as the day progresses. The nocturnal creatures take control as night descends; the diurnal parts of animal are more confident in the morning as day breaks. Hunger rises up and dampens down. Instinct battles against the confines of their form. The souls fight each other with ripping intensity. It grates on my own being, like a rake being dragged across a slate floor.

What would I do without Wensley's gobbets of knowledge? He states that he is an amateur, but I know no other who has devoted their time to the study of souls contained in the bodies of hybrid animals. They have been created by man to satisfy . . . to satisfy what? A need for some variety. Had we not enough variety already, created by gods (or evolution, whichever your leaning), placed on our hurtling globe for us to wonder at?

You have woken and reignited the fire. The paper from the presents we unwrapped curls and blackens in the flames. Beside me a beautiful silk gown with hand-stitched embroidery is laid out. Your gift to me. I feel like Cinderella when her fairy godmother arrives and announces—"You shall go to the ball." It is a feeling of expectancy with a fluttering of nerves.

I remember creating my gift for you. I had to wait for the right time of the month, then positioned the end of the pipette between my legs and drew the menstrual blood into the glass tube. It was a bit messy, I admit, but it looked magnificent when I had transferred it to the glass phial with the silver top and chain.

You smile. There is little more you can do. How I love your smile. It has become a rarity these past few months. You hold the phial up to the light, look at me, then fasten the chain around your neck, tucking it beneath your jumper so it can sit against your bare skin. There, it will become warm from your own blood.

You sift through the cards and unopened envelopes dropped off for us along with some supplies from villagers who have left their homes for Christmas. There is a long, thick cream envelope bearing the insignia of FdS. You run your finger inside the envelope flap to create a jagged edge and slide the card from it. Then with a roar you rip it up and throw the pieces of card and envelope on the fire.

I am startled by your sudden vehemence after your earlier tenderness. There can be only one person to incite such a reaction. I stare into the fire and watch as the shapes of animals form then disappear. Then the face of Felix leers out, grins, winks and is gone. I want to spit at him, but my mouth is dry and tight.

The stockings hang on either side of the fireplace. They are red and green felt with five-pointed gold stars dotted asymmetrically on the fabric. I try to count them but my vision becomes blurry. You take a swig of cider from a bottle and jab at the fire with the iron poker to shift the logs. Then you pace about the room, lifting up the pile of books and papers on the small table. What are you searching for? You find it and start ripping and tearing, screwing up paper and throwing it on the fire. Not just scrap paper–I spy a cover, large and hardback, a new book. I catch a glimpse of the image of the wolpertinger with its fangs and antlers projecting from a hare's body–it is Felix's book, Wolpertinger Dreams. You are destroying it. I want to encourage you but don't know why. The fire eats it up like the meal of some hungry demon who feasts on others' dreams.

Will you go so far as to add your own creations to this feast of destruction? Please, please–we can start again. A new birth. A shining star of promise in this gloomy hinterland. Perhaps it is not too late for us to be saved from our own mistakes. You sit with your head in your hands. A lull in the animal noises brings the illusion of peace. I stare at your body, searching for the shape of your spirit in the hunched figure before me.

$\mathcal{S}$EPTEMBER

In a quiet place, you realize how noisy the world is; it pulses and thrums. Past the periphery of the windswept branches, through gaps in fences, circling around buildings and benches and vehicles, the artifice of machinery and the endless rattle and scrape of plastic and metal, past the metallic hum of electromagnetic waves, even beneath the rumble of our bellies—the borborygmi of our digestive systems—there is another indistinct sound, a sound most human ears have forgotten to decipher. It is the nonverbal sound of life itself, and without it we would cease to have a purpose. It tells us who we are, and why we are.

Babies and animals are more attuned to this sound. Some call it instinct. But if you really notice this whisper of the void, in the space between the spaces, it is likely to make you question everything you've learned about this world. If you sit motionless for long enough, do you detach from the world or do you become a part of it? I had tried to remain still through the practice of meditation. Then I found the fidgets set in to my muscles. I was distracted intermittently by minutiae—dust on the edges of books and ornaments, a fluttering racket of a pigeon's wings on a branch, the changing pattern of light and dark on the inside of my eyelids as I tried to blink out the interruptions.

Outside, for example, everything moved. Even the apparent dormancy of the bulbs I had planted pulsed and slowly merged with the soil, waiting. They were active even in their resting state. We wait on the surface of this planet, compressed by gravity, but we are whizzing at huge velocities through space and spun constantly on the earth's axis like pinned moths on a board; our only reference point is the change we see around us, a cycle of never-ending revolution.

You likened me to a reptile, preferring to absorb the heat and light, assessing my environment, adapting myself chameleon-like to situations and people. Was I too adaptable or not enough? There are limits to how far you can adapt before you are caught by your tail and have to shed it to escape.

"Chameleons can see two things at the same time," you told me. "Their eyes rotate at three-hundred-and-sixty degrees independently." If I could roll my eyes backwards, could I see my brain? As a child, I used to think that would be an impressive trick; to examine the inside of my body with my own eyes.

You have touched the brains of animals, eased the moist, grey whorls of matter from the skull cavity; you have scraped the layers of fat from their skin, and discarded the skeletons and fibrous sticky tissue. You have touched death's glorious aftermath.

Once, I stroked a dead heron that lay on your work bench, smoothing over its prehistoric beak with my forefinger and touching the sparse tuft of feathers on the crown of its head.

"What if you could extract more than physical parts?" I said to you. I imagined you tentatively teasing out the soul of a dove with an olive branch or luring a heron's soul with the effigy of an eel. "Where would the soul reside? In the head or in the heart?"

"Solar plexus," you said.

"The what?"

"Where you feel butterflies, your tummy, that's where you'd feel it." You poked my stomach between my bellybutton and breasts, making me draw a sharp breath through my nose. I wanted to grab you but enjoyed the tension that played out between us in those moments when the air thickened like we were drowning together but didn't know it. It was like the time we had talked about my parents' death and I wanted to be alone, to wallow in my own memory in which you played no part. Yet, you were my rock when I hit the bottom of that particular watery well and all I could taste was stale emptiness.

"Stop being so hard on yourself," you said. "You were just a kid." But advice is not always easy to swallow. Not when you are being eaten up by guilt.

You left the door of your workshop open one day, and a waft of dried-out hide met my nostrils as I approached. That was the first time I realized the descent of my obsession, as if it had ripped through the boundaries of this world to the next. I thought I saw the creatures move, but the lightbulb was flickering and could've tricked my senses. You smiled at me, a wry silent smile of closed lips that had met contemplation but not tasted it.

"I don't want to intrude," I said.

"No," you sounded quieter than usual.

"Can I come in for a moment?"

"Scarlett?" As you softly said my name, I felt the distance disappear between us. You had been working for so long I didn't know if I could bear your absence any longer. It wasn't the physical absence; we still saw each other every day and shared the same home and bed. But you had gone someplace far away from the "us" we used to be. Something had come between us. Does that make any sense? We were fast becoming the strangers we were when we first met, and I wanted to draw you to me like I had back then.

"I've been thinking about Christmas," I said.

"Christmas?"

"Yes, just wanted to plan a few things, get organized."

"Of course, yes."

"I'd love a real tree this year."

That was when we decided we would pick and fell our own tree, trudge up to the woods and see it in its natural splendor. There were factors to consider: potential height, breadth, branch distribution, overall shape, and color. Once presented with numerous possibilities, how could we quickly decide? It was almost better to be given an option and be done with it. But no, we allowed ourselves a few hours to walk to the hills where the trees had been planted to stake our spot like settlers of the Wild West. We would find our tree and claim it.

A group of walkers trudged in our slipstream, following us on a single track through the woods. All the rain had meant the ground was sodden and fertile, yet that day was bright and warm. The sunlight played through the leaves like it was made of symphonies or liquid gold.

The disinfectant smell of pine, combined with early stages of leafy decomposition, rose up from the forest floor. I wanted to plaster my arms and face with it. You had persuaded me to wear boots and something to cover my legs. My thin jacket was tied in a loose knot by its arms about my waist. My arms were bare and my cheeks felt aflame with the first kiss of autumnal air, pleasantly warm but with an edge of the winter to come.

When we reached a small dip in the path that widened as if the bank had been carved away, we sidestepped in unison to let the walkers pass by in a rustle of sensible clothing. You stood next to me and we nodded our greetings to them as they stomped and puffed away down the track. It was rare to see people on this route deep in the woods, and they were the first sign of human life we had seen all that day. A woman with Nordic walking poles and a hat set at a jaunty angle thanked us in a loud, plummy voice, eyeing your moustache with a giggle.

Then, we were alone in the woods.

I felt strangely aroused by the tranquility as I pressed my back to your chest and you slipped your hands into the pockets of my thin cotton dress. We were standing alone and the pathway lay silent, stretched like a gash among the hard tree trunks and mad chaos of undergrowth. You nuzzled your face into my hair and started sucking my earlobe, kissing my neck in hungry mouthfuls. The world thickened with the thud of blood pulsing through my veins. I wanted you closer. I wanted you to strip me like you stripped the hide of an animal from its limp frame.

You pulled me around to face you and kissed me so hard I had to break free to gasp some air, but I felt heat spread up from my groin, and that thrilling pulse between my legs. You grabbed me by the hand and led me through the bracken at the side of the path, hacking with your free arm like a machete through the jungle. You were leading me to the dark interior of the wood.

Once through the mesh of undergrowth we found a clearing untouched by ramblers. The stillness purred all around us. It became our private domain. You pressed your mouth against mine, both hot hands clasping my cheeks. You tasted of salt and sweat and meat.

Then you were upon me like a wild boar, all teeth and spit. And your weight pushed me up against a fallen trunk, hoisting my dress up over my back. I steadied myself against the rough bark. You grunted a low, hard rhythm, the slap of your hips on my backside. I imagined steam coming off us, flames licking at our loins. We were rocking in madness. I thought I might explode.

My eyes were closed but I sensed the trees, our only witness, unmoved by our primal orgy. "We've seen it all before," they seemed to say, with leaves turned upwards to the light. "We've seen it all before."

It must've been over in minutes, but I felt like time had expanded, as if we had tumbled into a place long ago reserved for non-reason. I collapsed onto the moist red earth and layer of fallen pine needles, listening to your breath slow down to become a pattern of high and low, inhale, exhale. The world reappeared around us more vibrantly than before, pierced by our lust. A blackbird sang a noisy chatter and in the distance I heard the roar of a chainsaw. We were never far from life.

We said nothing to each other as you buckled up your trousers and I brushed my dress with my hands, retrieved my ripped panties and shoved them in my pocket. You held my jacket for me to enrobe like we were leaving a restaurant. I smoothed your hair back and you did the same with mine. Then we made our way back from where we had come, through the bracken, this time carefully holding the brambles between cautious fingers so they would not catch on our clothes. We returned to the path in silence. That was when we saw the perfect tree for our home this Christmas.

You carved the letters "S" and "P" onto its expanding trunk, and we sealed its fate.

There were a few fine days of sunshine in September. My body was winding down toward hibernation as the leaves mutated into autumnal oranges, ochres and yellows. One such fine day I was studying Wensley's taxidermy book outside on the lawn that sloped toward the trees.

I was about to turn the page when a tiny bug landed on the frilly edge of paper separated like a delicate fan. Instead of flicking it with my finger, I observed its movements. It was a small fly but none like I'd observed so closely before–striped with yellow and black but not furry like a bee. It was more like a manufactured piece of machinery, neat, squared off and shiny. Its eyes were black dots and a small proboscis made its head look eccentric, as if it were smoking a tiny cheroot. The legs were like micro-fine dark hairs and I didn't want to trap them between the pages of the book, so I turned it toward the light. The bug moved in unison as if it were on a revolving stage, its entire body getting its bearings. For a moment I worried it would fly at my face and become waterlogged by the liquid coating of my eyes, or enter my mouth or nostrils or ears to be ingested accidentally or retrieved by a clumsy finger that would most probably crush it. But it didn't fly toward me. When it didn't move, I spoke to it. "You're beautiful," I said, imagining my whispering voice a booming tannoy to its compact features. Upon hearing my affirmation, it lifted its wings and flew off toward the trees. A small piece of paper slipped from the pages of the book. I don't know how I'd missed it before then. Written in old fashioned handwriting, quite similar to the scrawling type in Wensley's book, was one sentence:

Never underestimate the power of love over death.

The book was over a hundred years old, and yet it spoke directly to me. I sensed the hold love had over the ages, and I hoped and prayed our love would never die.

Upstairs in our bedroom I went to retrieve the petals of the dying geraniums on the windowsill that had been placed there over the summer, but something moved next to my fingers. A buzzing sound met my ears, intermittent like a phone noisily set to vibrate. As I came closer, I could see it was a dying wasp on its back, the tail of its sting set into a rhythmic throb of anguish. It swam in mock upside-down flight, and I sensed its fatigue, the end of its days. Another two lay dead next to it, and as I surveyed this wasp Valhalla, another materialized and flew lazily toward the window, tapping fruitlessly against the glass. It seemed, that day, a visitation of insects sharpened my attention to the smaller details in our life.

Dying wasps were everywhere attempting to crawl slowly up the wall. As one landed, another appeared in a slow, steady flight toward the window, dropping down in exhaustion. Two, three, four were dotted across the duvet on our bed, some crawling, others expired. I shuddered and stepped back out of the room to fetch you.

⭠⭤⭥⭢

"You need to destroy the nest," the wasp man said, "or they'll keep coming back year on year. If the queen remains, you'll always have a problem."

He had dispensed his white killing powder and now *all* the wasps were dead. They had apparently set up home in the loft space above our bedroom. This was the buzzing I could hear at night, I thought. It wasn't in my head after all. It offered a brief respite from my fears, a rational explanation. Yet a few nights after, when I had cleared away all the dehydrated dead insects and aired the room of its chemical smell, the buzzing returned. At first, I was angry that the wasp man had not fulfilled his promise, and the poison powder had not worked. But it was not the wasps creating the incessant buzzing. I knew it was from another source entirely. Another dimension. No matter how hard I tried to ignore the creatures you had made, they continued to remind me that they would keep returning. They wanted answers just as much as I.

I flicked through Wensley's book and scanned the chapter headings: "Awe of the Exotica," "The Healing Power of Relics," "Conversing with the Dead," "The Transition of the Soul." There were hand-etched drawings of the specimens he had researched.

I returned to "Conversing with the Dead" and read:

Accounts of conversing with the dead are rarely recorded due to the invalidity of their authenticity or the intense personal link that the conversee and converser has or had. Deceased humans are most likely to be the recipient of first contact, not the initiator of contact themselves, unless there is direct association. On the rare occasion when a living subject is contacted by the dead, there will also be a strong, physical link, for example, an object or item belonging to the deceased, or, in rare cases, the deceased's bodily parts.

I was sure I wasn't the initiator of contact; those creatures were bothering me, not the other way. I thought of keepsakes such as hair or religious relics that were once regarded as powerful totems of healing or significance. I read on:

In the case of deceased animals, the principle remains. There is a physical body, which can be sensed with normal earthly faculties; the etheric body, which is the light transitional body that floats nearby after the physical's demise; and the astral or soul body, which traverses to the afterlife. In the cases of "taxidermic suppression" one has encountered, it is the faint etheric body of the creature that does not have the sufficient energy to travel alongside the astral body to the afterlife, hence a series of stages need to be enacted to allow the specimen to be free of its "ghost soul" should it be causing problems with live entities.

One would like to emphasize that traditional taxidermy does not seem to encounter as many occurrences of taxidermic anomalies as hybrid or mythical taxidermy, which one believes may be the result of soul, or astral, confusion that arises when species are mixed together shortly after physical death has occurred.

There was a picture of a rabbit with antlers and the legs and wings of a bird, with the inscription—*Wolpertinger,* just like Felix's front cover image of his book, *Wolpertinger Dreams,* which I hadn't actually read in full but just flicked through, fingering the glossy pages to see if there were any shots of him. There weren't, but the images were self-aggrandizing and fantastical, much like the man himself.

Wensley had published his book in 1898, and it was quite unremarkable in appearance at first glance. It was a thin booklet. The print was small and I imagined readers squinting in the yellow haze of candle or gas lighting. That's when I thought about the humming sounds, the wasps, and noises I had been hearing. There would not have been much electrical interference in Wensley's day, yet he referenced the buzzing sounds quite frequently and recommended candlelight as the purest source of *escalation*. It stated:

Escalation is a process whereby a natural source of ignition, such as fire or candlelight, can be used to help the etheric body transcend, or be released to the afterlife, and henceforth acquire unity with its astral body. The most successful escalation attempts have involved complete destruction of the physical matter in which the etheric body resides. The easiest and safest way to enact this process is to burn the specimen in a furnace or fire so only ash remains. The soul is then able to travel freely without being harnessed to the physical mount within which it has been tethered. One has witnessed cases where the owner of a taxidermied prize specimen, suffering from taxidermic suppression, has waved a lit candle before the subject in the hope that the etheric body will latch on and be removed. However, while this has the perceived effect of success, the light itself is not enough; it is necessary for the flame to touch the entire specimen in order to have an effect.

My thoughts turned to Parker. I had reunited the speck of fur with his body, but this was not enough. His poodle soul would still be tethered, and the division he had experienced with the swans meant he was doubly confused. I was confused too. What did all this mean for the mountains of creatures you had made? All those hybrids of cats, dogs, hyenas, cows, rabbits, birds, rodents and reptiles—not to mention the exotic creatures you had sourced. They would be struggling and gaggling and squawking and scratching and hissing and tearing and biting to be free, and it was entirely my fault.

All this had been my idea.

I checked my mobile. Three missed calls from an unknown number. No messages.

"You've lost your appetite," you said as we ate dinner in front of the TV. I was cross-legged on the sofa watching you devour a plate of ribs off a lap tray, ripping the meat from the bones and sucking the juices. I looked at my plate, picked up a bone and nibbled the end but nothing seemed to satiate me. All the food I ate seemed to have a metallic edge that coated my tongue; my enjoyment of taste had been affected as well as my hearing.

"I have a little surprise for you," you said between enthusiastic mouthfuls. I knew you sensed something was not right. I normally finished my food before you, wolfing it down and staring hungrily as you finished yours. I could clear your plate too like a ravenous scavenger ready to pounce on any discarded scraps. But now I placed my dish of untouched ribs back on the side table and sat back onto the cushions.

"What kind of surprise?" I tried to sound enthusiastic.

"You'll have to wait until tomorrow."

"You can't tell me I have a surprise then tell me I have to wait a whole day to find out what it is!"

"Scarlett, you are unable to muster any ounce of patience in that beautiful body of yours."

"I know. So tell me what my surprise is."

"No, I will not be harangued into submission." At first, I had a sinking feeling that you had created another hybrid like the Valentine's Day swoodle. So I decided a bout of tickling might get you to reveal the secret surprise. I grabbed your belly and made my fingers wriggle up to your armpits and down. You tensed up trying to grab my hands but I was too quick. "Stop–Scaaaarlett–no ho ho ho." You sounded like Santa. Then, as if jolted by a strike of lightning, you sat upright and almost flung me out the way with your bulk. I bounced back onto the cushions.

"Oh my God!" your voice boomed in my ear. Your shift in mood startled me as you leaned forward to get a better look at the TV screen.

"What? What is it?" I looked at you looking at the TV screen. I followed your gaze, but it was just a reporter outside a big stately home. "What's the matter?"

"Shhh, shush." You grabbed for the remote control and turned up the volume.

"... said to be one of the world's most famous artists, specializing in mixed-up taxidermy, also known as rogue or hybrid taxidermy, is wanted in connection with several inquiries. It is thought that he is the subject of an investigation in the illegal import of rare or exotic species of animals in order to create his multi-million pound artwork ..."

The camera switched to a close-up shot of a wolpertinger next to Felix's book.

"... De Souza has led a high profile, often controversial, life and police say they are keen to establish his whereabouts ..."

They flashed an image of the hybrid crocodile hanging from the ceiling of the exhibition. I recalled the slow, cool tear sliding down its cheek. The news continued but your face had faded to ash. You looked at me, then back at the screen, then back at me.

"What's the matter?" I asked you, "That's good news isn't it? He won't be number one in the taxidermy world anymore." A flicker of excitement was soon replaced with foreboding. You sat rubbing your hands over your face as if digesting something rotten.

I knew that look. I attracted that kind of energy. Call me a bright shining beacon of menace, a brilliant, dazzling lure that only knew one conclusion: trouble. I brought discord where there was harmony, doubt where there was true faith. I hardly knew Felix, but I knew his allure. You must believe me, my darling Peppercorn. He was nothing to me, yet he was the sort of man that held me captive like a wild cat in a cage.

You remained speechless so I had to ask you, "You haven't done anything—you know—illegal have you?"

You puffed out your cheeks, exhaling slowly, your face resuming some color, but I could see the shadows of worry working underneath your features. I had grown more and more sensitive to your moods. I thought back over all the exhibits we had documented, all the licenses we had received and the paperwork we had filled out.

"This could be your chance to knock him off the top spot," I said and snuggled up to you, pressing my shoulder up and under your arm so you could rest it around my back. You said nothing, but your hand lay heavily on me like something playing dead. You had offered me a surprise but had got one yourself instead.

<hr />

The morning after, I was still waiting for my surprise but it seemed you had been sidetracked by the news that Felix was missing. You had lit the fire early, way before I surfaced from sleep, and I noticed you had burned a stack of papers. When I asked you about it, you told me it was nothing.

I squeezed you and glanced behind at the rows of stuffed creatures all staring back at me with expectation. I scanned their body parts as if I could dissect them and reform them into what they used to be. A piercing pain shot through my head. I winced, but you took this as an affectionate squeeze and held me tighter with your big arms around my back, crushing the air from my chest.

The image in Wensley's book flashed across my mind—our etheric bodies were merging more tightly together like an unbreakable cord. I set out to buy plenty of candles and matches and start my experiment to release the stuffed ones' trapped souls.

This would be a new start. First, I needed to bring life back into our relationship. So, I spent the day preparing myself. After my bath, where I had defuzzed my entire body of unwanted hair, I rummaged around in my cosmetics bag. It had not been touched for months, and a light film of dust had settled on the contents. I found my tweezers and plucked out the hairs that had grown stray and ugly on my eyebrow line. When I finished, I scanned my face for any other unwanted fluff and plucked that in the same quick motion. I applied some foundation across my cheeks and down my neck. I now looked like a canvas ready for color. My skin tone looked more even, but I dabbed some lighter concealer beneath my eyes to blot out the dark shadows and down my pointed nose to make it seem smaller. Finding the only eyeshadow, a cracked green tablet, I used a little bud to paint my eyelids to the corners. My mascara was gloopy and thick, but I pumped it in and out then brushed the black liquid on to my lashes, opening my eyes like a surprised doll.

I looked at my face—more mature, but fake. It was as if I had reinvented myself. Finally, I retrieved my lipstick, the dark red I had worn when I met you on the beach. A mating call? You had remarked on its color then and said I looked very smart to be walking alone on a deserted beach. Only it wasn't deserted. You were there. And I. Predator and prey.

I carefully widened my lips to apply the color then instinctively pressed them together. Here was a different me to the girl I used to be, scavenging on compost heaps and running wild with Rhett across fields. I understood why Penny always wore make-up; it was empowering, like spreading tribal paint across your most visible features, stating who you were, declaring battle.

I sat for a while just looking at the transformation to my features and felt my back straighten up and my shoulders push back to accentuate my cleavage. My breasts became fuller and rounder. I was reclaiming the Scarlett I was supposed to be. Fearless warrior who always got what she wanted. And right then, I wanted you to want me more than those dead things.

It was nearly 6 p.m. I knew you'd be cleaning up and would come up the path through the back door, so I positioned myself in a place where you'd see me the minute you opened the door, wearing just the mink stole to cover my nipples.

"Holy crap, Scarlett?"

I was stock still and maintained my expression (I'm not sure how, as I was growing cold). But I felt like an actress with layers of make-up, and my nude body getting goose pimply from the evening chill. You stood looking at me, leaving the door ajar and smoothed your hand back over your receding hair.

"What's all this in aid of?"

I said nothing and continued to stare back at you. I blinked slowly like some sort of automated doll. You moved toward me and lifted the mink's head, which lay on my right breast looking down at my nipple which had hardened in the coolness of the kitchen.

"Are you trying to compete with my specimens?" you chuckled a little and ran your hand down one side of my body to my thigh, where you lingered before walking behind to my other side and surveying me as if I were a sculpture in a gallery. I had perched upon the sill and half regretted this pose, as my bottom was becoming numb and my ankles crossed over were making my feet tingle with pins and needles. My hands propped me up, pushing my breasts forward. I know it was suggestive and I wanted it to be. I wanted you to notice me like you used to.

How you used to study every inch of me and touch me with your hands, your lips! I felt moist from the stillness and the anticipation, the surge of power from your presence. Only an hour ago I had felt mad and angry that those creatures were taking over our lives, but now I knew how addictive they were. The precision and texture, the deep inner-being extracted and examined.

I could smell you and wanted you to move closer, but you stood to the side of me just out of my line of vision, waiting to see if I would keep up the pretense. Between my legs I felt the pulse of hot waves. It would've been easy to grab you and let you fuck me hard and fast on the kitchen floor, but I wanted this pleasure to last, to savor it and control it. It was a matter of battling with instinct, but I could not deny my physical body was reacting already without your touch. You smoothed the fur on the mink so I could feel it press against me. The edge of your little finger sent tingling down to my groin and up to my neck as if activating a chemical reaction.

"So Miss Scarlett becomes one of my exhibits," you whispered in my ear just close enough so I could feel your breath. "And what a fine specimen she is."

I shivered and blinked, wanting you more than ever to touch me. Still by my side, you let the back of your hand brush over my belly and down to my inner thighs. Then your fingers swept back up between my breasts. I tried to hold my breath as you continued your exploration up and down my body, feeling the wetness grow and the heat rise.

"This young skin is soft," you breathed in a heavy sigh and reached down between my thighs.

"I'll make you come alive," you said, lingering on each word, unbuttoning your pants. And I wanted to resist you, in my own battle. I wanted to gain control and excite you from just being near me like you had while you watched me sleep when we first met. But even though your breath was quicker, and I could sense a slight shake in your hands, I knew you had me on the tips of your fingers. In that moment I would do anything for you, I would give my life for you if you could hold me in that delicious, sweeping, pulse of glorious ecstasy.

"Would you like that, Scarlett? Would you like to come alive?"

I couldn't hold myself still any longer and turned to face you. You took your cue to plunge deep within me while I leaned against the sill. Once, twice, three times was all it took before we both collapsed into each other in a shuddering mess.

You looked at my face and said, "Why are you wearing all that make-up?" I burst into hysterical laughter. You had seen past my disguised outer layers. You always did.

Later that night, I removed all traces of the make-up that had not been kissed or licked from my skin and tipped the contents of my cosmetics bag into the bin. Why did we need all these fake coverings? I made a decision to clear all those unnecessary things from my life that I'd carried with me for too long.

CHRISTMAS DAY / TODAY

4 p.m.

I have always loved the comforting feel of fur on my bare skin. It feels like a creature in its own right, a rippling, glimmering ocean of follicles pushed up to trap warmth.

The creatures mime their moods. The swoodle twitches its two beaks, rippling its feathers as if the wind has rained words on his back and he is reforming them into runic symbols that tell me the secret of this place. I grasp at their lines and curves as if to decipher them through possession. I want to know what they say. Those words from the ballooning sky are like the decorations that drip from our Christmas tree. Beneath its luscious branches, on its trunk, are the carved letters, "S" and "P."

A bauble dropped from one of the branches lands near my feet. It mutates into a quivering mass of meat, womb-shaped, translucent pink and glowing like a jellyfish. Then it leaps across the floor as if an electric current has pulsed through it, charged with life.

I hear glass breaking.

My eyes are full of grit.

A hare is motionless on a wooden stand, gazing toward the cloudless, moonless ceiling.

OCTOBER

"Penny's having an emergency flood meeting. I think we should go."
You were covered in mud. It clung to your trousers in dark smears. You
took off your boots and washed your hands in the kitchen sink, splashing
brown soap suds onto the draining board.

"Do we have to?" As I said it, I remembered the candle experiment
from Wensley's book. "Where is the meeting going to be held?"

"At Penny's house. Why?"

"Will the puppies be there?" I thought this a clever ruse. I could
pretend to see the puppies but actually take my candle and see if Parker's
soul responded to the light. It was worth a try.

"Oh, I get it," you said, "not interested in our home getting flooded
but if there's a puppy, you're there in a shot!"

"You know me." I squeezed you and felt the cool wet of your clothes
seep onto me. I let it dry, like a second skin, and later picked at the crusts
of mud, dreaming up new ways to free myself of the darkness that seemed
to descend without any notice. I knew that to live in the middle of the
countryside meant a compromise of modern comforts and, even more so,

I realized that we were the unnatural invaders of the wilderness. It was we who encroached on what already had a natural order, not the other way round.

I flicked on the radio and pulled my cardigan tighter around me. It was getting chilly at night-time and we'd soon light the fire again. The lawn was sodden from the rain, the pond spilling over the sides and running down to the rhyne. The trees' remaining leaves clung on like chrysalises waiting for transformation. The fallen ones clogged together in clumps or adhered themselves to the window panes like opaque flat hands trying to feel their blind way through the glass. The birds looked disgruntled; the cows looked clogged and heavy, mud clinging to their flanks; the sheep had been taken in early to prevent their hooves becoming rotten; the villagers moaned about the river levels getting dangerously high and the authorities taking no action. The aquifers, last year, had been dried up, at their lowest level for years. Now it seemed they had miraculously filled over the past few months of rain. The rivers would soon reach their limit, teetering on the brink to push their swollen mass up and over the banks like fattened eels spreading onto the moor. A committee, headed by Penny, petitioned the Environment Agency to do something: dredge the rivers, position more pumps to take the water away from the properties, anything, but the waterways were already dangerously high by now. The lessons from the past had not been learned. We were riparian landowners too with our boundaries flanked by ditches that sported ancient willows in rustic rows and hawthorn hedges. Frustrated vengeful rumblings came up out the peat bog like Grendel's mother resurfacing. But I had decided nothing would spoil our Christmas, especially not the British weather.

<hr />

Half the village turned up at Penny's house. It sat higher than the curve of the river, where the brackish water bulged and rushed in strong eddies. Here, the kingfisher and heron observed and pierced the water with ease. St. John was lounging around in his role as "beautiful person" while Penny added to the urgency of the situation by skittering about like a startled goose. There were probably over fifty people packed into her amply sized dining room. She started the proceedings like a wedding speech, clinking a silver spoon on her wine glass before introducing one of the local councilors.

"People—people," she said as if she were about to deliver great insight. "Let's convene this meeting. We have many matters to consider. Over to you, Mr. Preece."

Mr. Preece had one of those forlorn faces that seemed to sag. Everything about him sagged. Even his beige jumper sat limply on his shoulders. He began droning on about river maintenance, the state of the environment, the weather, lack of response from the government, dredging, strategies and contingency plans. He held up a map of the flood risk area, blue patches covering most of the village.

"The water is coming—make no mistake," he said, "We need to be prepared for it. All of us need to be prepared." He looked about as prepared as a fish caught in a net. The grumblings from angry residents surfaced but died down as he continued to make promises of more sophisticated pumps that would not erode the river banks and reiterated that dredging *had* taken place since the last flood.

I looked at you and thought of your mud-soaked clothes. Were we prepared? With you I felt safe; you would not let any harm come to me. Your hand found mine and I felt your warmth seep into my own cold skin. After the lengthy discussions, some handouts were passed around in a paper-rustling frenzy, marking the predicted areas of a worst-case scenario and where to position sandbags. Were we naïve back then in October? Rivers did not wait for directives from the government; clouds did not wait for us humans to give them permission to burst; the sun would warm the ground again and far away on another continent they would be praying for rain to quench the wildfires. The meeting was nearly over and, with residents' hands raised for questions, I slipped from the room. I knew where to go.

Down the corridor I crept like a Christmas mouse. I heard the rumble of debating voices but didn't look back. I stealthily slipped into Penny's lounge and retrieved the matches from my handbag. Parker was still in the same position by the window. I swear he whimpered as I entered the room.

I struck the match. It snapped in half. I fumbled in the box for a second, struck it less violently and watched the flame splutter to life. It lit up the dark room and glinted off the glass eyes set into Parker's head. I slowly moved the flame, the short match petering toward my fingers. The whimpering got louder and turned to a low growl. His spirit could sense the flame and seemed to pull my hand toward it like a vacuum. But I steadied my hand so the flame wouldn't die. A touch may be all that was needed; I remembered the words of Wensley's book:

> . . . it is essential for the flame to touch the specimen in order to have an effect . . .

The flame was eating up the match, so I tilted it, but that seemed to make it burn more quickly. His fur would not catch. The match petered out before it burnt my fingertips. I lit another. This time I held it close to his leg and watched as the white fur curled inwards to create a blackened patch.

A whoosh, as if a pack of hounds were passing by, blew the flame out and the whimpering ceased. It felt too quick, too easy. Then there was just an empty silence and the drone of voices in the room next door. I exhaled slowly.

"What are you doing in here?" the plummy voice startled me. I was still kneeling in front of Parker, the scent of singed fur in the air. Quickly, I slipped the hot match back in my handbag and turned to face the voice. "Is that you, Scarlett?"

"I was looking for the puppies," I said, wincing at the transparency of my lie.

St. John moved toward me, his long limbs and wide gait reminded me of an orangutan. His arms were folded indignantly over his chest in a gesture that reminded me of Rhett. It made him look like a petulant child who had discovered some incriminating gossip but hadn't yet decided its worth. St. John seemed the sort of man to collect ammunition for later battles.

"What is that smell?" he said.

I stood up and moved toward the door, trying to distract him from what I had just done, but as I tried to get past him, he gripped my wrist, letting his nails dig in just enough to leave a mark.

"I know your type, Scarlett Pepper." His breath smelt of garlic and red wine.

"And I know yours," I hissed back at him and ripped my arm from his grasp. He didn't follow me. He stayed in the room, and I imagined him scouring it to find evidence, checking if I had stolen any of Penny's tat.

The meeting was over and a gaggle of people were vacating the dining room, chatting animatedly or silently shuffling past the bodies loitering in the hallway. Their homes were their lives; I understood that. And Penny had taken it upon her shoulders to spread the news. You saw me in the hallway and smiled. St. John appeared behind me with a thunderous look, but I felt satisfied I had done enough. It seemed that Parker was free at last, to roam in the afterlife, without being tethered to his taxidermied body. I couldn't wait to get home and try with the other hybrids that were slowly taking over our house.

You went to bed, tired from all your physical exertions. So I set up some candles and started work. Only it didn't go to plan. There was too much confusion. It was as if the light from the candle flames excited them into a frenzy and they were too muddled to leave their tethered frames. I consulted Wensley's book for more advice:

> If resistance is felt, often in the case of incomplete taxidermy, the physical parts of the specimen may need to be fully consumed by fire, as in crema tion, to enact the release of the trapped souls.

I looked around the room and, I admit, felt daunted. You had created so many different creatures of varying modifications. The cowstrich loomed in the corner upon large, muscular ostrich legs. The wallopea, too, had ostrich legs but the body of a wallaby and upper half of a peacock, tail feathers spread in full display. The head of a sheep attached to a badger's body; the three-headed turkey with a carp's modelled tail swam and gobbled air in a case on the wall. My head was beginning to spin. I needed space to think before my mind exploded.

I don't know why I did it, but I drove back to the blue house where I'd lived with my parents and knocked on the door. Some children's plastic toys in the garden had been shrouded by the tall grass and a swing set had moss covering its dirty seat. I peered through one of the windows and saw the kitchen had been refitted with a new range of cupboards, still the same shape as I remembered from my childhood. An island had been built in the middle of the kitchen. White marble worktops and shiny floor tiles made it look clinical. My mother would've hated it. There was a chrome oven and even the refrigerator was silver. It was sort of futuristic, nothing at all like the rustic, ramshackle kitchen I remembered. A row of shiny saucepans hung from the ceiling above the central island. There were a few dirty plates left in a pile with cutlery scattered on top and crumbs next to half a loaf of bread. I wanted Rhett. He would know what to say to make me feel better.

A gust of wind whipped up behind me. It had stopped raining but was still wet underfoot, so I stepped round a large puddle to look through the next window, steadying myself on the wall. There was a log burner where the open fire used to be, a faux leather sofa and a shelf full of books. Where I remembered the staircase, a door now sealed off the first step so it looked cozy and inviting. Rhett and I used to race up and down those stairs that led to the front door, chasing breathlessly until one of us was tagged then the chase would start again. I stood back and looked up to the second-floor windows. Our parents' bedroom used to be above the lounge. This was where they'd been found. Dead. The fire had gutted the lower half of the house, and they hadn't even woken up. The policeman told us they wouldn't have suffered. Just gone to sleep, overcome by fumes. An accident. The fireguard had not been put back in front of the fireplace, a burning ember, a candle, the rug, the flames, the smoke, the melting plastic toys. We never saw the cat again. I like to think she ran away and started a new life hunting mice and sleeping in barns, drinking the creamy milk from churns. I like to think the policeman was right. Although I would choose drowning over burning.

I heard a vehicle splashing its way down the road. So I dragged myself back to the truck and drove away. There was nothing more to do. I had seen where I used to live, the place my parents' souls had departed. They were gone forever.

At least I hoped they weren't suffering like those undead creatures we kept in our home.

⟵•⟶

The last day of the month and we had our birthdays to celebrate. Born on the same day, you, me and Rhett, even though there were many years between them. You were not quite old enough to be my grandfather, but with my elfish looks and your grizzly appearance the age gap must've seemed even more evident to others. I didn't care what others thought, even though I knew people talked about us behind our backs, chattering like nosy squirrels.

Rhett was unreliable but I could guarantee he would always remember our birthdays. He had hurriedly left in June and we'd not heard a word from him since. I hoped he had tried to reclaim some of his own identity instead of falling and failing with any woman who crossed his path. I worried about him more than you knew.

Before the phone started ringing, I knew it was him—sixth sense, twin telepathy, call it what you will. I answered quickly.

"Rhett."

"How did you know it was me?" The line was crackly.

"You're my favorite twin."

"I'm your *only* twin. And you are mine, Miss Scarlett."

"Don't start all that rubbish now." I pictured him pretending to twirl a moustache like his namesake, Rhett Butler, like he used to when we were kids. Was he now mocking our mother's belief that romance and passion were real objectives to strive for? Obsessed with that dream world of Deep South longing, our mother had wanted her very own Tara to ride a horse and live out her passions. As it happened, she was not much older than I am now when she died. She never rode a horse in her whole life.

"Where are you calling from?"

Rhett always called from a place of transit—a bus station or train station, in the boarding area of a flight, on the gangplank of a ship.

"I'm coming back, Scarlett," he said.

"What do you mean?"

"I'm tired of all this roaming around, it never gets me anywhere. I love it, don't get me wrong, I—erm—well—I just want a proper home. Like you."

"Well—that's a change from the Rhett I saw in June." Something must have happened. "Have you fallen in love? Or got that skinny bitch pregnant? Oh my God, you aren't going to die, are you?" I don't know why I said it, but as soon as the words were out of my mouth, the buzzing started up. Those incessant creatures. Like angry wasps in my head.

"Scarlett. I'm not ill and you won't believe it—I'm actually single. Have been for a while now."

"Christ, Rhett. Are you sure you're feeling ok?"

"I was thinking about how settled you looked with Henry." *Settled.* "How you've got this home in the middle of nowhere. As if you'd found peace." Peace? Was he mad?

We'd moved about when we were orphaned, but I was closer than we'd ever been to the blue house now that I lived with you. I wanted to tell Rhett I'd driven there not so long ago, but the words wouldn't come out. The phone line crackled and I thought I'd lost him but he was still speaking.

". . . Christmas . . . used to do . . . the fire . . ." his words were like patchwork hexagons waiting to be sewed together.

"Rhett—I can't hear you? You're breaking up."

". . . back at Christmas . . . you . . . enry . . . gether . . . old times . . ."

"Christmas—yes, come and stay. I really miss you." I had no idea what he was saying, but it was only a couple of months until Christmas Day and if nothing else, that was one tradition we seemed to keep.

The line went dead, but I pressed it to my ear as if being closer to the source of sound could close the physical distance between us. Nothing. Not a sound. Not even a crackle. But the buzzing in my head turned to a slow hiss, like air being released from a dying man's lungs.

<hr/>

I wanted our shared birthdays to be extra special, like a double celebration or triple celebration, even without Rhett present. Our Halloween birthdays were easy to celebrate. The shops were stocked with all sorts of party gimmicks, and I was a sucker for all those skulls and masks. I loved to dress up, much like you loved to dress a specimen with groomed fur or preened feathers. It seemed to me as if an anointing of skin on skin.

I thought the lights would brighten up the dull, wet days and craftily I planned to keep them up for Christmas and hoped you didn't mind.

"Any excuse for dressing up," you said.

"I've bought you an outfit too," I gestured to the bag sitting on the kitchen table.

Your expression faltered slightly, but I knew how you enjoyed roleplay. Spiced things up, you said. You tipped the contents of the bag onto the table as if inspecting a haul of stolen goods and pushed aside the lurid face paint, powder and accessories.

"—a mask?"

"Isn't it terrific?"

"Frankenstein's monster?" I could tell you weren't feeling the exciting vibe that was hammering through me like metal bolts. But there was more to dressing up; I saw you as the creator, Frankenstein himself. You were actually the inventor giving life to the dead creatures, not the creation itself. Even so, it was the monster that represented resurrection and here in the form of a rubber Halloween mask was something close to the truth.

"You want me to be Frankenstein's monster?" I don't know why you were so resistant at first. Perhaps you thought I was branding you a monster. But that was so far from the truth, my love.

". . . then I can be your bride—" I said, helping you pull the black suit from the bag.

"Are we having guests? A party?"

"No, just the two of us."

"Is that so?" You grinned. "Just an intimate, dressing up party for two is it?" Now you understood me.

"Let's just hope we don't get any trick-or-treaters come knocking then."

That possibility was far from my mind. We were in the middle of nowhere, down a long track. We would be gloriously alone and together in our fantasy world.

I set the heating high so a sleepy haze descended on the house. I didn't want you to see me until I was ready, so I locked myself away, cleansing my body and bathing in sandalwood oil. To make my skin appear pale, I applied powder to my face and arms and slipped into an ivory silk gown. I accentuated my eyes with black eyeliner and applied fake lashes. I fixed the black beehive wig complete with white zigzag stripes of hair, wrapped a fur stole about my neck and stood in front of the mirror to regard my transformation. I felt as if I was about to step onto a film set. My normally pale hair had been replaced by fake dark curls dashed through with a white streak of lightning. I felt like fire on water, like a bride preparing for her own funeral.

By the time you came in from your workshop it was already dark, but I waited expectantly in the room we rarely used: the big dining room with glass chandelier and large mahogany table. I had laid place settings at both ends of the table and lit the candelabra with black wax candles that flickered in the center. There were no windows open; it shouldn't have been too draughty. Even so, I'd drawn the heavy brocade curtains so the room was eerily lit, a gothic dream. Piled high in dishes, I had prepared some Halloween delights. Sweet cherries soaked in Kahlua glistened like balls of scooped flesh. Lychees stripped of their rough skin rested like eyeballs in a bowl. A marzipan skull was covered in liquorice spiders, and a bubbling cauldron held beetroot soup, thick and dark red like boiled blood. It seemed a shame that only the two of us would enjoy it, but you were worth all the preparation. It had been many years since I'd gone to so much trouble. The birthday before I met you, I had spent alone, Rhett unsurprisingly absent.

I heard you come down the stairs and look for me in the kitchen, the door creaking as if playing along with our game. Then your footsteps along the corridor to the end room where I waited. The handle turned slowly, and you pushed the door so I could not see you until it opened halfway. At first, I was startled by your height, but it was the shadow cast by the candles on the wall behind you. Your face was obscured by the mask, a monster's face, sad and scarred with unhealed stitches and green smudges. The only parts of your body that showed were your eyes and hands.

I stood up to greet you, and you walked toward me, your black suit rustling to create a sound like fallen autumn leaves. You held out your hands, big and muscular, and I placed my own slender palms on top of yours.

We gazed at each other as if meeting for the first time. I knew beneath the mask it was you, but I felt as if a stranger had joined me and I too was unfamiliar to his gaze. The clock struck ten chimes and we stood looking into each other's eyes until you led me to my chair, pulled it out for me to sit and reached for the carafe of red wine.

We sat in silence drinking our wine, observing the candle wax drip like molten tar down the shafts and into a solidifying pool on the table. You served me from the dishes and I delicately selected cherries and lychees between finger and thumb, letting the sweet juices trickle down my wrist, as if I were spilling my own blood in sacrifice. You did not eat. Probably because you could not negotiate the mouth hole in the mask, and I was not that hungry for food either.

I could not read your expression beneath your static, masked face. It was as if water had hardened to ice and left only its last movement there—a sad, silent replica of what might have been. Yet your fierce beauty shone through that façade. You were mine beneath it all, and in its pretense, I wanted you to also see me underneath the satin and wig and layers of costume.

Your violin rested on the table. It was a family tradition that you had kept, learning it at a young age. Your thick fingers were not the ideal player's asset but your skill was remarkable. The first time you lifted the instrument to your neck and tucked it neatly beneath your chin I wanted to laugh, because it looked so delicate compared to your bulk. But the way you commanded the strings made me more alert. I forgot that it was your movements that created the sound, believing instead that the violin was possessed by a specter capable of drawing sounds from a mystical place.

You lifted it and began to play. I closed my eyes and imagined my flesh and bones falling away, my spirit soaring to reach the notes. The whole room seemed to be filled with the vibration of music. I swam in it, bathed in it, sank beneath myself, and then resurfaced. It was as if I had found my wings, and the music you played gave me permission to fly. I was electrified, charged with a million bolts of lightning. Rocking and pulsing in rhythm with your rapid, bow strokes. You, the monster, emanated the sounds of heaven, cascading them down to earth through your hands, not impaired at all by that missing finger. A grand, final note was left ringing through my body as you lowered your violin and bow and held them at your sides. We were both as breathless as if we had just climbed a mountain together. Yet we were inside our home, waiting on each other's moves.

You gestured for me to join you on your seat. Like a true Frankenstein's bride, I responded to your beckoning by rejecting you. You beckoned again, this time by standing and curling your finger as if hooking my will and pulling it toward you. I remained seated. I could hear your breaths, even across the length of the table, above the sounds of the wind howling at the window. A storm was escalating. Behind your mask, the sound was viscous and throaty as if readying for battle. The air was heavy, not only from the heat of the room but the dense velvet darkness permeated only by candlelight.

You moved toward me and, although I knew it was you beneath the façade, I stiffened a little in my seat. I know you sensed my movement, as it made you more intent on having me. The more I resisted, the stronger your intention. From beneath the table I heard the clink of metal as you retrieved the chains. A long length trailed behind as you slowly walked toward me. As you touched my face, I couldn't help but flinch. This was our game but with the candlelight I felt transported to a castle in the mountains. Secluded and isolated, there was no one to hear my screams. The chains tightened around my body. Then you stood back and surveyed your bride. I struggled a little to incite you, and it worked, didn't it, my darling? I could've easily slipped your chains but didn't. To think you had me all to yourself in those sweet, dark days.

Outside I heard the screech of a bird or a screaming banshee flying above the roof. Perhaps the witches were out. Or the ghosts. The veil was thin tonight on All Hallows Eve, and we were on the threshold of piercing it.

The clock struck midnight and the games began.

⊷──∘──⊶

It was my most memorable birthday. Even when I count up all my childhood birthdays. My family never really celebrated birthdays. Most days in my childhood were catered with party food; it was all my mother ever prepared. When I was invited to another child's birthday party, I thought it a normal teatime, not an occasional treat. Mother used paper plates, so there was rarely any washing up, and we were forever sticking pineapple or cheese or pickled vegetables onto cocktail sticks. In fact, that may be where my obsession with using my fingers came from, an echo of the finger food introduced in my early years.

The morning after, I tentatively asked you about Felix. What had happened? Why was he wanted? Was there anything you needed to tell me? But you shrugged it off and left me to wonder. There were more pressing things to do. His fate had flashed up on the news a few times then disappeared beneath more saturated updates about the weather.

"... a sustainable solution to the rising waters, here in Somerset, is yet to be reached ... it is no surprise that feelings are running high ... some villagers in this small community have even gone so far as to purchase their own watercraft in preparation for what is thought to be another inevitable flood situation ..."

The water levels were getting higher with no sign of a break in the weather. You continued digging a trench around our perimeter, our very own moat. Just in case, you said. But I knew it was a private fantasy of yours. To create your own island set apart from the rest of the village. Were you keeping everyone out, or were you keeping us in? You started at the east edge of the pond and worked round the inner edge of the fence so a deep gully ran around us like a ring with the earth piled up to create an embankment. The only break was the width of the driveway that dipped down to the road. Potholes had already formed from the running water sitting on its surface.

I lit the fire for us as you scrubbed the dirt from your body. You joined me as I ate the left-over lychees from a bowl. I sucked the perfumed flesh until it gave way to the silky, dark red stone. The flavor reminded me of Turkish Delight, strong and rose-flavored, not fitting its almost dull grey hue. Lychees repulsed my mother. She said they looked like dead flesh. I suspect she meant they looked like eyeballs, but I had never been fooled by how things appeared. Having lived with Rhett and his scars, I could not see why anyone would judge by looks alone. It was only the surface after all.

I carried my own scars, but unlike Rhett's, they were mostly inside my head, out of sight. It would be good to talk to him, properly, about the night our parents died. I felt as if the world were speeding up to meet us, like a dam about to burst. I flicked the TV channels to catch more news.

"... the Environment Agency has upped the level of alert for the Rivers Tone, Parrett and Brue following an unprecedented amount of rainfall over the past few weeks. There is growing anger among the residents of one low-lying village ..."

The camera panned over the waterlogged fields and houses sitting like lonely, unopened parcels. I watched you snoozing and thought of how familiar you had become to me. When we first met, during those tentative exploratory days, it was like discovering a new landscape. You were not like the other men I had been intimate with. There were the physical differences, of course, but I mean you were somehow exquisite in your wildness, like a tree that had grown strong roots and gnarled branches but retained its beauty by being natural. You were pure to me; each wrinkle and hair was perfectly placed. They became landmarks I could rely on. I knew you, just as you knew me. Do you remember counting the moles on my belly and trying to create an image by dot-to-dot? You said it could be a diamond or a star. Like the one that led the Magi to Bethlehem. Christmas would soon be upon us.

CHRISTMAS DAY / TODAY

Dusk

It is getting dark outside and I feel the darkness inside me lurch and spin. I crave solitude but that is unlikely now there are so many creatures beside me. You are dozing on the couch with a bottle of whisky and I wonder if you still regard me as the woman you first set your eyes upon.

I am woman because of molded curves of flesh, because of secret curls of purple longing, because of acid tongue and saccharine touch, because of the debris of wave-lashed life-rafts abandoned on pure shores, because of the gold in my shadow, because of the sunbird-yellow highs and beetle-black lows, because of harmonic saffron-laced sultana dreams, because of tinsel-tacked rain-shower droplets of mercury on peat and leaf and breathless, boneless sorrow, because of woven willow baskets of stripped-back straightened reeds and rushes in dark, damp ditches lasting for eternity in ancestral memory, because of elderflower patchwork flowers suspended in sugary liquid, because of never-never take me home with you then release me from the cycle of the here and now, here and now, because of endless chatter shaped like the legs of insects tickling my feet, to the essence of my naked soul.

You snore loudly then mutter something in your sleep. I don't hear what you say.

#
$\mathcal{N}$OVEMBER

I hated winter and I hated rain. Both were a recipe for my mean mood. I couldn't shake off this dull, moaning ache of melancholia. The water seemed to seep into everything and even your stuffed creatures looked disgruntled, as if the damp had somehow crept between their feathers and fur and squatted like an unwanted guest.

I knew from your breathing when something was troubling you. It rattled from you in uneven throaty bursts, not just from the years of smoking that had lined your lungs but as a sort of cacophony of the creatures you had touched emerging from within, as if the stray feathers and hairs of the animals had lodged inside your chest and nested there. When you woke in the morning, you'd clear your throat, the night-time bubbling up and out just like it had stowed away inside you, then been expunged by your movements. Dust and ashes shifted, then settled. You were the vessel for all the souls that passed through your hands. Their maker. Their grave. Their cause.

Preparation for Christmas started well before Advent. The urge to shop and wrap and make lists overcame me. The weather had been so unpredictable all year, so I always kept the larder stocked full of essentials, boxes of candles and plenty of matches. The logs were piled high in the living room. We even had a generator so didn't need to rely on the outside world at all, provided we had enough fuel and logs for the fire.

A trip into town always made me feel more grounded, as if I needed to step out of the magic bubble we had created together and enter the real world. The dense, synthetic trappings of the commercial world brought me back with a whump. For all the time I spent in my own company, paradoxically, I felt more connected to the life around me, as if I had honed the skill of attunement through my sensitivity to others' rhythms and patterns.

At first, I found myself remembering the smell of my mother's hair, chamomile and geranium oil wafting about her and the deeper, sharper, synthetic scent of my father who worked away for months on end. He seemed to be made from an artificial substance that was molded to his transient life, rigid yet bendable, whereas Mother was soft and yielding, like a tall grass. I guess I took on both of my parents' traits, and that was how the battle inside me raged endlessly.

It occurred to me that Rhett and I would never have to deal with the slow demise of our parents in old age. We had lived through their horrendous sudden death when we were children. They had been healthy and vibrant one minute and gone the next. I had tried to talk to Rhett, but a steely look always came across his face. He would go pale and distant then make some excuse about needing to do something. He was good at running away. He had been running all his life. I guess I was his anchor, the place he came home to.

When I met you, I knew you were a combination of all the elements— fire, air, water, earth; an alchemical pot of deliciousness. You were the one to whom I always ran. Some days I would sense the fire taking dominance and you would whisk me up in your arms and we'd dance until the sweat poured from our bodies and we had to strip off our clothes to cool down—you lying like a starfish on the lawn and me spread across you, panting and laughing. Those were our summer days. On other days your presence would ground me, bring me back to earth to secure me to the physical world we inhabited. Then the presence of water seemed to make you fluid in these winter months, swimming in and out of my focus like a pike, stalking minnows through the reeds. Often, I would catch you looking at me, just breathing that slow, steady inhalation and exhalation as if you were studying a sculpture.

Our lawn had reduced to a slow growth; small patches of mud formed where the saturated ground was no longer able to absorb the incessant rainfall. Then the sharp spikes of frost appeared as the temperature plummeted, especially at night time. Everything seemed so dark and hopeless.

That was probably why November was carnival month in this part of the world. Not the showy, feathery street carnivals of South America, but a different kind of bright procession—a winter carnival illuminated and paraded at night time when all the natural daylight had vanished. It seemed to me that this was a good excuse to dress up and play the fool because anything was allowed. Men who normally sported conspicuous tattoos dressed up as little girls with pigtails and short skirts, secretly enjoying the feel of suspenders on their hairy thighs and reaching down to rearrange their sweaty balls in baggy synthetic panties. They would keep their make-up on long after the carnival procession finished, glittery fake eyelashes extended from their rough faces like trapped insects, lurid shades of lipstick bleeding over their lip line as they drank their pints of lager.

My parents took me only once—a spontaneous decision to have family time on a winter's night. The sky was clear black and dotted with stars. Although bitterly cold, we were cozy, wrapped up in scarves and mittens, padded out in layers of jumpers and coats and double-socked feet inside our boots. My father must've been home because I remember him lifting me up onto his shoulders so I could get a full view of the passing trailers (or floats, as they were called). A Hawaiian hula theme, a *Jungle Book* reprise with human-sized fluffy lions and dancing elephants in cartoon costumes and the haunting grey ghost ship with human mannequins, carnivalites painted up like chalk and ash with staring black eyes, cutlasses held aloft in mock battle and dry ice billowing out around their legs.

The winter carnival—a great parade of illuminated floats piercing through the dark night like a slow-moving, giant centipede. All coyness dissipated like the hot vapor puffing out from the onlooker's cheeks. The floats were pulled by tractors or lorry hubs and decorated to match the theme—the drivers sometimes sported hats or full-face masks like the one you wore at Halloween. The music rose up from speakers on a continual loop. The generators spewed out dark spluttering fumes. Outsiders might wonder why a mass of people would want to stand on the pavement for hours on a wintry, November night watching vehicles decked out in colorful, costumed, dancing troops of adults and children.

The smell of diesel from the generators mixed with the fried fat from the burger stands and saccharine hit of candy floss on sticks—it all stuck to the inside of my nostrils. The myriad lightbulbs screwed onto the carts in neat rows sometimes shorted out and were left reflecting the lights from other carts, dull and lifeless. Sometimes the spectators would clap as they passed, much the same way a paraded coffin is applauded as it makes its final journey.

Floats had been worked on all year, stripped back from the previous year and re-kitted out with new sculptured fittings, repainted and sprayed, decorated by volunteers' hands. All this work paraded in just a few days of the year, in the dark. The bystanders, mostly static, watched and sometimes pointed, clapped or just stared in awe at the butch men painted up like hairy geishas exposing more flesh than was decent, or the misjudged costumes implying sexual promiscuity among farmers and their livestock.

On the night my family attended, Rhett was keen to get home so he could play with his new dartboard. He kept asking if it had finished and could we please go. My brother, so unlike me, always looking to the horizon.

Your taxidermy creatures were not so different from the painted mounts of animals on those carnival floats, hyper-real but poised for action. Yet they were fake and did not feel the music as it bounced off their artificial frames and effused into the night air. They came to life through some other intervention.

Mention of the carnival procession triggered some dark memory in my soul, as if the concentration of scenes had unleashed a furious recognition of what my life would become. It was a parade of dead souls, a slow-moving compulsion toward an ending where the lights would go out and we would return to darkness.

There was no way we could go to the carnival this year, unless we swam across the moor and reached the town by the waterways. I was not disappointed. We had Christmas to look forward to after all. We had returned to ancient times, where the land had become a watery grave, but I had you, and you had me.

<hr />

We stood together in the attic room and looked out toward the river. For days now its swollen edges had been widening. Then, as soon as the land could no longer absorb any more water, its course was set. The river crept stealthily toward us after bursting its banks, coming a little nearer every day. I would measure its progression by landmarks that still poked above the rising flood water. Four fields, then three, then the nearest gatepost level with the big old beech tree, or the top of the submerged road sign that warned of crossing deer.

The mass evacuation of farm animals had set a frenzied news team upon the village. Farmers from across the country were spurred into action to help their kin save threatened livestock. Loaded up onto lorries and trailers, the cows and sheep and horses were shunted to makeshift barns and a big agricultural center near the higher ground of the motorway. Meanwhile, sandbags were positioned around the houses, possessions moved up a floor and provisions stockpiled so people would not have to make too many trips across the floodplain. We were becoming a ghost village set apart from the rest of the county.

There was indignant horror that this could be allowed to happen again after the floods only a few years before. Campaigns for the drainage of the land, early warning systems, new pumps and the dredging of rivers did not stem this cruel deluge. Water would find its level, its way; it would always seek the easiest course. No amount of human intervention could stop it.

Some people had already moved out of their homes, predicting the same devastation that had wreaked havoc before, but some resilient stalwarts stayed put. Penny was one of them. Speaking daily to the local and now national media who circled the floodplain in noisy helicopters. Angry clusters of villagers met in wellies on the puddled higher road with hastily drawn placards berating the government for ignoring the plight of residents who lived on their own doorstep.

They blamed them for not doing enough, for sacrificing the few for the many, for putting money above lives, for not learning the lessons of the past.

Meanwhile, you finished the moat and came into the house looking disheveled.

"I've taken the dogs to Penny's—she's leaving the village," you said. "There's no sign of the water receding. In fact, I think we should prepare for the worst." If Penny was leaving, it must have escalated more than I imagined.

"What do you mean? What's the worst?" I said. We were higher up on an elevated mound of land, and the water was only just at the edge of the village. We weren't cut off. Yet.

"Scarlett. It's time to be realistic. We either sit it out here or we leave. In the next few days. Maybe tomorrow—"

"No, I can't leave," the feeling of dread swam over me. I couldn't go. There was no way I'd be able to cremate all those poor trapped creatures if we uprooted and left them to the floods. This was our haven. You were my foundation, I know, but I couldn't bear to leave the house for fear I would be plagued forever. My temples began pulsing and I felt sick. Besides, if I left, how could Rhett find me if he decided to turn up? *When* he decided to turn up.

"My darling," you held me tightly, "it won't be forever, just until this flood situation eases."

"But where would we go?" I know I sounded like a spoilt child.

"There's nothing to stop the flood if the other river bursts, and that one's on red alert too. You saw how quickly that water moves."

"But—the moat, isn't that enough to hold it back?"

"It might be—I don't know. It was bad before, but no one expected it to happen again so soon."

I looked out toward your workshop. The place where I had presented my dreams before you, not knowing they would turn into nightmares so quickly.

Next to it, under the buddleia, was a small shrine of stones and beneath that our child, who came into this world already dead. Had he survived, would we be facing a different decision to protect our offspring, to put them first? But it was just the two of us. Would things have turned out differently if I had agreed to leave at that moment, left our home and the creatures who harangued my every waking moment and sometimes my sleeping moments too?

That night, ferocious winter storms hit the South of England with such force that buildings were battered, roof tiles flung like frisbees, untethered objects were relentlessly smashed, glass shattered. Whirlwinds hurled leaves and rubbish and dirt at any permanent structure. The water that lay like a silk sheet on the Levels turned into a giant lake, waves breaking on its surface as if it remembered its tidal cousin, the sea. The wind was visible; it had form and substance like a raging angry bull charging full speed and goring all that got in its path. The sky hurled down arrows of ice and snow—thundersnow—as we watched in disbelief. It felt like punishment, like prophecy.

We battened down the hatches. We secured all the windows and moved some of the irreplaceable antiques to the top floor of the house. We sat in the lounge with a pile of logs in the big basket against the wall and the old sofa as our refuge. The creatures seemed to implore me, wanting some answers to this tempest that they could not outrun. I turned away from them, tried to ignore their frustrated whimpers and groans.

You had positioned the binoculars in the bedroom upstairs so we could look out across the moor toward the main road out of the village when we went to bed. I looked through the lenses and saw only chaos: swamped abandoned cars, the tops of trees reaching up through the muddy floodwaters, showing where the ditches used to be, the windows of houses staring like empty-eyed orphans left to fend for themselves The wind screamed through the house. It was angry, without definite rhythm, and turned my muscles into a knotted mess.

Perhaps I had done too much over the past month. Purchasing all the Christmas goods and presents, storing the food in the freezer, sealing packets of dried food in plastic containers and placing high up in cupboards. We would not be hungry if, or when, we got stranded.

We had been glued to the local news reports dominated by the flood. An aerial view of our house panned round, a helicopter shot. *The house with the moat* flashed across the bottom of the screen. We were called the eccentric couple who decided to face the flood. Some even likened you to Noah. They said you were creating a stationary ark for all the species you had stuffed, a sort of makeshift home filled with taxidermy animals. They kept showing a clip of Penny struggling to get all the dogs—our labradors, her poodles and the labradoodle puppies—into her Range Rover. St. John was nowhere in sight.

In bed I snuggled into you, burying my head beneath the covers so I created a sort of soft cocoon. Your snores were drowned out by gusts of raw wind buffeting anything in its path. You seemed unaffected by the raging storm. My body ached, more with each passing day, and even though my mouth was dry, I didn't want to leave the bedroom to fetch a glass of water.

Each squall of wind seemed to threaten the rafters with destruction. At one point I thought it would be better to sleep downstairs and risk waking in a pool of stinking flood water than stay upstairs and be wrenched from the house if the roof blew off like Dorothy's in the *Wizard of Oz*. I could hear the trees bending and groaning, their branches like motorized whips in the wind. Even the trees sounded like rapid water.

I heard glass breaking and tried to wake you. But you only stirred slightly and turned over. You must've been exhausted, all that physical labor and the flood taking its toll.

I left you. That's right. I got up and went to the bathroom. No, I went downstairs first to see what had broken. It was definitely glass, but there was no draught and the windows in the lounge were all shut. The wind died down to a steady howl, less gusty but still strong enough to worry me and make me tense.

Then I saw the movement. I thought a bird had got in somehow, but now I know I was just kidding myself. I knew what it was. There was no mistaking its sleek black feathers and luminescent white fur. The crabbit was moving about, flapping its ungainly wings; it had knocked a glass vase from the shelf. It moved in circles like a wind-up toy, not sure of its bearings. I felt sick, watching the way it stumbled and flapped, too weighed down by the heavy haunches of the rabbit body. Its crow wings could never take flight again.

A deep bovine cough startled me. I spun round to see the cowstrich lift its cow head at me, taking a tentative large-toed step on ostrich legs, tilting like an overloaded crane. A flick of its legs backwards made me bolt out of the room. I slammed the kitchen door, frantically trying to think, but the lack of sleep had dulled my wits. Now I had trapped myself in the kitchen and there was no way to alert you. I scrabbled in the kitchen drawers and the cupboards. A knife—what use would that be? They were already dead. The force of their souls had reanimated them. I had to set them alight and cremate them fully. The touch of the match was not enough to free them. All it seemed to do was make them more agitated, as if I had given them a taste of freedom and cruelly snatched away.

I grabbed the shed key off the small hook and opened the outside door. A gust of sharp air penetrated through my dressing gown. I was barefoot so stepped into your big boots, still muddy and damp. Shuffling outside, holding my gown about my waist, I kept my head low to protect my face from the lashes of icy rain that sprayed me like bullets.

I felt in my pocket for the matches. Inside the outhouse you kept a couple of spades, a fork, an ancient petrol mower, shelves full of rusty tools. I stepped over the unopened crates next to the bottles of wine covered in dust, some broken furniture, an old engine sticky with black oil, a used tractor tire. Spent cartridges from your shotgun littered the stone floor, and cardboard boxes of live rounds were stacked together next to plastic bottles of tomato feed and slug pellets.

The roof rattled as the wind drove through it. The building groaned like an old ship. My flashlight lit up a bright red container on the floor. I shook it, gauged by its weight that it was half full, and opened the lid to sniff the fumes. This was my only option. To douse them with petrol and set them on fire. They'd be incinerated, their souls would be released, and we could go back to how we once were. Untroubled. This was all I needed, and while the adrenalin was rushing through me, I knew I had it in me to set them all alight. That was all I could think of, so I didn't even hear you appear.

"Scarlett?" I remember the tenderness in your voice as you faced me. "Scarlett?" You said my name again. We could only see by flashlight, but you looked from my face to the petrol can and back. "What are you doing out here?"

"It's—you must've seen—did you see?" I pictured you striding confidently through your creations, unconcerned by their re-animation.

"What's wrong?" you took a step toward me as if I were a wild animal and you needed to keep your distance.

"You know what's wrong," I said. "All *this* is wrong—those bloody creatures. Are you blind? They're trapped, Henry. You've trapped them in those grotesque bodies."

As I spoke, your shoulders slumped slightly, and you rubbed your face as if to wake yourself up.

"Come back inside. It's freezing out here."

"They need to go!" The flashlight flickered where my hands were shaking with the cold.

"Okay, okay. Calm down."

"They want to be free. And—and—I have to do it. Now."

"We'll get rid of them. I'll sell them. Is that what you want?"

"No, Henry! They need to be destroyed." I spat the words at you.

"That's absurd. Do you know how many hours I spent working on them?"

"They need to burn!" My voice tipped into a scream. The words flew from me like poisoned arrows. My hands were becoming numb. It pains me to remember how I spoke to you. My thoughts, my headaches, those creatures feeding off my energy—I wanted to blame them. But ultimately it was all my fault. I admit that to you now. It was me who encouraged you to stray from the path you knew best. I made you create them. A little knowledge is always dangerous.

"Scarlett." You held out your arms to me. "Come inside and we'll talk."

"There's nothing to say," I said through clenched jaws. My teeth were chattering from the icy wind.

A sudden strong gust shook the outhouse. I gripped the petrol can and could feel the stony cold creeping up my legs, thickening the blood in my veins. My head was thumping with rage. You moved toward me. I shuffled back, still looking for the best way to exit, but you were blocking the only way out. I shook the petrol can at you, but you still kept moving toward me. It was not a fair match. You outweighed me by over half my body weight. And even though I could out-run you, there was no way I'd get back to the house without you catching me. I pleaded with you, wanted you to understand how this was something I had to do. For both of us.

You lunged toward me as I shuffled about shivering and clutching at the petrol can. Just as you reached me, I heard a large crack like the sky had broken open. Your weight on top of me winded me as the noise escalated.

The falling timbers from the rotten roof narrowly missed us. I screamed at you to let me go as you pinned me to the dirty stone floor of the outhouse. But you held me, crushing your hot body against mine. All my words were crushed too.

"Leave it, Scarlett," you said, "You'll destroy us both if you carry on like this."

"I—don't—care!" each word uttered with immense effort; my taut frame collapsed beneath you.

Then darkness.

And my words to you were like acid on my tongue—*I don't care.*

But my darling, I *do* care. More than you can ever know. Believe me when I honor our vows and, even before that, our promise to follow one another into the afterlife and beyond.

<hr />

The next day I woke with a thumping head, all glue and sawdust. My neck felt like it had been concreted to my spine. You must have left me to sleep and gone outside to inspect the storm damage. I rubbed my eyes then peered around the room. Morning must have crept up and leaned into our home like a weary traveler taking a rest. A familiar smell, toxic and metallic, lit up my senses. Petrol. I had wanted to set fire to those wretched creatures but you had stopped me.

It infuriated me how you could use your bulk to overpower me. I was helpless, and all those moments I felt protected or sheltered by your strength were crushed by the fact that you simply knew I could never be physically stronger.

I recalled you leading me back into the house, avoiding the crashing timbers of the outhouse, half carrying, half dragging me. I must've passed out from my exertions. None of my efforts had paid off. The image of the crabbit and cowstrich flashed in my memory, and I shot out of bed to lean over the bannister and listen for any noises that would indicate they were active. Nothing. Just the stillness of the house after the night's storm.

"Henry?" I called but received only the echo of my voice as an answer.

<hr />

Your confession came as a relief. I knew that honesty was always going to be our saving grace.

"I couldn't keep it hidden from you any longer," you said.

"Why didn't you tell me when I asked you?"

"I was embarrassed."

"Why?"

"Because I thought you'd think less of me. When I found out you'd been talking to Felix and when he found out you were my wife—it made me angry. I thought he had told you what we were doing."

"Felix was just using me?" I asked, a sudden taste of cherries on my lips.

"He was using you to get at me."

"But how?" My mind was racing about in circles.

"We'd set up a business arrangement way before I met you. He'd approached me to do rogue taxidermy and I kept saying no, but he kept raising the money he'd pay. In the end I gave in. It went against all my training. Taxidermy uses only the skin and outer layers of the specimen. Anything else is just molding."

"So when I suggested for you to make them—you already were? And you didn't think to tell me?"

"I couldn't risk you knowing. He loved all the limelight—I made the best exhibits. He had contacts in the art world—I could carry on living my quiet life. You know I hate all that attention. We were the perfect combination, or so I thought."

"But why didn't you tell me?"

"I don't know, Scarlett. I'm sorry I didn't, but that's why I had to work so much. I was fulfilling our orders and all of his too. Penny was keeping them at her house so you wouldn't find them."

"Penny?" My intuition was right. You were keeping secrets from me, but not what I imagined.

"I love you Scarlett and only you. If that idiot hadn't messed up . . . If he hadn't got greedy. He used others who didn't stick to the rules. I had to burn all those papers that connected me to him. He's in big trouble. Luckily Penny had got rid of all the exhibits before she left."

"But what about all yours?"

"Mine are fine. Not as sought after but I don't care anymore. All that matters is us."

"I love you, Henry. Only you."

You stopped me with your finger to my lips. "You sweet thing. We'll never have any more secrets."

I wanted to confess to you then about Wensley's book but the words wouldn't come. You still believed they were inanimate objects. I knew they weren't.

CHRISTMAS DAY TODAY

Early Evening

I want to taste your skin
Midway between my thoughts
And your touch, your skin untouched
My thoughts unsaid, unsunk midway
Between the distance of your skin
And my lips unkissed, unexplored
Midway between us, your skin
On my skin merging magnificent
The colors blessed by mist
Between my thoughts and your touch
Midway. I want to taste your skin.
I hear swans with salted feet
Stuck dead midway between feed and flight
You have an island in your thoughts
Midway between the here and now.
Your touch. My thoughts. My skin.

⟵———⟶

You have removed my heart, dear love of mine. Can I now claim yours? Will you know my arms when they are wrapped around you as if wishing with all my might that they can? Did I wish for wings? Did I wish for a tail? Be careful what you wish for.

You mumble as you sit beside me. You drift in and out of wakefulness, sleep tipping you closer to me as I wait patiently. Dive with me, my love, into the rusty waters. Roll my transparent song about your body. I'll sing to you in riddles 'til you wake. Drown out those human voices, drown out the fear of the unknown. I am here, waiting for you. Arching and stretching through feathered strands, leaping and laughing as we used to. After the fire there comes only ash and air.

I'm sure I can catch the smell of chemicals as you lay beside me. Perhaps it is the memory of your work smell that greets me so vividly. You tell me you love me a million times a day. Today, Christmas Day, you tell me you love me more than any other day.

The memory of you inside me is a recurrent one, like a pomegranate seed in my teeth, gritty and persistently stubborn. It sticks even though I know it is moveable. Then, once loosened, it tries to slip down my throat, grating a little.

I can dance over seconds, minutes, hours, then knit them back together with hands and feet and lips that no longer move. I am a feathered trap. Beware my scorched feathers; they may cut.

DECEMBER

I must've drifted off because there was a stillness that encompassed me. You notice how loud it has been when the silence falls, the absence emphasizing the memory of a vibration. For a moment I felt calm and free. Then I recalled the night before; that incessant wailing of troubled souls clamoring at my consciousness. I couldn't remember how I'd got there, but I was perched on a high-backed chair in your workshop, flopped over to one side, among the wood wool and wire.

I know this because I could see myself—not by reflection but as if I were another person looking back at me. It was a peculiar feeling. Much like the accounts Wensley recorded in his book. A passage from the book flashed across my psyche as if I had tattooed each word in indelible ink onto the inside of my eyelids:

> . . . at first there may be disorientation as the soul tries to readjust to the disturbance caused by lack of physical function. There may be gaps in consciousness. But these will soon pass to give way to greater clarity. The soul will return to its true nature unless . . .

Unless what? The soul will return to its true nature unless . . . I tried to patch together what I could remember: We had eaten a light supper. The storm had started. We shut windows. I needed to find petrol. No, that was way back in November. There was no storm outside. The storm I felt was inside me.

You did something with the generator and came up to bed soon after. We were both tired, but I couldn't sleep because of the noises and thoughts of Christmas Day worming their eager tendrils into my brain. You told me not to worry and that we'd be prepared, and it would be our best Christmas ever regardless of the weather.

My head had been thumping as if a dam of blood were trying to burst free from my temples. Then there was no more pain, more a sensation of tethering. Then, I awoke in your workshop. But the hours after I had gone to bed, and the awakening in the chair, were hard to stitch together. I would get a sense of longing to inhabit my body then a deep repulsion, like I wanted to tear myself away in blind panic at its uselessness. You were weeping and moving my heavy limbs, then laying still beside me on our bed. Once, I recall your face pressed against mine. Then you were gone. Or I was gone. But your love held me in that space with you. I could sense you there with me at an unspeakable level. You had kept your promise and so I had to keep mine.

I met each soul of the departed creatures head on as if they were waiting for me in their limbo world. They recognized me instantly as one of them; they knew I had passed on to their side. The crabbit came hopping and flapping, and the cowstrich inquisitively peered at me and shook its feathers. Even the more cautious creatures acknowledged that my soul was in their world and not just on the periphery.

You sat for hours looking at my motionless body. Sometimes you would touch me or tip my torso, repositioning me. Other times you would place your head on my chest, as if listening for the workings of my heart, or lift my static eyelids with your thumbs. At first, I was with you in our bed, draped over you, reanimated only by the racks of your sobs lifting your chest in a motion like a boat on the open sea. You kissed my shoulder, my forearms, my hands, wiped the tears from your face and stood. Then you sat again, as if you couldn't bear to leave me on my own. Your face collapsed and reformed, collapsed and strengthened, then twisted in recognition as you woke and saw my body still where you had left it. I could do nothing but wait. *I'm waiting for you now. Please come to me. I know you can hear me as I sit like a specimen in this chair.*

You must've carried me to your workshop at some point. I was wrapped in the bed sheet, naked and unwashed, but sitting upright in the old chair. I knew it was cold but it did not affect me anymore. There were other things to occupy me in this state.

I could spend what seemed like a lifetime watching a droplet of water hang from a branch. Then, after the paws of a thousand tigers padded over my bare skin, I would sprout wings from the creases of my shoulder blades and unfurl them like a papery concertina. It was like switching channels on a television, except I was the screen and the viewer at the same time.

I would dip and dive with the swallows, hover like a kestrel, glide over endless oceans like an albatross. But each time I found myself in motion, there was a lingering ache that I needed to return to the shell of my body that I had left behind. And it was you, my darling, who beckoned me home with your tender fingers.

I witnessed you all those days and nights that followed as the deserted village swam in its own effluent mixed with the downfall and spill-water, overflowing drains and detritus. We were cut off on our makeshift island. Then the deep freeze solidified all the movement around us. You hardly noticed, as you were so focused on treating my body with care and precision. *You knew I always wanted wings and a tail.*

I couldn't leave. The longing was too deep. A dark ache weighed upon me like the untouched sides of a forgotten well. Your tools slipped beneath my skin, gently turning me to extract the parts that no longer served me. You had told me once that there was no mystery in skinning a primate, and I suppose humans were a less hairy version. Your tools were employed to master a hybrid no man had ever attempted. Those mummified remains of ancient Egypt were wrapped and preserved by dry air in tombs. You were more skilled.

The careful extraction and disposal of redundant parts became your mantra; the slow scraping of viscera so my body's outer layer became a shell ready to be reborn. You were so careful not to stretch my skin as you divided it left to right, putting cotton and paper on my body, sprinkling powder to absorb the fluids that leaked from me like the land we inhabited. There may have been a witness soaring above us like a buzzard gaining height on the thermal air currents, a circling wide-winged motion, as you fed those parts of me back to earth. The parts consigned to rot, that spirit has no need for.

You looked exhausted. The damp from the surrounding landscape had infiltrated everything in our home, creeping up our walls like guilt. The floods had not escalated since the rains had ceased in their relentlessness. But the damage was done, both outside our home and within. We were cursed by our naivety to think that we had power over death. It does not play by the same rules as life. Once a spirit has been carved off, dissected, there are few opportunities for healing. *The soul will return to its true nature unless . . .*

You will know what I mean when I say you drowned me and saved me all at once. This was just as well in this peaty paradise we chose to live upon, the wetlands shifting beneath us then constrained by freezing temperatures. We were the only remaining residents after the burst rivers had spread and stopped short of our door, forcing all but us to flee. The temperature had plummeted to create this wintery wilderness. The Big Freeze, as predicted, held us captive in this place.

Just three weeks before Christmas, the final deluge of icy rain had forced the few remaining homeowners from the far end of the village to evacuate on motorboats and amphibious vehicles supplied by the army, creating great crackling waves as they crashed through half-formed ice to reach higher, dryer ground. The cattle had been saved and the pets shipped off to catteries and kennels. It was ironic that the so called North and South Drain did not live up to their names, with water saturating the fields and lying like a dark skin over the Levels. There was nothing draining here—wet, dank, bog, sludge, silt, effluent. This biblical flood was a sluggish stew of hopelessness.

Did you wish you had built an ark, measured cubit upon cubit, committed long-term to a redeeming project such as Noah's? Your moat had been infiltrated by some flood water, but thankfully our house sat proud on the mound. We were surrounded by miles of patchy ice but we had faith that we would overcome these difficulties together.

I remember how you sighed and nearly wept as I read my vows to you at our wedding all those months ago. There was never any man I wanted to be joined with more than you. And I can say I knew that from the first time we met.

After we'd met on the beach, it only took two more dates and I was in your bed. We would have self-combusted in our own lust otherwise. Yes—I worried it was a momentary fascination. Why do people fluff about at the periphery of passion, dancing in choreographed coyness? Honesty was the only way to save time, and we were not a couple to pussyfoot about where displays of affection were concerned. If we removed the social constraints of this time we live in, you would have had me there and then on the beach. I can picture you there sniffing the sea air, puffing out your chest to mark your stake on me (believe me, you didn't need to do this—you had my attention). I was crouching, metaphorically and literally, like a ferret on heat. Perhaps as a species we had gone too far into the subtle realm of pheromones; those tasteless, silent signals that are blamed for animal attraction. Who knows what it was? We were prisoners to one another. I believe you saw the riot in me—raw and ready like a split, ripe fig.

There were a whole string of reasons and not always connected by knots tied by our own hands, but tangled like twine or fishing line or those strands of cotton that twist themselves to infinite union without any intervention when laid together over time. We were faced with endless possibilities angled toward their own truth. Which is why, once, I chose to explore your workshop when you were out. And what I found changed me forever.

When you think you know every vein of another, every scar and blemish, a shock like that can force you to re-evaluate every assumption you ever made. Your finger, for example—was it really chopped off by a lawn mower blade? A common enough injury, fingers get in the way. But you are left-handed and this shortened finger of which I speak is the third of your right hand. Severed to the first joint, an uneven, shiny, blunt end. I'm not even sure I noticed it the first time we met. There were too many other interesting contours to take in—the angle of your cheekbones rushing into the unruly craft of your beard, the bulk of your shoulders matching the curved boulders on the beach, the stretched fabric of your trousers across your buttocks—so how could I have missed what was already missing? A part of you I love so much—your hands, the part that has palpated every inch of me, inside and out.

Forgive me, my darling, for my disjointed ramblings. Time slips and slides as I sit here waiting. Time seems endless, limitless, like your love for me. You have made me into something new, once again. I can see and hear and taste and smell, even feel, but not in the sense you imagine. It is heightened and freed from the limits of a body, yet I am tethered too strongly to shift far. Imagine my perception as a holographic image that lifts and moves when the light refracts from my surfaces—that is how I feel I must move in this new limbo state.

It wounds me to say it, but my wish for wings was unfounded. I can no more fly than you can. They are a part of me, now you have stitched them with such accuracy to my back, like the angels you see on the ceiling of a cathedral, set proud, feathers spread in a fan. But I cannot fly. Believe me, I have tried. There is a sensation of pulling, like a sticking plaster being slowly removed. As for my tail, I feel heaviness behind me, at the base of where my spine used to be. I know it is long, a white horse's tail to match my white swan's wings. You had carefully stored those items in readiness for me. *The soul will return to its true nature unless . . . unless . . . unless it is tethered to . . .*

That was what it said. Of course it did. I knew all along that by messing with nature there would be a price. And Wensley had written it down to warn anyone who'd want to try. My greed and selfishness had allowed my judgement to be clouded. I thought I was special. You made me feel special. That was how our love had been founded and I let it escalate into this twisted mess.

I do not feel the chill here in this place where my consciousness slips from inside to outside my shell of a body. There are no goosebumps on my preserved skin. I am freed from physical pain or sensation. I am within myself, but without, like all the animals you have touched. They want to source their identity through the parts they are made from. At first, I was too preoccupied with my new shape to take much notice of them squabbling and fighting for order. But they are brutes only interested in the one thing I seek too. They seek to find out what they have become. They seek freedom to be their true selves.

Their souls veer toward the flames of the candles, knowing they may provide a momentary release. Then they draw back, tethered like a kite to a string set aloft on the currents of a strong breeze. I see the flames now. There is clarity in my current state that I had not experienced before now. Now I am dead. They call it dead, yet each death is as unique as each life, so please don't quote me on this. All I can tell you is how I am. I still *exist*, my darling Peppercorn. I am still your beloved wife. You have kept me here and I am so, so torn between the love I remember (I say remember because my feelings are stripped back to the core) and the love of onwards and away from this restricting, physical form.

Do not panic. I was not sickened by the processes that I know you must've gone through to keep me in this state. The scrape of flesh and bone and application of chemicals to prevent my spoiling. It does not bother me. There is no pain, as I said. I drift between what you would call wakefulness, what I would call "the now," and the in-between that threatens to come calling for me when I least expect it. It wants me more than you want me. That is my fear. How strong is your love?

No heat runs through my veins (I have none) but I remember those hot, passionate moments we shared where my blood pumped in vibrant rhythm with your own breathy yearnings. You have formed me from my own skin, my outer layers and the choice pickings of my favorite creatures. I have become your fairy tale, but there is no way of telling you if there is a happy ending in sight. If only you could reach me.

I've coveted the caving of your features, the rise and fall of your shoulders, as you twisted and cut, sawed and bandaged and stitched my motionless body back into being. You did not falter in your service to me. But you did not give me air to breathe. You have given me new life, yes, but a life where you can longer play a part. And this, my darling, makes me sad and exasperated all at the same time.

CHRISTMAS DAY / TODAY

Evening

A match strikes and my eyes see the great beyond beckoning. You puff on your pipe. The flames lick and curl about the logs in the hearth. We are bathed in orange. I feel the pull of all the creatures around me, as if they are making a massive effort to reach the flames. They do not fear the fire as they would in their living state. They have become accustomed to it and crave it like a drug. It is their portal, their destiny, their redemption. Their glass eyes twinkle with expectation. Touch me, they seem to say. Burn me up. Set me free. I sit on the chair you have positioned like a throne among our Christmassy scene and weave my mind back over the year to tease out some meaning, to understand how I got here.

Wensley's book was no accidental find in a dusty bookshop. I had meant to find it, so I could put right the wrongs that you had done. I do not shirk from my own deliberate actions in the creation of all those poor, wretched hybrids. But I found out how desperate and cruel it had been. And now I have become one.

You once mentioned the eyes. I remember your words: "The eyes," you said, "they never quite show what was once inside." Yes, the eyes are not needed, my love. They are mere fancy. For it is the soul that sees who we truly are, not the eyes. It is the soul that knows who we are. This inescapable fate ties me with sinewy strands of hope, like the workings of your fingers through to the un-beating hole where my heart should be. Wrap me in your arms, sink into me, remind me what it is that keeps us bound together.

I don't expect you to answer me as I speak to you. I doubt my own story. I doubt my own existence at times. No one has been able to scrap together evidence, the real proof of what happens when our bodies cease functioning. Even Wensley's attempts are crude and borne from a longing to explain his experiences on the living side of the veil. I am telling you how it is for me. I am the fathomless proof.

There are theories and philosophies about life after death in the religions I have encountered. Most extol the afterlife, the future, the better life. They swim with infinite symbolism: the Hindu wheel; Nirvanic cycles of reincarnation into body after body until life lessons are learned; resurrection and ascension; silver cords; karma; judgement; heaven; Valhalla; torment; hell; limbo; confinement; purgatory; descending worlds; ka and ba; the Fields of Aaru; your heart weighed on the scales counterbalanced by the feather of truth; sarcophagi; mummification; doors; tunnels; veils; rivers; ferrymen; Elysian fields; the underworld; Sheol; graves; tombs; pyramids; cemeteries; the world-to-come; extinction; rapture; battles; salvation; atonement; sleep of the soul; isthmus; the dream world; ghosts; change of form; freedom; bridges; Summerland; time.

There is time here, but it runs differently to how you would perceive it. It does not flow like the hands of a clock or the linear dates of a calendar. I am now. It is now. There are flashbacks and coherent patches, but I am a riddle.

1. I am not dead.
2. I am not alive.
3. What am I?

Time here is like a big slice of cake gobbled up and ingested by a greedy old hag. She stuffs it in her puckered, salivating mouth with gnarled dirty claws and hardly chews. I plead with her for some crumbs but she ignores me, sucks at her misshapen fingers, licks her cracked black lips until a glittering bolus shifts to the wet abyss of her gullet, down her esophagus, then into the churning acid of her stomach where time dissolves and joins the other morsels of time she has swallowed so mercilessly. Then it molds in her dark gut and descends to the underworld of her bowels as a sticky mass ready to be excreted.

CHRISTMAS DAY / NOW

I hear you in the kitchen again. Other men's voices. Yours and others, maybe three? No, just your gruff voice reasoning with another familiar, higher-pitched male voice. I catch some words like flakes of papery ash alighting on my grey skin:

"... she said to come at Christmas ... always come ..."

"... not convenient ..."

"... but, I always ... where is she? Scarlett?"

"... having a lie down ..."

"... freezing ... can I come in? Henry? Henry—what's happened?" I recognize the voice. It's Rhett. My Rhett. Like I said, he always turns up at Christmas. I try to stand. I urge my stationary body to move. I will it to move. I pray to the other souls to help me. They carry on cacking and squawking and kicking and spitting. But my soul remains tethered like a tick to my own remodeled body, held fast like a suckling demonic babe. I am my own useless parasite.

Rhett! Rhett! In here! Come in out of the cold. Share this festive day with me and my lover. But of course, Rhett cannot hear me. Neither can you. But you, my darling, seem to dissuade my brother from entering the warmth of our Christmas bubble. You attempt to turn away my own flesh and blood. You are the cruel, selfish inn-keeper, unwilling to share your space with a weary traveler.

"It's fucking dangerous. Do you not realize how serious this is? Do you know how difficult that was, coming across the ice?" Rhett's voice rises as he confronts you.

"We—are—fine." I love your stern tone, but I want to see my brother. I *need* him.

"Where is she? Where's my sister?"

"Rhett, stop . . ."

Your voices are coming closer to the door of the lounge. The door swings open and nearly crashes into the wall. Rhett's eyes flick about the room. He is motionless, like a stunned rabbit. The air is fractured around all three of us. His realization has turned it to glass and imploded in slow motion. Rhett turns to you and then back to me, his hands clenching into fists then splaying out again as if he is grasping at an invisible rail to steady himself.

He keeps swearing but not actually finishing the words, his mouth gaping open, so it sounds like "wah—tha—fah." I want to speak to him but obviously can't in my current state; my consciousness is so flaky, locked inside this redundant body with animal attachments. I try to reach him in some other way, some signal that he may understand, but he is rubbing his eyes and squinting back tears and panting as if something has caught in his throat. Here is my brother, my twin, witnessing his sister as a work of art.

The taxidermist's lover—taxidermied.

The irony may reach him someday, but for now he just coughs up a mouthful of sick and doesn't even try to catch it in his hand. He spits it on the rug and you look at it in disgust.

He must appreciate the workmanship you have so beautifully and lovingly crafted, but the strange hue of my scaly skin and my fake resin eyes, not to mention the large wings that poke through the slits you have cut in my dress are probably not a sight he has imagined in all his years. I am a queen on her throne, a beautiful swan chameleon woman with the tail of a white mare swept round onto my lap. My hands have been positioned on my thighs like a stately heiress waiting for her loyal subjects to serve her. There is nothing uncomfortable about my pose. You have even arranged some tinsel around my wrists and neck, so I complement the Christmas scene.

"You've fuh—fuh—fucking stuffed her!" he manages to blurt out, shock turning to hostility in his croaking voice. He is shaking. You try to reach out to him, but he snatches his arm away, backing toward the door. "Sick bastard." Something bordering on hysterical laughter bubbles up from his throat. He is moving away from me but there is something I need to tell him.

Rhett—Rhett it's me, I'm ok, it's all ok, I want to tell him. I want to hold him. I want to enfold him. I want to swim back in time and tell him it's alright and there is no blame and it was me who did it. It was me who killed our parents. I set the candle alight. I started the fire. I left it to burn. I burned the house down. I killed them. It was me. But how will he ever know? How can I ever tell him to release all the guilt that forces him to travel around the world, purging himself in the pleasures of flesh like a mad dog dipping and diving into a rapid river but always coming out thirsty?

"Rhett, it's not what you think." You hold out your hands to him as he continues to back cautiously toward the door like a man who has discovered he's landed in a pit of sleeping dragons.

"Sick, fucking sick . . ." Rhett's temples pulse like they always do when he is battling some complex emotion that forces him to feel something other than lust.

A door slams and he is gone. My Rhett. My twin has gone back out into the icy void, and I cannot bear it. Think, think. What did Wensley say? What was the other way to release the tethered soul? Fire. I know fire can help, but I cannot move. How can I set myself free if I cannot set myself on fire? But there is another way, the manifestation of fire by spontaneous combustion. A poof of smoke and all that is left are a few charred limbs among blackened ash—as quick as mercury. I focus on my center to build the heat within. My glass eyes are staring ahead, but within I am squinting and squeezing with the greatest effort. Pleeeeeeeeease!

Nothing.

I jostle with the other souls to reach the flames that are licking higher in the fireplace from the draught that has entered our home. The crabbit is cruelly pecking his way forward, the jackalope whomping his paws, the cowstrich and wallopea are scraping back their strong, sinewy legs in readiness for a race. As for me . . .

Nothing.

I hear you lock the door from the inside, the one that Rhett has just backed out of. He is retreating outside into the now darkening day. You grab a bottle from the kitchen cupboard. The sound of liquid being poured into a glass. A slurp. The glass noisily slammed back down onto the worktop. The creak of the lounge door hinge. And there you stand.

You stand in the doorway with a bottle of scotch, swaying slightly and look directly at me.

"Merry Christmas, Scarlett!" You grimace. "Always one to get what you want."

You raise the bottle in a toast and take a full mouthful of whisky, letting some slop down your beard. *Do not descend to the darkness, my darling*—I send out a feathery message like a scribe scratching scrolls of black ink onto parchment—*Merry Christmas, sweet love of mine.* I sense troubled waters bubbling up within you. When they talk of veils and thresholds, of tunnels leading to light, of ascension into the great white sky above, what do they know? They are living. I'll tell you how it is.

Imagine who we were: each cell as a boat on a lake without oars, ready to be plunged into repetitive cascades in search of a destination that is out of sight. Imagine the liquid that silently and secretly slips in perpetual motion within the veins and arteries and capillaries of our bodies. Imagine the secretions, that which has been washed away to join greater rivers, solidifying and becoming gelatinous. Imagine those sensations of ebb and flow, heat and stiffness, rise and fall, petering out to stillness.

A flicker of movement through the window pane. And another. At first, I think it is a bat, at this late hour, sweeping over our island. But again, I sense light. You do not see it as your back is to the window where you sit and face me, swigging and swaying as you study me: your creation. You reach forward to caress my cheek, but as you do, the window is smashed with deafening force from outside and the fire splutters in response to this invasion of wintery air. Another smash, and another, in quick succession. The flicker was not a bird. I see light hair and pale fingers. A petrol-soaked rag tied to a log is lobbed toward you and lands with a scattering of flames as the fire is sent inside our home and brightens the interior.

You leap up and turn, but your reactions are slowed by the alcohol. Then another whump as the next flaming missile narrowly misses your head and lands near the creatures. Their dry fur and feathers are ideal incendiaries, and I hear them shriek in delight as the flames take hold. I am jealous. The unfurling of the souls from the mixed-up hybrids tease me as they unpeel themselves from their harnessed bodies. It is like watching ectoplasm swirl among the smoke in spiral patterns. My own wings seem to twitch and lurch, my tail is as restless as if the horse to whom it belonged has been spooked into action.

"Bastard—" You lunge toward the window to see Rhett running away, then you grab at the curtains to beat at the flames, but there are sparks spitting from the flammable creatures. The rug lights like a cartoon bomb wire spreading in a straight line toward me. The thin, bare skin of my feet are positioned neatly on it, soles pressed flat like I am about to stand. I urge the fire to reach me, reasoning that the touch of fire will set me free from the animals you have stitched to me.

You are swearing and cursing and flailing about. You stagger and cough. Your bottle of whisky falls and adds to the fuel, like an electrical circuit made live. I watch the journey of liquid across the floor.

Then, a banging and rattling and a hard whump against the door. Rhett is breaking it down. You are losing your battle with the spreading flames that lick and catch the edges of the frayed furniture. It blackens and sizzles as more flames take hold. Flimsy metallic decorations disintegrate and dissolve, folding up and in on themselves as the heat reaches the ceiling. The tree ignites and spits like an angry camel, its dangling ornaments popping and falling to the floor. There is black smoke everywhere and you are on your knees, choking.

You know how I love you, my darling, but I must be free.

The sweet burn of fire reaches the skin of my back. It catches my new tail and sizzles and curls as the horse hairs are eaten up, turning the white to black. My skin is peeling back to reveal the metal body shape upon which you have mounted my skin. My wings are alight. I see flaming angels fall from the sky. You flap at my body to try and extinguish me with your jacket like a maddened ringmaster. But Rhett appears and bulldozes you from behind. He is smaller than you, but fast, and knocks you to the ground. Before you can scramble up, he is trying to lift me. I am lighter now than when I was living, stuffed with wood wool. My body is no longer my own, stitched together over wires that you have fashioned so perfectly to match my body shape. Out through the flames we go, Rhett holding me over his shoulder, as if I am a precious mannequin being transported to a designer store.

You are coughing and crawling behind us, but Rhett moves quickly. He reaches the door and carries me outside into the wintery abyss. Surrounding us is a lake of ice with the ragged gash where Rhett has powered a heavy motorboat through the thinner patches. He drops my smoldering body into the boat and jumps in. The mists are set around us; it has become dark quickly. In the distance, Christmas lights dance in the air.

Rhett is fumbling with his phone. "Police," he shouts. "He's killed my sister . . .

"No, I said police . . . and fire brigade . . .

"Yes—a fire . . .

". . . the house with the moat . . . flood . . .

"What? No, I don't have the fucking postcode . . .

"God knows who else he's killed . . .

"Yes of course I'm in imminent danger . . .

"Look—she's definitely dead—just send someone—he's dangerous . . ."

"Come on, come on." Rhett is now swearing at the boat, pumping the throttle, but the cold has stalled it and the water has started to harden like icing on a cake. He hits the motor with the palm of his hand and swears again, a strangled cry coming out of his mouth. "Why is this happening?"

I want to hold him. I want to caress my twin brother. But I'm an immobile beast, the bride of Frankenstein's monster. He shifts my stiff legs, covered in the soiled silk of my wedding dress, and tries again to start the motor, but it merely judders. The fire has affected me. I feel untethered, lighter, but not yet free enough to float away from my body. Something draws me back. It is you.

When I said I found something in your workshop, you knew what it was, didn't you? The end of your finger. You had kept it as a token, preserved in a jar of formaldehyde, hidden behind all your other jars. A slice of it attached to my own expired body completed our connection. You gave a dead part of yourself to me upon my death, and my part of the bargain would be to live with you for eternity. I saw those labels too, in your workshop, attached to the swan's wings and the horse's tail—*For Scarlett! X*—in your bold, sweeping handwriting, the aptly tied luggage labels dangling from them as if they were destined for someplace faraway. You always knew where we were headed, and, I suppose, so did I. It was the "X" that touched me most, as if you were actually writing a gift tag and sealing it with a kiss.

Rhett gives up on the boat and hauls me back out and onto his shoulders. He is grunting and puffing in the cold night air. There is a loud bang as the door slams against the frame and you appear. The sound of the operator still squeaks from Rhett's phone, "Hello? Hello? Can you tell me what's happening now?"

"Stop there, Rhett," you say. A regal steadiness oozes from you. Rhett continues to stumble toward where the driveway once was, now covered with a long sheet of ice, toward the silhouette of low hills in the far distance.

"I said stop!" There is something in the tone of your voice that makes Rhett turn and he sees your shotgun pointed level with his chest. Dark clouds of smoke billow from the doorway, and I hear the hiss of the fire as it takes hold of the fabric of the house. The creatures must all be burned by now, their souls freed from the stitched terror of their afterlives. I am envious of them as they rise above me. A Chinese water deer leaps away up into the night sky like a magical Christmas reindeer. All the parts that have been consumed by the fire are free. Yet they soar and swoop around me before dissipating into the night sky. I watch them go and feel like weeping with joy. My half-life is clinging to this sorry state, a charred body with grey smoky wings, and a blackened tail clinging like some frayed piece of cotton from my behind.

"Turn her loose," you say. I catch the slur in your voice as you gesture with your gun.

Rhett stares. I am still on his shoulders but feel the pull toward you. Even now I want you. I know what I have become. What you have made me. But I want you; I want you in all your glorious madness.

Rhett lowers me to the ground. One of my wings angles awkwardly from my back. He stands up straight, looking down at my stiffened body, his brow furrowed, a streak of smoky ash across his cheek, like a boy playing at cowboys and Indians.

"Come on, then, if you're going to shoot me. Want to stuff me as well, do you?"

"You don't understand."

"What is there to understand! You've killed her, you've killed my sister and done this to her. All this freaky stuff—" He rips at the half-detached wing and tears it from my back, launching it into the night toward the moat.

"No!" You watch a wing bounce away like a crashed kite.

"She's dead, you bastard. Look—" Rhett gestures at my flaccid, hollow body, pale and broken on the lawn, and reaches for the other wing. He tugs sharply at it so white feathers strip off and start floating like snowflakes across the frost-hardened mud of the lawn.

"She's *not* dead." You walk slowly toward me. "My Scarlett can never die. Can't you see? I've kept her alive. I found her in bed . . . the cold, pneumonia . . . It was too late but I had to try. Don't you see? She can never die. Not like this. I couldn't bear it. I love her more than life itself. You must believe me. I would never harm her." All this comes out in a garbled impassioned plea.

Rhett shakes his head and looks at you while scrunching up his nose in that way he does when things don't go his way. But you are right, my darling. I am not dead. You have kept me alive with your magical hands.

There is a light coming out of the fog and a pulsing, vibrating sound that hammers the air in thick waves. The sound echoes around the house, bouncing off the walls. You look up toward it, so does Rhett, and he takes his chance to attract attention by waving his hands over his head. You put your gun down as he runs after the helicopter waving at the beam of light as if it might lift him up to the heavens.

Then you are kneeling by my side. I sense your mortal earthiness as you effortlessly lift me and caress me. *Won't you join me, my love?* I am slipping away from this limbo world. The fire has touched me, and I yearn to be released. You lift me so I am sitting on your lap and you cradle me in your arms. The light is getting closer and swoops around us, picking up the smoke rising from the house, the flames licking like orange ribbons from the windows. Then the light finds us and the pulsing hum is above us. The waves of air push at us, and you lift me up and walk toward the ice.

"*Stay where you are!*" A loud, tinny tannoy echoes from the light in the sky. The helicopter hovers and tries to catch us in its beam, but you keep moving steadily, striding toward the expanse of ice that begins where the bottom of our drive ends.

"*Keep away from the ice. Move away from the ice.*"

But you keep walking. Me in your arms. The helicopter circles and catches us again in its spotlight.

"Bring her back," Rhett is shouting at you above the noise of the helicopter. He aims at your back and fires a shot from your gun. You are blown flat onto your face, and my body tumbles from your arms. I search for your soul in the darkness which weaves its winnowy fingers around my wreckage. My own twin has shot you, laid you out cold on this Christmas night. We lie together. Shall we die together?

Rhett peels me from beneath your heavy body, swearing and spitting and sinking to his knees.

"Scarlett," he whispers, "my sweet sister—what have you become?"

If I had a heart it might beat faster at his soft words, but it is you who I yearn for with every cell of my remaining skin.

Rhett looks to the sky as if the answers may fall upon him. Is this retribution, an eye for an eye? Rhett kicks at your boots as you lie still. I want to kick him. He drags me with him like a child possessive of a toy. He is skirting round the edges of the lawn away from the climbing flames that spit and churn from the burning house. We are heading back toward the boat, the warmth of his breath making patterns in the cold air. Then he lurches backwards, tugged from behind. You have risen again. Your arm compresses Rhett's windpipe as you hook it under his chin.

"Thought you'd got me, eh lad?" you rasp in his ear, saliva dripping from your bottom lip. He tries to unhook your arm, but you are stronger. "Knocked me off my feet there. Not a bad shot, eh?"

"How?—Why?" Rhett splutters as he struggles to break free.

He tries to hit your head from behind, but in a single movement you crush his arms against his chest as if you are hugging him. His feet kick toward your shins, but you wrap your leg around him and push him easily to the ground. He lies there rubbing his neck, looking up at your towering bulk.

"I don't want to fight you," you say. "I just want to be with Scarlett. Can't you just leave us alone?" I sense the fire in your eyes as you lock your gaze upon him.

Rhett is rubbing his neck and looking up at your shining, demonic face as if you have transformed into one of the creatures he has burned.

"B—but I shot you. How did you . . . ?"

"Corn." You grin to reveal blood on your teeth.

"What? You are totally insane."

But I knew what you were talking about. The cartridges were filled with corn for the wassailing all those months ago at Penny's. How time flies. And here we are, fighting in the muck and flame of Yuletide armed with grains of corn. Rhett leaps up and tries to punch you, but in a reflex movement you backhand him and he falls to the ground without a whimper.

You lift me tenderly, nuzzling your face into the charred remains of my neck, and walk steadily toward the dip where the running water normally meets the road. A loud crack signals a weakness. Then another, as the ice takes our full combined weight. You stumble and slide but manage somehow to stay upright. All around us, the frozen landscape seems to speak to us.

You step further onto the ice. The helicopter moves off swiftly and arcs back round to catch us in its spotlight. You stand still and raise your head to the heavens. The ice can no longer hold us both, and you crash through, feet first. I feel you gasp as we are sucked under by the cruel fingers of icy water. You hardly fight it. Yet your final breath feels like a hurricane to me.

Your body grows heavy with liquid. I am still entwined around you; my head resting on your shoulder, my wedding dress draped like a fabric anchor around your legs.

And we sink as only lovers can.

TWILIGHT

"*Scarlett. My favorite name.*"

   Earth. Air. Water. Fire. Ice.

   Death and rebirth in magnificent cycles.

   A promise made. The power of intent.

   "*Will you stay with me—ever after?*"

   "*Always, my darling Peppercorn, always.*"

ACKNOWLEDGEMENTS

There were many people who encouraged me to write this book or nodded enthusiastically when I told them what I was writing, so I would like to thank the following:

The MA Creative Writing cohort who offered feedback and constructive criticism throughout the early stages.

Lucy English, my MA manuscript tutor, who guided me through the dark, dirty scenes and told me to write a book I didn't want my mother to read! (Sorry mum!)

For putting up with my madness as I wrote the first draft, Rich Gregory.

For gently championing my writing from way back, Genista Lewes.

Thanks to Mr. Henry Royston Wensley, for being my writing buddy and mentor. I will always be your No. 1 Fan!

To everyone in the Somerset Writers Group, especially Dixie Darch, for your inspiration, laughter, fun and the most delicious home cooked delights (fuel for writers!).

To Mr. Rose, who showed me a cabinet full of false eyes, among other treasures, in his fascinating taxidermy workshop.

To Dave Webber for showing me the Somerset countryside through your eyes.

To Dorothy (Dee) Pochon for generous support and encouragement to be myself and live my life.

Many thanks to the Art Bank Café in Shepton Mallet for welcoming me into your quirky love nest of arty delights, feeding me cake and listening to my stories.

To all my friends—I am blessed to have you in my life.

Thank you, Mum, Dad and Stu for your unconditional love.

To Lucy Banks for keeping the faith and encouraging me to persevere.

And most of all to the team at CamCat Publishers especially my editor, Helga Schier, for making this such an exciting and enjoyable process. Thank you for making my dreams come true.

FOR FURTHER DISCUSSION

1. What do you think of hybrid taxidermy?
2. Give the story an alternate ending.
3. Create a playlist of songs to complement the book.
4. If you were making a movie of *The Taxidermist's Lover* who would you cast?
5. Why do you think the author includes references to *Gone With The Wind*, *Thunderbirds* and other popular culture?

ABOUT THE AUTHOR

Polly Hall has been published in various anthologies and won competitions for her poetry and flash fiction. She holds an MA in Creative Writing from Bath Spa University.

A longstanding member of a Somerset writers' group, she also teaches creative writing workshops. *The Taxidermist's Lover* is her debut novel.

She lives next to a cider factory with her cat, Vishnu.

You can find out more about her writing projects at www.pollyhall.co.uk or @PollyHallWriter.

AUTHOR Q&A

Q. How did you get the idea for *The Taxidermist's Lover?*

A. There used to be a museum of curiosities, at Jamaica Inn in Cornwall, featuring Walter Potter's taxidermy. The stuffed animals were dressed in clothes and portrayed in anthropomorphic scenes such as a kittens' wedding, rats smoking and gambling, and thousands of other animals and birds in tableaux form. Sadly, the collection got split up and sold off in 2003 but I remember visiting as a child on our family holidays to Cornwall. Most of it was really bad taxidermy but the bizarre creations really appealed to me. There are some fantastic taxidermy artists out there who I greatly admire: Polly Morgan, Kate Clark, Iris Schieferstein, to name a few.

Q. Water and fire feature heavily in the book. Is this intentional?

A. Yes. I guess this relates to transformation, and the elements of water and fire represent this so beautifully. Water can destroy or cleanse, fire can destroy and cleanse. Taxidermy, love, water, fire are all ways to transform one thing to another.

Q. Why did you choose to write about taxidermy?

A. Taxidermy is fascinating and provokes a strong response—you either like it or hate it. Preservation of animal skin has been around for centuries. The word taxidermy comes from the Greek taxis (to arrange) and dermes (skin). It has evolved as an art form for traditional cultural objects and during the height of its popularity in the Victorian era to display wealth and prowess by modeling animals in their natural habitat; effectively domesticating the wilderness was the height of fashion. The advancement of taxidermy continued to include some of the most famous exhibits in museums, depicting a lifelike representation of the animal. Popularity waned in the mid-20th century but has reignited as an art form that not only employs trophy specimens but hybrid taxidermy, where different species and synthetic elements are combined to create new creatures. Humans' preoccupation with death plays a part in the fascination too.

Q. How does the place you write about influence the characters?

A. I chose to set *The Taxidermist's Lover* on the Somerset Levels because it is a place I know well and I never tire of its natural beauty. The moor is made up of wetlands and peat marshes, an area of biodiversity and conservation.

There is a sleepy ethereal quality here which comes from the moorland's relationship with water; it shifts like the tides or the cycles of the moon or the seasons. Although, the flood in the book is fictional, it is based on real events in living memory when many areas of Somerset were affected by the rising flood waters. Living alongside the tidal rivers and estuaries of South West England involves a constant monitoring and evaluation of the changes in environment. I think this clearly indicates the fragile and oftentimes devastating inter-relationship between man and nature.

The county of Somerset, in England, is also known as the Land of The Dead and has many mythical and spiritual connections, so it corresponds with the dramatic irony of taxidermy representing life through dead things. Because the book covers the whole year from January to December, I wanted to represent all seasons through the experiences of Scarlett, the narrator, who is immersed in the changing landscape.

"An epic, romantic fantasy where the desert meets the sea, about the magic of wishes—and their unintended consequences."

Available February 2, 2021, wherever books are sold.

![CamCat Books logo]

CamCat
Books

VISIT US ONLINE FOR
MORE BOOKS TO LIVE IN:
CAMCATBOOKS.COM

FOLLOW US

CamCatBooks   @CamCatBooks   @CamCat_Books

CPSIA information can be obtained
at www.ICGtesting.com
Printed in the USA
LVHW111513061220
673490LV00021B/725/J

9 780744 300376